DARK HOLLOW ROAD

Karen Ann Hopkins

Books by Karen Ann Hopkins

Serenity's Plain Secrets
in reading order
LAMB TO THE SLAUGHTER
WHISPERS FROM THE DEAD
SECRETS IN THE GRAVE
HIDDEN IN PLAIN SIGHT
PAPER ROSES
FORBIDDEN WAYS (a romantic companion novel)
EVIL IN MY TOWN
UNHOLY GROUND
SWEET REGRETS (a romantic companion novel)
BLOODY TIES
THE WIDOW
WICKED LEGACY
BLOOD ROCK
THE OFFERING
SERENITY
NIGHT SONG
DEVIL'S EYE
LOST SOUL (coming fall 2023)

Wings of War
in reading order
EMBERS
GAIA
TEMPEST
ETERNITY

The Temptation Novels
in reading order
TEMPTATION
BELONGING
FOREVER
DECEPTION

Willow Creek/One Kiss Is All It Takes (in partnership with HarperCollins/One More Chapter)

The Fortuna Coin

The Possum Gap Novels
The series has future ties to Blood Rock and Serenity's Plain Secrets.
FREE FROM SIN
DARK HOLLOW ROAD
NIGHT SONG

In Night Song, Sheriff Serenity Adams teams up with Sheriff Mills to solve their most chilling case yet.

If you enjoy this book, we invite you to read Serenity's Plain Secrets where Sheriff Serenity Adams solves crimes in rural Indiana. With 15 books, over 25,000 Amazon global ratings, and a 4.4 overall average, crime fiction/mystery readers say it's an unputdown-able series that will keep you flipping the pages way past your bedtime.

ACKNOWLEDGMENTS

Many thanks to Heather and Katie for editing and proofreading this installment.

Appreciation to Melissa from The Illustrated Author Design Service for this gorgeous cover. I think it's my favorite cover art yet!

EbookPbook provided the formatting of this book.

When I'm not writing, I'm rescuing dogs and cats from crowded shelters and lonely roadsides. We're experiencing a crisis of unwanted pets across the United States and rescue organizations are stressed to the max. The best remedy is to spay and neuter your pets. Also, please adopt, don't shop.

Heartfelt thanks to all my rescue partners!

1

LUCINDA

A gust of wind rattled the maple tree, spraying burnt orange across the yard and pelting the side of the farmhouse. The air was still and warm, but dark clouds on the horizon promised cooler temperatures and rain.

"Well, it's about time autumn arrives," Martha said. "I, for one, am ready for chilly days."

I took a sip of coffee, then looked over the rim of my mug, holding in a smile. At forty-five, Martha Mast was nearly fifteen years older than me, but I still considered her my closest friend. She was more opinionated and louder than the other women in the community, and she didn't much care what the others thought. Being a widow and having married off the last of her four children at the beginning of summer, she had a lot of spare time on her hands to sit on my porch swing and keep me from my chores.

"Autumn is my favorite time of the year, although, I am not a fan of raking leaves." Martha's rosy round cheeks puffed out with her scowl, making me laugh.

Then, the gulp of my coffee went down the wrong pipe and I began coughing.

"Do you need my assistance?" Martha set her cup down on the floorboards and started to rise.

I held up my hand and managed to say between gags, "No, no...I'm fine." A moment later, I had recovered and could talk normally. "Martha, you do this every turn of the season." Martha's brows lifted and I added, "Welcome the warmer temperatures or colder ones, then immediately complain about it."

Martha made a huffing noise. "It was an exceptionally humid summer, I think. Wouldn't it be nice to have days pleasant days like this without the constant wind or falling leaves?"

I shrugged, then carefully sipped my coffee. "There's always good with the bad. The Lord never sends us weather we cannot withstand."

We fell into silence and the wind lessened to a stiff breeze. The horses grazed in the nearest field beside the road and where James had already plowed under half of the garden. There were still a couple baskets worth of late-growing tomatoes that I should be picking right now. Only then I could begin canning them, but it would have to wait until morning since my limbs were tired and my mind was restless. No matter how many times I'd thought about rising from the rocking chair to shoo Martha on her way, I couldn't find the gumption to stand up. Phoebe was still napping and Martha didn't seem in a hurry to leave. Josh and Sarah wouldn't be home from school for several hours.

I surveyed the jagged hills in the distance and sniffed the air. The signs were all there. The trees were awash in splendid colors and when I inhaled, the earthy scent of damp earth and decaying leaves flooded my nose. We were only a few days into October, and I already dreaded the fast-approaching snow and ice of winter.

"Bah." Martha swatted the air with her hand before using it to smooth a few loose strands of chestnut hair back into her cap. "I appreciate the Lord's choices, but that doesn't mean I can't show my displeasure at times." She winked and her mood suddenly lightened. "Will you and James be going to this year's Apple Festival in Possum Gap?" Before I had a chance to answer, she rambled on, "I'll ride along with you all if you don't mind. We can share the cost of a driver."

The idea of hiring a driver for the eight-mile trip into the English town was pleasing. It would be more comfortable than the buggy. The traffic and crowds always made me fear for our horse, Goliath. There would be plenty of room to stow packages if we purchased any of the arts or crafts that were for sale in the booths that lined Main Street as well.

I tilted my head, returning my gaze to the tomato plants with their abundance of late season fruit, feeling guilty. Still, I couldn't manage to rise. "I'll speak with James. He's been stingy with trip money lately, but he may make an exception because of all the trouble it is to find a place to park the buggy during festival days."

Martha puckered her lips and nodded. I could tell that something else was on her mind.

My friend finally let her thoughts flow freely. "How are the children and James doing, Lucinda? It's been nearly six weeks since that horrible girl came into the community with her devious and violent heart."

An image of Charlie Baker sprang to life in my mind and lingered there for a few long seconds. Her enormous, widely spaced eyes held a faraway look in them. At the tragic moment Sheriff Sadie Mills pulled the trigger and the sound of gun blasts exploded inside my ears, I knew the teenager wasn't spiritually with us anymore. Charlie was somewhere far, far away, and she was smiling. Her sins were grievous—she'd killed her mother, stepfather, younger sister, and even Vivian Hershberger—but I still prayed for her brittle soul each night when I closed my eyes. I wouldn't dare let James or even Martha know that I did such a thing. Charlie had kidnapped my very own children and even tried to kill James. Thank the Lord, they all survived the evil power that had taken hold of that girl.

Charlie still terrorized my dreams, but not in the way you might think. She came to me at night riding a large black horse that looked like our Goliath. She was still rail-thin, but her straight brown locks shined in the sun. Daisies poked out from her hair, tucked behind her ears. She'd turn to me and the corners of her mouth would lift high. Then the horse would whirl around and gallop away, disappearing into the tall grass.

I wanted to ask her so many questions, but she'd be gone before I got the chance. Was my mind playing tricks on me or was it something else—a vision of sorts? I shouldn't have been so stubborn when the sheriff tried to arrange a therapist to visit the farm. We could have all used some worldly guidance during the dark days that followed Vivian's murder—especially me.

I let out a long, shaky breath, feeling the urge to discuss the matter with Martha for the first time. "Children are resilient. Sarah's nightmares have ended, and Josh never speaks of the girl. Phoebe was the most unaffected, it seems. Their routines have returned to normal."

Rubbing a wad of blue material from my dress between my fingertips, I caught Martha's sympathetic gaze and glanced away. I didn't want her to see my eyes water. I was too emotional and angry with myself for how easily tears flowed these days.

"And James?" Martha asked in a coaxing voice.

"He acts the same as always, but I notice he's much more vigilant about the children's whereabouts. He isn't so carefree about things as he used to be."

"I'd say." Martha let out a long sigh and one of the horses whinnied.

When I cocked my head, I heard a horse's hooves striking pavement in the distance.

"And you? Lucinda, how do you fair?"

I swallowed the hard knot down my throat and my mouth went dry. I forced my mouth to open and then the words tumbled out. "Some days are better than others. I can't help but wonder at the Lord's purpose for dropping Charlie Baker into our lives to wreak havoc upon us, but it's not my place to question His intentions."

I couldn't look Martha in the eye, fearing she'd see how my faith waivered.

Martha snorted. "We can do our best to stay the course and act wisely, but there's nothing to be done about the corruption of others. Unfortunately, those individuals can easily taint our lives. No matter the outcome, if we cherish our Lord and follow His word, we are saved. Vivian's death is shocking for sure, and she left this world in such a brutal way, but never fear that she's in a perfect place."

Anger swelled in my heart, and I finally turned to Martha. "Do you think Samuel and Louisa Hershberger feel the same way about their only daughter?" I hardened my tone. "Louisa walks around with a vacant look in her eyes and James says that poor Samuel rarely speaks anymore." When I saw Martha's cheeks redden, I plowed on. "No matter how hard I pray about it, peace evades my heart. I cannot understand why Vivian had to die the way she did and that her killer was a ragged and abused girl. It makes no sense!"

Martha leaned back and continued pushing the swing back and forth with her feet. The squeaking of the chains soothed my nerves. I closed my eyes and tilted my face to the sunshine and breathed in the sweet smell on the breeze. If I tried hard enough, I could push thoughts of Charlie and Vivian out of my mind for a moment or two. But I didn't try very often. It was my cross to bear.

"There is no way to make sense of such things. They are from the depths of hell—"

"Then hell has come to this place. Whatever tormented Charlie did not die with her. I fear it's still here."

Martha made a *tsk, tsk* sound. "Don't speak of such things, Lucinda. You are still carrying the shock of it all—"

"It's all my fault!" I began to shake all over and buried my face in my hands.

I knew Martha had left the porch swing in a hurry when her palms were immediately pressing into my shoulders. "Now, now, dear friend. That's nonsense. You helped a girl in need, that is all. I would have done the very same thing if faced with the same choice."

As emotions rocked my body, I looked up with wet eyes. After sniffing and wiping my nose while Martha rubbed my back vigorously, I could finally speak properly. "Are you saying the truth, Martha? Or just trying to make me feel better?"

Martha straightened up and placed her hands on her hips. "Don't you think I can do both at the same time?" When I nodded slowly, she continued, "The way I see it, everything you did was with good intentions."

Another sob rolled through me as I swallowed down burning juices in my throat. It was strange to speak of things that I'd held inside for weeks, not even sharing with my sweet husband. "Louisa won't even look at me. I doubt she'll ever forgive me for harboring the girl who killed her daughter. And I can hardly blame her."

"It is only the Lord's forgiveness that you should be concerned with, and I am sure you have it." Martha returned to the swing and plopped down, suddenly looking tired. She began pumping her feet and the chain squeaked again. "I'm sure Louisa and Samuel don't blame you. They're consumed with grief, and it will be a long while before their hearts mend enough to interact with you normally. When they see you, they're reminded of what happened to Vivian. It's a natural response." Her voice became sterner. "No good comes from fretting over something which is out of your control." She grunted loudly. "My oldest brother, Aaron, used to say the phrase all the time. As I've grown older, I believe he was right."

After dabbing at the corners of my eyes a few more times, I leaned back in the rocker and exhaled. The heavy feeling in my heart hadn't left but talking to Martha had lightened my spirit a bit. The breeze on my cheeks was pleasant and the hills, awash in autumn's splendor, were quite beautiful. Phoebe was still sleeping, and I had some quiet time with my friend. I would embrace the moment and hopefully it eased my troubled mind.

"You rarely speak of that particular brother, and I can't recall him visiting Possum Gap before," I said. The change of subject was just a distraction to help collect myself.

"Ack." Martha swatted the air in her usual manner when she became annoyed. "The age distance between Aaron and myself is great, as he was the first child and I the last. He moved away from the community in Ohio where we were both born long before I came about. Still, he's a memorable character, that's for sure."

"Where is he now?" I asked out of politeness.

"Indiana—in a settlement called Blood Rock. He's the bishop there," Martha said in a flat voice.

My interest piqued. "Isn't that the community where all the drama has been?"

"If you call kidnappings and murder, among other terrible things, drama, I guess it is."

"James grew up in Poplar Springs, Indiana. Have you heard of it?"

"Several of my cousins live there. I believe it's a good haul north of Blood Rock," Martha said, still pumping her legs to keep the swing moving.

"Yes, that's where I heard about Blood Rock. We

haven't visited in a while, but James' family said a lady sheriff assisted one of the local families when barns were being lit on fire. A woman's body was even found in one of them—an outsider. I don't recall all the details, but I do remember the sheriff who helped solve the case came from Blood Rock."

Martha snorted, then chuckled. "My oh my. Another female sheriff? I wonder why a woman would want to do a dangerous job like that?"

I thought about Possum Gap's sheriff, Sadie Mills. Never having met the woman until Vivian's body was discovered in the shed, I was impressed by her courageous heart.

"In the outside world, a woman can do anything she wants. It certainly wouldn't be a dull job." I drank the last bit of coffee and finally stood up. Those tomatoes weren't going to get picked and canned by themselves. "Thank you, Martha, for the advice." I let out a jagged breath which I wish had been smooth. "I'll try my best to forget the disturbing events of last summer."

Martha rose with me. "That's not exactly what I meant—"

I stepped up to the porch railing, interrupting Martha. "Look, someone turned into the driveway."

Martha joined me, resting her hands on the rail. "By the looks of the horse, I'd say it's Susan."

Quite right. The bay horse trotting up the driveway had a wide blaze down it's forehead and a thick, long black mane. When the slender hand waved out the window, I knew it was Susan Miller, Bishop Zeke's wife.

Martha lowered her voice, leaning close to my ear. "Now, there's a resilient woman. She acts like nothing at all happened." Martha grunted, catching my eye. "After the relationship between her son Marvin, and that girl Charlie, your behavior is reasonable. Hers is not."

Leave it to Martha to say exactly what I was thinking.

The buggy came to a stop in front of the hitching rail. I quickly straightened my cap, smoothed down the front of my dress and jogged down the steps to grasp the horse's head.

After engaging the brake, Susan jumped out of the buggy. Instead of smiling my way, her round face sagged which was uncharacteristic for the auburn-haired woman.

"Is your youngest napping?" Susan asked without a greeting.

I tied her horse to the post and answered without looking back. "She's been down for over an hour. I have the window cracked to her bedroom window just above our heads. When she wakes, I'll know it."

"A good day for you indeed," Martha said.

She must have just noticed Martha leaning over the porch railing. "Oh, hello, Martha. Fine day it is."

"A little windy to suit my taste." She made another rude snorting noise. "And if you ignore the dark clouds looming on the horizon."

I shot a look of disapproval Martha's way. I couldn't

understand why she prickled so much in Susan's presence. The women were similar in age, and I'd never witnessed Susan say or do anything to warrant Martha's attitude. Yes, Susan had a pushy personality and usually got what she wanted, but it often worked to the advantage of the women in the community when she did.

"I like to focus on the sun shining above my head. Perhaps you should as well, Martha, dear."

Before Martha could reply, I quickly asked, "What brings you by? You were moving at a fast clip." I paused for the right words. "I hope everything is all right."

Susan wiped her hands on her apron. "I dare say, yes. But one never knows these days."

"That sounds ominous," Martha said, walking down the steps. Her own horse stood in one of the stalls and her open cart was parked in front of the barn.

Susan threw her hands up. "More than likely it's nothing, but better safe than sorry, right?" When I nodded vigorously and Martha crossed her arms, Susan continued, "You know how Albert Peachy has been causing his folks grief lately?"

The fourteen-year-old boy had blue eyes, pale skin, and a head full of curly blond hair. I always thought he resembled my idea of what an angel would be like. Many little boys went through the cherub-looking phase, but a now-teenaged Albert hadn't outgrown it.

The boy, who had always been polite and helpful to me, was known throughout the community to be a handful.

Martha spoke up. "The lad takes after his older brother, Gunther. I wouldn't be surprised if he went English as well."

In a rare instance where both women agreed on something, Susan nodded. "Yes, I fear that is the direction he's heading."

I glanced between Martha and Susan, frowning. "He's too young to be labeled. Many of our youth straighten out before they turn eighteen. He has time."

Susan's brows rose before a gust of wind smashed into us. We clutched our caps and turned our backs to the onslaught. "Come inside, Susan. We can talk once we're out of this wind," I said loudly to be heard over the rush of air.

Susan kept her feet firmly planted on the ground and shook her head. "No time, Lucinda. I want to visit most of the community before I return home." The wind softened a notch and Susan stepped closer. "Albert argued with his father late last night and when the boy didn't arrive at the breakfast table, Tina went looking for him."

It felt like my heart dropped into my stomach. "Is he still missing?"

"Run off is more like it," Susan countered. She saw what must have been a look of shock on my face and quickly added, "The boy told William that he didn't want to be Amish any longer and would leave at the first chance presented to him."

"What got the boy so riled?" Martha asked.

"Albert is not happy about having to give most of his wages from working at the Glick's dairy farm to his parents. When he tried to negotiate a higher percentage to keep money back for himself, the conversation became heated and William struck the boy in anger."

My hands went to my mouth and Susan rushed to William's defense. "It was nothing but a swat to the cheek for Albert's foul language. Tina confirmed it to me personally. Albert's cheek was red, but that is all."

I understood how Albert felt about his hard-earned income. We all went through the process of entering the workforce straight out of the eighth grade and giving around ninety percent of the money we earned to our parents. The teenagers helped sustain the family until they married, and then, most parents returned the favor to their children with a gift of land and a large wedding present. It had always been that way and always would. But I too had been frustrated handing over most of my paycheck from babysitting and cleaning neighbors' homes. It was a hard pill to swallow as a youth.

I glanced at Martha's face to see her reaction, but her brow was furrowed in serious thought and she remained silent. Turning back to Susan, I asked, "Do Tina and William want us to look for Albert?"

"Not yet—"

"After what happened"—I paused, sucking in a breath—"to Vivian, don't you think we should call Sheriff Mills?"

Susan took my hand into her warm ones and squeezed. "Hush, Lucinda. Do not speak of that poor girl. This situation is completely different. We will not live in crippling fear, paranoid every time a teenager acts out. It happens all the time, and you know this."

Susan's voice was kind, yet firm. She was right, of course. Amish teens ran off for short periods of time, usually with an English acquaintance. Rarely did harm come to any of them.

Martha finally found her voice. "What does Marvin think of it? There's a four-year age difference between them, but I've seen the two riding horses together."

"I spoke with my son this morning and he wasn't at all surprised. It seems Albert has been sneaking off and spending time with a neighbor boy—an Englisher living in the trailer at the corner of the settlement on Dark Hollow Road."

I remembered seeing the boy she spoke of in their yard, playing cornhole by himself. "How did he become tangled with him?"

"His father is a sometimes driver in the community. That is probably how they met," Susan replied. Before I could respond, she moved past me and untied the reins. "I stopped by to alert you of the situation, that's all. If you see Albert, please reach out to Tina. She's concerned." Susan offered a small smile before she climbed into the buggy. "I expect the boy to be home by nightfall—or the end of the week at the latest. But he'll not stay. That one might look like

15

an angel, but he has a rebellious heart and a reckless spirit. He's doomed to go English, no matter how hard his folks try to make him stay." She paused to take a breath. "Have a good day, ladies. Pass the news along."

Susan turned her bay horse around and clucked to the gelding. He was off and less than a minute later, turned the bend and was gone.

I stood next to Martha, staring at the rough terrain rising out of the wilderness to the east of the community as a chill passed through me.

"I hope this foul wind hasn't brought dark mischief with it," Martha said softly, almost to herself.

My optimistic nature, which had been hiding for weeks, emerged. "Albert is probably playing video games with his new friend and oblivious to the worry he's causing at home. He'll be back when his belly starts grumbling for some of his mama's fine food."

"You're right," Martha agreed through gritted teeth and with a weak voice.

"Susan shouldn't talk about the boy's destiny. I've known some to have a change of heart about the Plain life."

"As have I," Martha agreed.

When Martha began walking slowly toward the barn, I joined her but didn't say anything else. My mind was far, far away.

Was the prickling discomfort in the pit of my stomach because of Albert? I certainly hoped it wasn't. This community couldn't take another tragedy.

2

SADIE

A shadow fell over Main Street and I looked up. Fast-moving dark clouds blotted out the sun and were building to the west. As cooler air touched my cheeks, I inhaled deeply. Mixing with the scent of grilling burgers and fried chicken was a touch of rain on the breeze. A quick glance around made me sigh.

The street overflowed with townspeople. The Apple Festival was Possum Gaps' biggest event of the year. Vendors lined the sidewalks, showcasing every kind of craft a person could think of. The Cliftons, the richest family in town, had personally hired a local bluegrass band to play for the crowd. Their music trickled through downtown from where they were set up on the lawn next to the courthouse. Several rows made with bales of straw formed a half circle around the band and nearly every inch of seating was taken.

The wind picked up and the trees lining Main Street shook, scattering orange, yellow, and red leaves everywhere. Kids laughed at the onslaught and their moms grabbed onto their hair. My gaze lifted to the hills looming over the town. Even though they were awash in fall colors, strands of shifting shadows blotted out the beauty, reminding me that behind the stunning mountain view was a dangerous wilderness.

A light touch on my arm made me jump.

"Mom, I see Hayley. I'm going to hang out with her," Chloe said.

"It's about to rain. Stay close to the store fronts—or the food tent—" I didn't get to finish my sentence because the sixteen-year-old had already started walking away.

Chloe looked over her shoulder, holding her long brown hair away from her face. "You worry too much." She pointed toward the sky. "Look, it's sunny!"

Then she disappeared into the crowd, and I was left with a prickling feeling of annoyance in my gut. My daughter was a distracted teenager, so it wasn't surprising that she didn't notice the dark clouds amassing in the distance and the damp air blowing into Possum Gap. All the adults strolling leisurely by seemed oblivious to the approaching storm and that was just as annoying to me.

People were rarely aware of their surroundings and as the sheriff of this rural Kentucky town, I knew firsthand how much trouble that caused.

"Hi, Miss Sadie." Jeremy Dodd threw up his hand as he raced past me.

His mom, Rachel, who had been two grades below me in high school, paused from chasing her ten-year-old just long enough to say, "Oh, hi, Sadie. I'm having a baby shower for Samantha next Saturday. I hope you can make it."

I nodded and mumbled, "I'll try."

Baby showers, bridal showers, or any kind of domestic gathering that involved party games really wasn't my thing. When I wasn't with Chloe, I spent the little spare time I had with my first deputy, Buddy, or best friend, Tanya. There just weren't enough minutes in the day to keep relationships up with a lot of people.

Another gust of wind returned my attention to the hills. Darkness spilled over Dalton's Peak, the highest mountain in Possum Gap and my heart skipped a beat. The chill that passed through me made me suck in a soft breath.

Wicked things were on the wind…

"Me and you are the only people here paying attention to the weather."

I turned to find John Dover standing next to me with a lopsided grin.

I'd met the man six weeks earlier following a shoot-out at a single wide trailer that killed three men, including his cousin Jax Dover. I still got heartburn thinking about having to confront his clannish—and angry—relatives in Jewelweed Hollow. But the source of most of my nightmares since that terrible summertime week were of a teenager named Charlie and the moment I pulled the trigger, ending her life. The girl was a lost soul who had been raped by her stepfather while her mother had ignored the abuse. Charlie was bound to blow and when she did, she shot and killed her parents and younger sister. She ran away from brutal memories and guilt right into the arms of a man twice her age who sex trafficked her. Her murderous appetite didn't end with her family. She added an Amish teen to the list of lives she took, nearly succeeding in killing an Amish father and his young children before I intervened.

Seeing John Dover again stirred unpleasant memories. I gave my head a small shake to rid myself of them before speaking to the hillman.

"I didn't take you for the festival type," I said with no emotion.

The corners of John's mouth rose even higher. He snorted softly. "I was kind of thinking the same thing about you."

When his eyes swept over me from head to foot and back up again, I experienced an uncomfortable fluttering in my belly. It had been a very long time since that had happened. My face warmed and I looked the other way, trying to focus on random people moving up and down the street, but seeing only a colorful blur.

"Who doesn't like apples?" I glanced back at the man and his brow shot up.

My shoulders slumped a little. The feeling of foreboding I'd experienced a few minutes earlier had sucked the energy right out of me. I crossed my arms over my chest, suddenly thankful I'd worn the green sweater, jeans, and suede knee-high boots. My original plan was to dress in the tan uniform, but Chloe had complained about me intimidating everyone and said something about having fun, and I'd relented. Now, with John Dover, a man whom I had to admit was handsome—in a rugged, back-to-nature sort-of-way— staring so intently my way, I was glad I'd taken her advice and stuffed the uniform into the duffle bag and left it in my car.

John was close to my age, very tall, and wearing a faded blue old-style jean jacket over a t-shirt sporting a large marijuana leaf on the front. A hunting blade was holstered to his belt loop with a strip of brown leather. His dark brown, shoulder-length hair was tied back in a ponytail and a few strands flapped at his forehead. He was not my type, but I could still admire his muscular arms and the rough growth of dark stubble covering his defined chin and jawline. John could pass for one of the guys who spent time in the county detention lockup, but from the brief conversations I had with him while investigating the trailer killings, I knew he was definitely a step off from the usual dangerous men I came into contact with from the back country. This guy was articulate and polite. John Dover wasn't afraid to look me in the eyes, either. He'd taken up residence outside of the Dover compound in Jewelweed Hollow, making it appear that even though he was loyal to his kin, he wasn't overly close to them, which made me wonder what his story was. John Dover was a bit mysterious for men in these parts.

John didn't respond to my apple comment, continuing to smirk and stare at me. I wasn't easily flustered, especially by a Dover, but this one had my stomach in knots. Lifting my face to the cool, stiff breeze, I finally admitted, "I'm here for my daughter. In the past, I enjoyed these things more than I do now."

John's face sobered and he lost the grin. "I get that. Everything's better when we're young'uns and haven't been touched by death."

I cocked my head towards John. *What an odd thing to say.* Strings of tension pulsated between us. The sounds from the fiddles in the courtyard and the friendly conversations all around us disappeared. Depending on the lighting, John's eyes switched colors between green and hazel. Right now, they were a shade resembling creek moss and they looked sad.

Needing to break the tight energy and to erase the troubled look in his eyes, I asked, "If this isn't your thing, what are you doing here?"

I didn't like the uncomfortable feelings rippling through me, but weirdly enough, I liked talking to John Dover. I had no idea what he would say next, and that kind of spontaneity suited the turbulent weather rolling in.

"Calvin Holloway's maple syrup." John smiled big, relaxing for the first time since he'd suddenly appeared at my side.

"You better be on your way then. When I passed by his booth a half hour ago, he only had about twelve bottles left."

"In a hurry to get rid of me, Sheriff?" The lopsided grin returned, and his eyes didn't flinch as he held my gaze.

What game was John playing? It annoyed me to no end that I couldn't figure out if he was being flirtatious or mocking me—and that I gave a damn about which one.

I shrugged, trying to appear disinterested. "Just trying to be helpful. My three bottles are already bought, paid for, and tucked away beneath Calvin's table. I wouldn't dilly dally if I were you or you'll have made a trip into town for nothing."

The corner of John's mouth twitched, and he nodded slowly. "Oh, even if ol' Calvin sells out, the trip wasn't wasted." My eyes grew round, and his grin deepened. "I hope you have a raincoat stowed away somewhere close." He lifted his gaze to the gloomy sky where jagged, dark layers of clouds blotted out the mountains. It was already raining in the hills. "I give it about four minutes before it hits."

He winked and aimed straight towards Calvin's booth. I admired his no-nonsense, long-legged stride. He moved like a coyote—loose and all too confident.

With John's departure, I was suddenly aware of the wave of cool, fresh air.

I shouted out to the nearest townspeople, "Seek cover! We're about to get a soaker."

My voice woke most of the festival goers from their leisurely wanderings. Even without the uniform, they all knew who I was. That's the way it was in a small town. As people started moving quicker, I surveyed Main Street for a sign of Chloe and Hayley. A downpour wouldn't hurt the teens, but the motherly side of me worried about Chloe getting sick and missing school.

The drizzle lasted only a few seconds before the sky opened. Everyone scattered, running for cover. The cold, clean rainwater striking my face made me feel alive and chased away residual thoughts about Charlie Baker and the sense of foreboding that had squeezed me all day. I smiled. John was wrong. The downpour only took two minutes to arrive.

"Sadie! Sadie Mills! Over here!"

I knew the sharp, bossy voice and dashed toward the sound. A moment later, I was standing soaking wet in Miley Meeker's jewelry tent. I dabbed at the water in my eyes until I could see Tanya clearly. She dropped her bags onto the grass and shed her white wool jacket.

"Why did you stay out there in the rain like that?" Tanya chastised me while she draped her jacket over my shoulders.

I didn't feel the chill.

"I'm fine, really," I said, blocking her hands when she tried to button it up.

"Have a seat, Sadie." Miley pointed to two empty chairs in the corner of the tent, then went back to talking to a client at the table.

When we were seated, Tanya frowned at me. "You're still not yourself. Ever since you had to shoot that poor girl, you haven't been thinking straight." Tanya had been my best friend since elementary school and knew me better than anyone else. She leaned closer and lowered her voice. "You had no choice, Sadie."

My eyes drifted to the deluge taking place outside of the tent. The street had emptied, and currents ran alongside the curbs. The sound of the rain beating the canopy was so loud, I could barely hear Tanya and I couldn't help craning my neck to look for Chloe or to see if John Dover was stuck in Calvin's tent.

I didn't turn toward my friend. "It's not that. I have my mind on other things."

"If it helps, I saw Chloe and her friend in the café a few minutes ago." She stretched to reach a cup of brew on the table with jewelry display boxes nearest to us. I caught the aroma of my favorite cappuccino and sighed contentedly when she handed the cup to me.

"Are you sure?"

Tanya swatted the air in between us. "Of course. You need it more than I do."

I hadn't yet swallowed the first sip when Tanya,

added, "Or maybe you were just looking for that sexy mountain man."

I nearly choked, coughed, and swallowed the warm liquid down without tasting it at all.

By the look of it, Tanya's round face tried hard not to chuckle and her large brown eyes sparkled with mischief. High humidity caused her shiny black curls to be frizzier than normal, but Tanya liked the artfully wild hairdo. The dangly gold earrings shined against her dark skin, and even though she was dressed casually in jeans, a purple blouse, and black boots, she was too stylish for a place like Possum Gap. Tanya was the best realtor in town and as of a few months ago, a single woman. Nothing got her down, and nothing got by her either.

I glanced around. No one was paying attention to us and with the downpour, I was sure no one could hear us. Still, I scooted the lawn chair closer to her. "Were you spying on me?" I tried to sound stern, but obviously failed when Tanya grinned back.

"Of course! Girl, you never stand that close to anyone." She smacked her lips. "He's a fine one, but I never dreamed you'd hook up with a Daniel Day-Lewis, *Last of the Mohicans* type."

I swiveled in my seat, checking for eavesdroppers before I hissed, "Hush, I barely know the guy."

"But you want to get to know him, don't you?" She sat back and folded her hands in her lap. "Oh, come on. You can't fool me."

My mouth opened, then snapped shut. The rain continued coming down hard and when I shivered, I was glad for Tanya's jacket. I could lie to myself, but not to Tanya. "If you get bored of the real estate thing, I'll get you a job on the force. You really should have been a detective."

Tanya's smiled deepened. "So, I was right." She chuckled, shaking her head. "I have a heightened sense of awareness but only in matters of the heart, Sadie."

I held up my hands. "Wait a minute. I admit, the guy is easy on the eyes, nothing more."

Tanya made a *tsk, tsk* sound. "It's been an awfully long time since you divorced Ted. Maybe your busy mind could use the right kind of distraction."

Tanya's brow raised suggestively, and I felt my cheeks burn for the second time today. The problem was, she wasn't wrong. It *had* been a very long time since I'd been intimate with someone and lately, I'd been thinking about it more than usual. The problem with sex was it wasn't like buying a fizzy bath bomb that amused you for a few minutes, then disappeared. Men could be clingy, and the last thing I needed or wanted was an actual fully-fledged relationship.

I took a sip and then grunted. "I don't have time for a fling. Besides, I don't trust John Dover. He's got a secret. I can tell."

"I didn't see a ring on his finger, but does he have a girlfriend?"

27

My friend was thorough. I blew out a breath, wishing she'd stop talking about the man. "He was single the last time we spoke, for whatever that's worth."

"Relax, Sadie, I'm just teasing you," Tanya's said with a softer voice as she toned down her assault. "Come over to my place tonight. I'll open a bottle of bourbon and we'll watch a sappy romance, how does that sound?"

"I'd rather watch a thriller or sci-fi." An evening at Tanya's sounded good.

"I have to warn you, Darcy might be there. She's been coming over a lot lately—and romances are all she wants to watch." Tanya rolled her eyes. "Even though she starts crying five minutes in."

The rain subsided, and a shard of sunlight poked through the clouds, slicing the street in half. People started leaving the tents. The smell of smoke from the grills still floated on the wet air. I pulled out my phone and checked the radar. There would be a lull in the rain for about an hour, just long enough for everyone to do the last of their shopping and reach their cars, wrapping up the last day of the festival.

But the weather wasn't the only reason I checked my phone. Seeing there weren't any new emails or text messages, I put the phone away and returned my attention to Tanya.

"Is she still pining over Raymond Russo?"

"She's not like you or me, Sadie. Darcy is tender hearted and to her, relationships are more about love and romance than sex."

"They're having sex?" I leaned forward, holding my breath.

"Of course not!"

Tanya was protective of her younger sister, although Darcy was twenty-four and certainly not a virgin.

"I didn't think they got past a couple of lunch dates."

"They didn't. Darcy has a crush on him. I think it's the appeal of someone new to town, and that he actually reads books. It's nearly impossible to find a fellow around here who goes to the library."

I nodded. True. Poor Darcy had been looking for her Prince Charming since she was ten years old and she thought she might have found him in our new coroner, an east coast transplant. "She should forget about him."

Tanya's eyes flared. "Has he finally contacted you?"

I shook my head. Now that it had stopped raining and the sun had popped out, the air became thick and steamy. The band struck up again and people moved along the street as if they hadn't just been nearly washed away.

Russo was a sore subject and a recurring question for the past several weeks.

The Yankee transplanted to Kentucky at the beginning of summer, did a brilliant job and even helped solve a few cases until he requested a week or two off to head home for some undisclosed family matter. That was nearly six weeks ago and in all that time, he hadn't called or texted. From the beginning, I'd thought the appearance of the smart young coroner had been a miracle, and one not likely to last. After all, who moves from a civilized place to Possum Gap? Still, for all my reservations about hiring Russo, he'd kind of grown on me during his short stint here.

I was sure Russo was gone for good. For whatever reason, he'd needed a break from city life and after some time in the wilderness, had decided to move back east for good. It would have been nice if he'd emailed me a resignation letter or at least made a damn phone call so I knew what was going on. After four overdose deaths and a drunk thirty-eight-year-old who drowned in his swimming pool last week and having to send all the bodies to neighboring Wilcox County for autopsies, I was saltier than ever over Russo's ghosting.

"For whatever reason, Russo decided not to return. I gave him the benefit of the doubt for a few weeks, but I'm done being patient. It's time to start hunting for a new coroner," I said.

"I understand why you've been so distant lately. Like Darcy, you miss Russo, but for different reasons."

"That about sums it up." I finished off the cup and stood up. "Thanks, Miley." I waved at the blonde-haired woman from across the tent, then turned back to Tanya. "Do you want to walk with me? I better find Chloe and see what her plans are for the evening."

Tanya joined me as I stepped into the sunshine. Dark-rimmed clouds circled the town, but the sun shined on Possum Gap like it was in the eye of a hurricane.

I handed her back the jacket and she bumped into my side with her hip, snorting. "Haven't you heard of a cell phone?"

"Yeah. I actually want to sneak up on my kid and see if she's with Lucian Denham."

"Oh, is that cute boy in her sights?"

"I don't know. Her phone rang the other morning and when I picked it up and handed it to her, I saw his name."

"What did Chloe say?" Tanya had the rare ability of being able to have a conversation without looking where she was going and not fall flat on her face.

"She mumbled about a school project and ran out of the room." I pressed my hand into my forehead. "I'm not ready for dating."

Tanya rubbed my back. "It's inevitable—and so is that glass of bourbon."

I cracked a smile. Since my parents were both gone and I had no siblings, Tanya was the next best thing to family I had. I felt a sense of comfort that she would be there for me when things got tough with my kid, and at Chloe's age, there were bound to be rough days ahead.

Tanya looped her arm around mine tightly and jerked me to a full stop. "Turn left, left—go!"

"Sadie!"

Tanya's warning came a few seconds too late for me to look up and see my ex heading straight for us.

I didn't care about being rude to the father of my kid, but since Ted was Possum Gap's county attorney, it would be unprofessional to run the other way. But boy, oh boy, did I feel like doing just that.

"I'm in a hurry, Ted. What do you want?"

My ex was six feet tall, had a soccer player's wiry body, and his wavy hair was always perfectly styled. As far as human beings went, he wasn't the worst. Ted had been my high school prom date. The night went too well, and we had Chloe nine months later. We married because we thought it was the right thing to do. We found out quickly that, other than sex and fishing, we had nothing in common and couldn't stand each other. Ted also drank too much and had a roving eye. Supposedly, he was reformed from both vices, but I didn't believe it. His new girlfriend, Sandra, was just as fake and irritating as he was. They were perfect for each other.

I heard her perky voice before I spotted her. She wore high heels, and a blue floral dress, and stood in a tight cluster with her girlfriends, chatting up a storm and completely ignoring Ted as he lengthened his strides to catch me. Who wore heels to an apple festival?

"Hello, Tanya," he asked in breathless voice, quickly facing me. Ted was frightened of Tanya, even before our divorce. "Did you get my message?"

"What message?" I really didn't know what he was talking about.

His eyes closed for an instant as he sucked in a breath. He hated when I didn't respond as quickly as he thought I should. I avoided him like a summer cold and he knew it.

"Sandra and I are going to Gatlinburg tomorrow and we'd like Chloe to come along." His words tumbled out of his mouth in a choppy fashion. For a man who was cool under pressure in the courtroom, he sure was a mess when it came to his daughter.

Tanya made a humming noise, squeezed my arm and mumbled, "I'll meet up with you in a few minutes at the ice cream truck."

I gave her a curt nod without taking my eyes off my ex. Even though it had been years since our divorce, speaking to Ted still gave me heartburn. I wouldn't let him know that, though.

I kept my voice pleasant. "It's up to Chloe. She's old enough to make up her mind about taking a last-minute trip with her dad."

"I messaged you a week ago—"

I cut him off. "Do you think a week is enough time? Really, Ted? She'll miss three days of school."

Ted leaned in. For a change, he wasn't giving up so easily. "Did you even mention it to her?"

"Actually, I did. I don't think she's going to join you, but if you want her to go so badly, why didn't you ask her yourself?"

The idea of Chloe being away for a few days was unsettling, but it was kind of a relief at the same time.

Long hours at the department left me feeling guilty that my kid was eating dinner alone when I couldn't make it home on time.

Ted let out a long, ragged breath, shifted his weight back and forth, and stared at his tennis shoes before looking back up. "If you tell her she should come with us, she'll do it." He blew out again. "Come on, Sadie, I want to make a connection with our daughter before she's grown up and gone. Can't you help me out this once?"

I almost laughed. Ted had waited until Chloe was sixteen to finally pay attention to her, and now he wanted me to make it all better. I probably wouldn't be so salty if I hadn't juggled work and raising a child by myself while my ex spent years running around with women until he finally settled on Sandra. I had completely given up a social life for Chloe, and Ted had put her second to his drive to have a good time.

For all of that, I felt a slight tightening of my chest when I looked at Ted's droopy face. He still had a chance to repair some of the damage he'd done, and Chloe needed a father figure in her life. The deciding factor was that deep down, I knew it was best for my daughter and had little to do with Ted's change of heart regarding fatherhood.

"I'll talk to her, but she's sixteen, Ted. She doesn't listen to me anymore."

Ted's face lifted and he smiled. For an instant, I saw the star soccer player I'd had a crush on in high school. The vision faded and the older version of Ted stood in its place. "You're wrong about that. That girl respects you greatly. She's just at an age where she doesn't want you to know it."

Praise from Ted made me uncomfortable. I turned on my heel. "I'll tell her to call you either way."

"Thank you!" Ted said to my back.

I'd taken a few steps when my phone buzzed in my pocket. It was my first deputy, Buddy Gallenstein.

"What's up?" I asked.

"You better get down to the river at the old dock off Fleshing Road, and right quick," Buddy said. The usually laidback giant of a man's voice was edgy, and I began taking long strides in the direction of my truck. I would text Tanya later. She was used to me up and disappearing because of a call. I could count on my best friend to bring Chloe and my maple syrup home.

"What did you find in the water?" It was an assumption, but given his location, it was my first thought.

"A body, Sadie. A teenager's body."

3

LUCINDA

Rays of sunshine pierced the thick clouds making the sky look like heaven's glorious gateway. As I flicked the reins sending Goliath into an extended trot, I lifted my chin to catch the warmer breeze. Indian summer was attempting to push back the rush of cooler temperatures of the day before. Inhaling the sweet smell of damp earth and decaying leaves, I settled into the buggy seat and smiled. It was always nice when I had the opportunity to travel without the children. I could enjoy my own thoughts and the peace of being alone for a change.

The rhythm of Goliath's hooves striking pavement lulled my senses and I swayed from side to side, catching glimpses of neighbors doing their evening chores or children playing in yards. On the seat beside me was the blue and yellow crib quilt I'd made for Diana Coblentz's newborn and on the floorboard beneath it was a pot full of freshly made chicken and dumplings. When I tilted my head and sniffed the air, I caught the scent of the cherry pies that were wrapped and stored next to the pot. Diana already had five children, ranging from three years up to fifteen, and the food would be a pleasant surprise for the family. I'd purposely waited to visit my friend until a few weeks after the birth because it was about the time when the rest of the community's support began to dwindle, and Diana's husband would be working longer hours to bring in their pumpkin harvest.

The smile on my face grew. I couldn't help it. The thought of holding Diana's baby boy was appealing. My Phoebe was fast approaching two years old, although it seemed like just yesterday that she came into the world.

If James had his way, we'd be working on our fourth, but I wasn't so sure about another baby. I was blessed to have a patient husband who honored my wishes above his own. But when I spent time around newborns, the desire to have another one blossomed in my mind.

Saretta King waived a hand as she collected mail from the box, and I returned the favor. To the left of the King's farmhouse, stretching for several hundred acres, was a field of sunflowers. The giant yellow petals flicked in the wind as the clouds parted, spraying a fine glow over the glorious plants. "Such a lovely time of year," I muttered to myself.

Diana's family farm was one of the last Amish properties you passed before exiting the settlement. As the
large, perfectly manicured acreage slipped away, the
land became hillier and the earth rockier. More and
more trees popped up and English households became more abundant.

I tugged on the reins, slowing Goliath to make the
turn onto Dark Hollow Road. It was a shortcut that
would shave several miles off the trip so that I could
reach my friend's home before dusk. But I had never
traveled this way before without James.

Taking another glance at the sky, I reckoned that
I had another thirty minutes or so before the setting
of the sun. I knew the trip back would be in the dark,
but I hoped to unload the buggy with some daylight
to spare. I did however make a mental note of how
quickly the days were shortening. The change of season was a mixed blessing. On the one hand, there were
less hours to finish outside chores, and on the other,
I suddenly was gifted with another couple of hours of
reading time in the evenings. There was a particular
book inside my nightstand drawer I'd bought the previous spring and couldn't wait to dive into. It was labeled as a historical family saga and was set in Ireland.
I enjoyed peeks into other places and times, but what I
really looked forward to was the romance.

I wouldn't tell anyone, not James or even Martha.
I'd always been fond of romance stories, the kind
with impossible relationships and couples who faced

challenges that were ultimately overcome and they found their happy ever after.

I'd married young and could easily boast to have picked the perfect man. Other than the interest of an older man, who eventually became Possum Gap's bishop, my love life had been nonconsequential. My husband was my soulmate and I was content, so my interest in romance wasn't because I missed something in my own life. No, it was because my relationship was neat and tidy, and it was fun to read about those who weren't so blessed as James and me.

Hearing Goliath's heavy breathing, I tugged the long reins, slowing the black gelding down to a walk. Glancing around, I realized I hadn't planned the trip well. True to its name, Dark Hollow Road darkened as we entered a place where large poplars and oaks stretched across the roadway, their branches reaching to touch each other. They swayed with the breeze, dappling the pavement where the last spurts of the day's sunshine managed to break through the canopy.

It felt oppressive to suddenly leave the open farmland and be surrounded by forest. I had planned this impromptu change of course all wrong. In my musings, I'd lost track of time. Now, Goliath was tired and he had to walk for a while. His slower speed would triple the time it would take to pass through the dreaded stretch.

I snapped my head around, peering into the shadows on each side of the road. The birds were quiet here

39

and the still air beneath the trees had a stale quality. When we passed the gravel road to the left, I frowned. Several dented mailboxes were lined up on a board that was attached to a pair of weathered-looking posts. Paint peeled from the boxes and the numbers were barely distinguishable. Golden rod plants filled the gaps below the boxes and the colorful weeds managed to give the rundown appearance of the mailboxes a happy pop of color.

Wrinkling my nose, I wondered why some Englishers didn't mow their properties when they had fancy, motorized riding machines to do so. Laziness, I assumed.

James had told me that the potholed road led to Jewelweed Hollow, a place where a number of Englishers from the same family resided. He had warned me to never dally here and to be wary of approaching vehicles from behind or ahead. I usually did as he asked and in my mind, I could hear him scolding me for my silly daydreaming.

Movement caught my eye, and I gripped the reins harder, ready to snap them on Goliath's rump to get him moving in a hurry. I saw a flash of tan, then white spots. Letting out a sigh, I chuckled. Only a fawn and her mama trekking through the woods.

Sweat trickled between my breasts and I wiped the wetness away by rubbing the fabric of my hunter green dress into the crevice. The hills on either side rose, turning the roadway into a narrow, winding channel through dense vegetation. I held my breath as I passed the mailboxes, only exhaling when they grew small in the side mirrors.

I could see the light ahead, past the leafy branches and the sight was wondrous. Beyond the gap were color-splashed hills, the same ones that I could see from my kitchen window. The sight settled my nerves somewhat, but then my mind drifted back to Charlie Baker. This part of the woods was younger and the trees scraggly, like the place where the hunting cabin was located—the one where the poor girl lost her life.

The air was similarly heavy here, almost as if it was closing in around me and my horse. The next mailbox looked the same as the others, only it rose from a mound of dry dirt in a lonely fashion. The box tipped forward and I wondered, with the flip door hanging open, how the envelopes didn't fall out.

Unlike the driveway that led into Jewelweed Hollow Road, this was a narrow one that was partially covered in overgrown grass and weeds. Tire tracks flattened the grass and when I peered up the lane, I could just barely make out the front porch of a cabin, tucked back into the woods. In the front yard was a rusty old blue pickup truck and articles of clothing hanging from the porch rafters, obscuring the cabin's door from view.

I caught a whiff of something dead and blew out a breath then held it again. The prickling sensation along my arms and the back of my neck made me wish I'd taken James up on his offer to drive me over to

Diana's. But that would have meant bringing the children and staying only a short time. When the offer had been made, I had wanted some time to myself and now, I regretted my selfishness.

The sound of wings flapping and a sharp screech directed me to where the awful stench came from. The bloated carcass of a deer lay several feet past the tree line and only a stone's throw from the cabin's driveway. One, two, three—I counted seven buzzards hopping over the deer, ripping at the rotting meat with their black beaks.

A screaming howl made my heart stop beating.

Out of nowhere, a pair of large brindle-colored dogs streaked out of the woods, aiming for Goliath's hooves. The gentle giant came alive, tossing his head and breaking into a trot as the dogs yapped and snapped at him. The bigger one jumped up, planting its front paws onto Goliath's side. The great horse sped up more and shook his body, causing the buckles on the harness to clink loudly.

I half stood up from the bench. "Shoo! Go away you beasts!"

Never needing a whip on Goliath, I didn't have one handy, but I did have the bushel of apples in the back seat.

Grabbing for one, I nearly lost my balance, bracing my legs further apart and planting my feet firmly on the floorboard. I let it fly and my aim was true. The dog yelped but didn't stop attacking. I tossed another apple and missed, then another, hitting the smaller dog's back. My tactic riled the dogs even more.

Goliath kicked out, striking the larger of the two and it made a sickening yelp before dropping away from the black horse and falling to the ground. In a flash of red, I saw blood coming out of the dog's mouth. With only one dog snapping at his belly, Goliath surged forward causing me to flop backwards onto the seat.

I didn't try to slow the horse. I wanted away as much as he did. Craning my neck, I looked out the window where one dog lay prone on the pavement.

A pang of sympathy for the dog constricted my chest, but I couldn't focus on my emotions. The smaller dog still chased Goliath and when a gunshot boomed, my horse broke into a canter. I started pulling back to slow him down before he hurt himself or both of us.

"Damn fucking Amish! Look what your fucking horse did!" a man's voice shouted from behind and the speed of time slowed as my heart pounded in my chest.

In the side-view mirror, I saw a tall, thick body and a scruffy black beard. The man's chest was bare except for wide band suspenders stretching over his shoulder blades. The pants he wore were faded denim and his boots were as black as his facial hair.

The man whistled and the remaining dog stopped its attack, running back towards its owner. My gaze returned to the road and a second gunshot rang out. My heart dropped into my stomach, and I felt ill.

He shot his own dog.

Goliath broke from the tree cover, which gave way to a cornfield on the right and grassy field on the left.

Goliath didn't mean to hurt the dog—he was protecting himself from the dogs and reacted as any horse would.

I should go back and apologize—that is the right thing to do.

But I didn't get the chance to. My usually well-behaved horse was still agitated and lurched forward, throwing his head to the side. He grabbed the bit in his mouth and flipped it and all of my tugging didn't do any good. The giant horse sped up, breaking into a gallop.

"Goliath!" I shouted, sitting down and planting my black tennis shoes firmly on the front wall of the buggy.

Wind gushed in through the open windows and my heart pumped so wildly, I feared it would explode. The colorful hills blurred before my eyes. My only thought was for my horse's safety when suddenly, there was a roar of an engine and from out of nowhere a red pickup truck appeared.

Using the shoulder, the vehicle overtook us. I only caught a glimpse of the man driving. His brown hair was tied back in a ponytail. He didn't have a proper beard, just a dark covering growth around his jaw.

The truck shot forward, swerved, and was in front of Goliath.

The horse threw his head up as the truck slowed.

With fencing on either side of the road, Goliath was hemmed in and could do nothing but reduce his speed in order to avoid hitting the back of the pickup truck. There was a certain amount of finesse in the way the driver kept the truck steady and adjusted speed to accommodate the horse. Finally, after a minute of doing this, Goliath dropped his head and I let the reins loosen.

Goliath slowed to a bouncing trot and by the time we reached the quiet intersection of the road that Diana lived on, he was breathing hard and walking again, fully under my control.

I realized I hadn't taken a breath the entire time and quickly drew in a huge gulp of air. The sun dipped below the hills and a breeze blew through the windows as the sky became streaked with swaths of pink and orange. It was quite a sight, one I was glad to see while still seated on the buggy's bench and looking beyond Goliath's large, flicking black ears. Besides exhaustion, my horse appeared to be fine after his explosion of speed.

The red truck pulled over and when the buggy reached it, I stopped Goliath. His sides heaved, but he was beginning to breathe easier.

I leaned out the window. "Th-thank you, s-sir. You…saved the day!" I swallowed the rush of adrenaline, forcing a smile.

Judging from the thin lines crinkled around the man's blue eyes and his muscled arms and shoulders, I gauged him to be a few years older than me. He wore a faded gray t-shirt with a funny-looking leaf on the front and even if he hadn't just assisted me in slowing down my runaway horse, I would have liked the nature-loving man.

"Glad I could help," he said with a drawl. Where I was still breathy and shaking, he was as calm as an old man out for a Sunday afternoon drive. I envied his composure.

"What made you think you could slow my horse with your truck?" Now, Goliath hung his head. The way it was turned to the side, and I saw one of his eyes close.

The man's grin deepened, and I wondered what he thought was so funny.

"Ma'am, I rescue damsels in distress on a regular basis. That's why I installed a turbo engine—for situations just like this one."

He winked and I stared back at him, replaying his words in my mind.

When I didn't immediately answer or laugh or whatever he expected, his smile disappeared. "I pulled out of the lane back there"—he gestured with his head—"and saw you galloping past me, I thought you needed some help." The grin returned. "It seemed to me if the gelding didn't have open road in front of him, he'd settle down."

I swiveled in my seat and looked back at the way we'd come from. Tree branches curled around the road, making it appear small. With twilight upon us, it almost looked like the entrance into a black hole.

"I'm Lucinda Coblentz. My husband James will want to thank you for your assistance." I spoke without turning my head toward him. I was still staring back into the woods. "Won't you stop by our farm to meet him tomorrow? I'll make you a pie and send you home with a roasted chicken dinner."

"That's mighty tempting. I do love pie."

I hardly heard him answer when I glanced his way. "You spoke of a lane? The one next to the trailer over there?"

I had been so caught up in stopping Goliath, I hadn't noticed the Englisher's trailer—the same one that Albert Peachy liked to visit.

The man sat up a little straighter. His smile was gone and his jaw tense. "Aw, yeah. My cousin and his teenaged boy lives there." I continued to stare, and he offered more information. "I stopped by to check in on the family. The boy is there alone most of the time because of Dale's work schedule."

He scratched his chin and added, "Not that you care about any of that."

I jumped at the opportunity. "Actually, I do." From this distance, the trailer looked even smaller and unlivable than I remembered. There were several dented-up cars in the yard, and one had the hood up. Weeds grew tall in front of the front porch—more of a slanted stoop. An ancient oak tree in the front yard had branches that spanned far enough to shade both the trailer and the road. Its yellow leaves fluttered and it struck me that even though the Englisher's home was shabby, the tree didn't care, standing just as brilliantly as it would anywhere else.

"Was there an Amish boy there?" I asked. The man's face became slack, and I knew he was confused. "Or have you ever seen one of my people—a fourteen-year-old boy—hanging around the trailer? I heard your family might have befriended him." The man dipped his head and I began to feel silly. "Sometimes our young'uns rebel. And when they do, it's usually to an Englisher's home to watch TV or listen to music."

He shook his head, puckering his lips. The firm set of his jaw gave me the impression he was very serious. "No, ma'am. I haven't seen any Amish kids hanging out with Wade. But that doesn't mean they don't. I only drop by every so often."

I nodded, letting out a breath. "It's probably nothing, but one of our boys didn't return home the other night. Even if the boy changed into English clothing, you would notice him. He has curly blond hair and a"—I searched for the best way to describe Albert—"pleasant face."

The man nodded. "I'll ask around." His eyes shifted back towards the ever-darkening tree line. "Mind me asking what set your horse off? Buggy horses are usually so well behaved."

I frowned as the memory of the dogs attacking Goliath and then the ugly, bare-chested man screaming came to life inside my head.

Then the gunshot…

I shook my head to clear the troublesome thoughts. "Dogs chased after Goliath. He normally wouldn't have been so vexed by the beasts, but they were ferocious. His kick injured one of them and then a man came out—" I abruptly stopped talking and licked my lips, before drawing in a deep breath. The roadway was quiet except for the frogs that began croaking in the ditch. The air turned a wispy gray color. "He was angry about what my horse had done." I looked my savior in the eye. "He shot his dog, sir. I think the noise affected my already agitated horse and that's why Goliath got away from me."

The man grunted and scowled. He looked like he'd just bitten into something foul tasting. "You must be talking about Cooter Calhoun. He's a piece of work. And don't go fretting about his dogs. They're dangerous. Last spring, one of them took a chunk out of Wade's calf when he rode his bike by Cooter's place." The man made a humming sound. "It caused a row with my kin. Grandmother Gerrie was fit to be tied. The only reason Cooter didn't have to put the dog down was because his mama and Grandmother are distant kin and were friends when they were kids." He offered a small smile. "Your horse did everyone in the hollow a favor."

The man sure seemed appreciative, but I felt terrible and my hands continued to shake. The sky grew darker by the minute. "I must be on my way. Please stop by for the pie and chicken, Mr. ..." My cheeks heated. "I never did get your name."

"John—John Dover," he replied politely.

"I can hardly believe you're a Dover, you're so nice." The words slipped out of my mouth without thinking and I sucked in a breath at my rudeness.

John Dover's eyes twinkled, then he began to laugh. It wasn't just a chuckle either. He erupted into a full-blown belly laugh. Even Goliath perked up, turning his sweaty head towards the Englisher's pickup truck.

"I shouldn't have said such a thing, Mr. Dover!"

Mr. Dover's hand shot up. The other he used to rub his mouth, trying to control his mirth. Once he'd settled down, he said, "You only said the truth, ma'am. And please, call me John. Mr. Dover makes me feel old. I'm only thirty-four."

The man's smile was contagious, and I smiled back. "Will you stop by to meet my husband and for the food?"

John looked sideways at me as he put the truck into drive, and it began rolling away. "I might do just that." He hit the brakes and swiveled in his seat. "Ma'am, I wouldn't drive back by Cooter's. No reason to rile him further."

Sage advice. "I'll take Brimstone Road. It's three miles further and I was in a hurry to reach my friend's farm." I glanced at my wristwatch. "And here I am, running late by fifteen minutes. Shortcuts aren't always the quickest way, I reckon."

"Lesson learned. Stay safe." John's hand went out the window. He waved as he slowly pulled away.

A glance at the floorboard brought relief. The pot and pie were not disturbed. I drew in a deep breath and blew it out before I snapped the reins, sending Goliath into a trot. I wouldn't mention any of this to Diana. She had a new baby to concern herself with and it was my fault for daydreaming and deciding on the shortcut.

As Goliath trotted along and the wind stirred through the cab, I risked a glance in the side-view mirror. The forest was dark, and the vegetation created a natural wall. It was almost as if nature herself kept intruders away.

I wasn't welcomed in that place and would stay away from now on.

4

SADIE

When I stepped out of the cruiser, I had to hop several puddles to reach Buddy. At least the rain had stopped. Although the wind stirring the trees sent dribbles of water onto my head. A hawk screeched from somewhere overhead, but I didn't see it. The tree cover was too thick here along the Puissant River. Pushing aside the wet branches, I stepped carefully, searching the ground for tracks—either from a person or vehicle. The heavy downpour had erased any evidence that might have been present that morning. Of course, finding the body at this bend in the river certainly didn't mean the corpse had originated here. It likely traveled some distance, maybe even miles, before it became lodged on the boulders below the embankment.

Buddy's patrol car and the ambulance were the

only other vehicles present, and my first deputy and the pair of EMTs were standing on the edge, looking down the slope when I arrived.

Afternoon light filtered through the clouds onto the rocks below. It was easily a thirty-foot drop and I had butterflies in my stomach as I looked over the edge. I didn't do well with heights and the inside of my head felt like it swelled, then my vision started to spin as vertigo threatened to force me back from the edge.

I kept my feet firmly planted in the dirt and swallowed the queasy sensation down as I surveyed the scene below. The pale, puckered skin stuck out against the grainy gray of the boulder it rested on. Following a dry summer, the river level was low, exposing rocks that normally wouldn't be visible. The body was positioned face up. The river had softened the limbs and the head was bent sideways. Water lapped over the feet. A young male, probably a teenager. Fair hair, slender physique. Just a kid. Damn.

"Do we have any idea who it is or how long he's been in the water?" I asked, still staring at the body. Now that I was distracted, I forgot about the height and my stomach settled.

Buddy answered. "I made a few calls to the adjoining counties, and no one matching this kid's description has been reported missing."

David spoke up. "I'm not a coroner but considering we can determine the sex and approximate age, I would guess he went into the river fairly recently."

David had been with Possum Gap's emergency response team for seventeen years. His gray eyes had seen all kinds of crazy shit, and I valued the sensible, calm way he went about his job. I agreed with his assessment, but I had so many more questions. I needed Russo.

I lifted my gaze and searched the hillside. "How are you going to bring the body up?" I asked no one in particular.

Bran made a whistling sound. "Might be better to try to reach it from the water. There's a dock about a half mile north of here. We could put a canoe in and get the body out that way."

Bran was twenty-four and spent most of his free time camping, kayaking, and hiking. He used to run track on the Possum Gap High School team, but sometime after graduating, he'd decided the wilderness was his thing. For two years he'd tried to grow a beard and only managed to sprout a few crinkly hairs on his chin. I was sure he'd love to spend some time on the river even if it was to retrieve a corpse in the process.

"Not a bad idea," Bobby mused.

"The body has been contaminated by the water anyway. Won't make much difference, I reckon," David added.

A dozen thoughts crossed my mind. We had a teen, probably a drowning victim, who hadn't been reported missing. The Puissant was a wide, ragged river that was accessible by the Glory Acres Lake system and a handful of smaller tributaries. This stretch was by far the most treacherous. During the rainy season, there were Class 4 rapids upstream from here. Downstream, the river quieted and roughly three miles away there was a campground that would be closing for the season the next week. If the body hadn't gotten hung up here in the bend, it might have washed up on the stony little strip of beach where kids played.

"If we go that route, the next place to pull a canoe out of the water is the campground." My gaze skimmed each of the men. "Do we really want to do this in such a public way?"

"The campground is full, that's true," Buddy said as he scratched his fingers through his white hair.

Buddy was fifteen years my senior and could have been elected to the head position if he'd been more motivated. The burly man towered over everyone in town at six foot seven. His full head of snowy white hair with matching beard contrasted in a startling way with his tanned face and broad features. For as long as I could remember, Buddy had white hair. Someone had told me that not long after his own brother drowned in the Puissant River, Buddy's hair turned snow colored. He had been only fifteen at the time of the accident. I often thought that if you combined Clint Eastwood's and Santa's DNA, you'd come up with Buddy. At first glance, he was intimidating. Once you got to know him, you quickly found that Buddy was a great big softy who would give you the shirt off his back in a snowstorm.

Buddy had no interest in leadership. Being a good soldier came naturally to him. He was loyal to a fault and had an opinion about everything.

I wondered if seeing this drowning victim brought up unpleasant memories about his brother's death, but when I studied his weathered face, I saw only determination to get the current job done. Buddy was like that. He had the ability to compartmentalize his life in a way that I only wished I could.

I stretched my neck as I inched closer to the edge to get a better view of the terrain below. "Couldn't we bring a stretcher down over there?" I pointed to a narrow path that was probably a deer trail. Branches blocked the path in several places, and it was steep enough that if you tripped, you'd tumble the rest of the way straight into the rocks bordering the river's edge.

David whistled. "Going down will be a little rough. Coming back up is what I'm worried about."

"I think there's less chance of evidence being contaminated and it will be a lot quicker if we keep him on land." I turned to Buddy. "If the four of us work together—"

"Five."

Russo stood right behind us. He wore his usual blazer, khaki pants, and crooked smile.

"The possibility of turning a canoe over in the river is too great to chance. If there are any clues on that body, I plan to find them."

Russo slapped Buddy on the back as he walked past him, so close to the edge that the toes of his loafers hung over the edge. Buddy snorted and was about to speak, but I finally got over the shock of Russo materializing out of nowhere and found my voice.

"What the hell, Russo! You've been gone for weeks, haven't answered your phone or replied to emails, and you suddenly show up out of the blue along a riverbed?"

Russo spared a few more seconds to look down at the body before he went straight to where I'd just pointed out was the only place to descend from.

"I wasn't expecting my first day back to be so exciting." Russo spoke with the same controlled edginess I remembered. "I arrived in town an hour ago and my first stop was the department to see what I'd missed. When the call came through dispatch, I jumped in my car and headed over." He snickered. "Thank God for GPS."

We stared at each other. Russo's face was lit up and expectant, as if he found my agitation entertaining. The northerner had probably prepared for this meeting and rehearsed exactly what he'd say. The wind was blowing again and the clouds shifted, concealing the sun which was already low over the eastern hills. We'd run out of light soon enough. And there was a body below that required our immediate attention. This conversation with Russo would have to wait. We had much more pressing matters to deal with. My heart rate was steady and strangely, for having a mysterious corpse on my hands, relief flooded my insides. I didn't think Russo would return to Possum Gap, and yet, he was back.

I snorted, then turned back to Buddy. "Russo and I will head down there. Call Darcy and tell her to get back to the office. I want her to reach out to every jurisdiction within a hundred miles and to check the national database." Pausing as I walked past Bran and David, I told the guys, "Better make sure you have some tread on your shoes. You're going to need it."

It took all of ten minutes to traverse the rocky bare patches that led to the river's edge. I spent part of the time on my butt and even Russo slid right into me at one point. My heart raced the entire way, but I kept my eyes locked on the body and that kept me from losing it. Once my feet were on sort of level ground, I blew out a sigh of relief and stopped to catch my breath.

Russo jumped ahead and didn't stop until he knelt beside the body. I was impressed when he pulled out a small notepad and pencil and immediately began taking notes.

When I joined him beside the body, he already had surgical gloves on and he started talking. I listened, focusing on the sockets where eyes should have been. It didn't take a doctorate to know fish had nibbled them until they were gone.

"To answer your earlier question"—he glanced up and flashed a grin—"that I heard when I arrived, this is a young male." Slipping the eraser end of the pencil into the corpse's mouth, he continued, "Thirteen to sixteen years old." He poked the skin over the chest a couple of times with the same eraser, making me sway back a little and grimace. Like most coroners and morticians, Russo was cavalier around dead bodies.

"This young man hasn't been in the water very long. Less than a week, but longer than forty-eight hours." Sitting back on his heels he looked up. "Other than today, when was the last big rain in the area?"

I recounted the previous days in my mind before I answered. "Monday, so five days ago." I lifted my brow guessing on the significance but wanting to hear what Russo had to say.

"See these bruises"—he pointed to several large spots along the torso and then the legs—"here, here, and these right there? I believe they're postmortem and caused by the body striking objects in the river. But they had to happen fairly soon after he died to bruise to this extent."

"How do you know he didn't enter the river this morning or last night?" I studied the body with morbid fascination. The soul had left and what remained was a shell of a person I didn't know. Of course, I felt bad for the kid, but he was past saving and now the only thing I could do for him was to figure out what his story was and, if foul play was involved, bring the kid justice.

"I've kept track of the weather here in Possum Gap." He saw my brows rise and added, "It's a habit of

59

mine. Weather conditions affect decomposition, and this part of Kentucky has been relatively cool over the past week so I'm sure the water temps follow suit. The body is bloated and the skin has a rubbery texture, indicating some time in the water. This time of year, there isn't a lot of fish activity in the river, but enough for creatures to go after the eyeballs, which they have in this case. The hair follicles are also starting to come loose." I leaned closer to see as he gave a gentle tug to a wad of hair that would have pulled right out of the boy's head if Russo hadn't let go. "Someone might have tossed him in on Monday through Wednesday is my guess."

I threw up my hands. "Whoa, wait a minute. What makes you suspect he was murdered and this isn't just some kind of accident?" For good measure and trying not to rush my words together, I concentrated on speaking slower. "Or…a jumper. The Puissant bridge is about eight miles north of here. Every few years someone picks the bridge as their way out of a crappy life."

Russo's lips thinned and he sucked in a large breath making me want to argue my case further.

"Besides, Buddy immediately began making calls before I even arrived and no one matching this kid's description has been reported missing. If you're correct and he's been dead for several days at the least, wouldn't you expect a report to have been filed if he disappeared under shady circumstances?"

He smiled tightly and rose to stand next to me.

"He very well might have jumped to his death, but that would be too easy."

I sighed. He was right about that. Seemed here lately, nothing was easy. My mind drifted back to my earlier conversation with Ted. I might have to talk Chloe into going on the trip with her father and Sandra. Even if this kid's death was by suicide or an accident, it was going to be a busy week. If Russo's instincts were correct, my every waking moment would be consumed with the case.

Buddy shouted down. "Sadie, I have someone on the line. You'll want to take this call."

Russo's brows arched before he spoke. "And so, it begins." Then he cracked a smile and bent down to the body.

I trudged back up the steep and rocky narrow path, sparing a glance over my shoulder at Russo. He had a notebook in hand and as he knelt next to the dead youth, he jotted down notes. I could see his lips moving. He was talking to himself.

Russo was an odd bird. He did his job well and even in his thirties, he knew as much about the coroner business as Johnny Clifton had, who'd been at the helm for more than fifty years. I actually liked the Yankee. Russo's dry wit was amusing and although his curious nature could be annoying at times, it was that insatiable thirst for knowledge that made him a great coroner. But there was something about him that hadn't sat well with me from day one. My gut had never steered me wrong, but in Russo's case, all I had to show for my usual sharp instincts was a slight clenching of my stomach. Why had Russo been gone so long, and an even bigger question was why did he come back?

I was out of breath when I finally reached Buddy and he handed his cell phone to me.

Not recognizing the number, I looked up questioningly at Buddy while the phone was away from my face.

"Sheriff Adam Crawford from Wilkins County," he whispered loudly enough that I figured Adam had heard him.

"Hi, Adam. What's up?" When Adam began speaking in his tired, raspy way, I could easily picture his huge bulk spilling over the chair in his office.

"When I got off the phone with Buddy a little while ago, I mentioned to a few others in the office what you all are dealing with over there in Possum Gap and Becky, our secretary, reminded me of a case from about four years ago."

Adam paused to catch his breath. I'd known the man since I was a young'un myself and frankly, I was surprised he'd lived this long. Adam waddled when he walked, which was something that he rarely did. But for his large girth and terrible eating habits, he was a smart guy and an honest man.

He coughed, then cleared his throat into the phone, making me grimace.

"Four years ago, we pulled a boy out of the river, remember?"

I certainly did. "He was sixteen, right? Drowning victim?"

"That's correct. Orville Walker. Billy ruled it an accident, but he was incompetent half the time. That's why I fired his ass last year."

Everyone in these parts knew Billy Dunham was a drunk. I was surprised it took so long to get rid of him, but that was just a passing thought as the entire conversation sunk in quickly. "Okay. What of it?"

"I always had my doubts Orville drowned. He was a straight-A student at Wilkins High and he ran cross country. He was an athlete."

I searched my memories for what I knew about the case. Wilkins County was our neighboring county to the south. The Puissant River flowed from Possum Gap straight through Wilkins. "Didn't Orville go missing a few weeks before he turned up in the river?"

"Four weeks. Billy's report was flawed."

"Because he was under the influence?"

"Something like that." Adam chuckled. "I had a feeling the boy was already dead when he went into the water but didn't have any evidence. Once Billy released the report, the case stopped there."

My mind raced at the possibilities of what he was saying. "So, you think our cases are connected?"

"I have no idea. I just want to put Orville on your radar. I think we fucked up his investigation. It's been four years and there's been nothing here in Wilkins to cause us to reopen the case."

"Ok-ay," I drew the word out. "Where do I begin?"

"Chrissy Coleman. She's a reporter at the *Citizen's Review* newspaper here in town. She followed the case closely." Adam coughed again. It took him several seconds to clear his throat. "Chrissy pestered me to death about the case. She didn't think Orville had drowned accidentally. If I were you, I'd talk to Chrissy."

I nodded my head, gazing down at Russo as he assisted David and Bran load the body onto the gurney. He certainly wasn't afraid to get his hands dirty.

The three men worked quickly as raindrops started falling. It was going to be a bitch getting the body up here, but Russo was right. It was the quickest and safest way to move it.

The already wet branches drooped even more, making the forest seem like it was closing in on us. Mist rose from the rushing water, hovering over the river. I caught one last glimpse of bright golden hair before Bran zipped up the body bag.

"Adam, is there anything else that makes you think our dead kid is related to yours?"

"Buddy mentioned your boy was a blond. Orville was too."

5

RUSSO

I inhaled the crisp, sterile smell of *clean* and glanced around the examination room. Everything was just as I'd left it and I couldn't help smiling. Sheriff Mills might act nonchalant about my sudden reappearance, but she'd missed me. Who wouldn't? I had the kind of skills that were hard to come by in a remote location like Possum Gap.

The room was windowless, but I'd left the door slightly ajar, and I could see the window in my office. Dark clouds covered what the locals affectionately called "hills." They were mountains to me. And the thick vegetation that covered them was impregnable in most places. Sadie laughed when I called Possum Gap the wilderness, but it was true. A few hundred feet behind every business in this town was forest, and the feeling of claustrophobia was strong.

That's probably why I liked driving west into the narrow swath of cropland in the county. Somehow, the farmers managed to keep the jungle at bay and that rather impressed me. Possum Gap's citizens were tough and fiercely freedom-loving individuals, but they always seemed ready to lend a helping hand. You couldn't walk down Main Street without a string of hellos and smiling faces.

The sound of rain pelting the window made me glance up. My office had darkened considerably. Trails of droplets raced down the glass and a flash of lightning made the lights in the examination room flicker. I swallowed, thinking back to the Dover Clan in Jewelweed Hollow. Now, those were some unfriendly types. A real-life clan of hillbillies resided here and even though they grew marijuana, made moonshine, and were probably murderers, they also had a strange sense of honor and loyalty that reminded me of my own family.

Sure, they were dangerous people, but there was order to the chaos.

I shook the thoughts away and slipped on surgical gloves, then pulled the sheet back. Seeing the gray-skinned body sent adrenaline shooting through my veins. *Drowning my ass.* I would bet my Porsche that the kid didn't just fall into the river. The answers to his story might be somewhere on or in his body—and all I had to do was find them. I couldn't wait to tell the sheriff that I was right.

"What do you have for me, Russo?"

Seeing the sheriff grimace, I pulled the paper sheet over the opening to the boy's stomach.

Sheriff Mills was a few years old than me and several inches shorter. Her brown hair was thick, shiny, and shoulder length. She occasionally cracked a joke and smiled often, yet she was a private individual. The sheriff had deep thoughts—her mind was always working things out—and I liked that about her. Because there wasn't an ounce of flirt in her serious body, it was easy to miss her bright blue eyes and high cheekbones. If the woman relaxed for a couple of minutes, she'd be a real looker. But Sadie Mills wasn't a fun kind of person. Her kid and her job were the only things that mattered to her.

The look she gave me now held a hint of expectation and was glad I wouldn't let her down. Turning the tables, I asked, "Do we have a name for him yet?"

She shook her head. "Darcy is working the database and I've shared his postmortem picture with the state bureau. No hits yet."

"For the time being, we'll call him Vic." I picked up my clipboard and glanced over it to find the sheriff standing with arms crossed and feet slightly apart. "We have ourselves a murder case."

Sadie Mills had a great poker face. Calm and collected. The lady sheriff of this hick little town was one cool customer.

"It will take a few days to culture the blood sample,

but because of this," I pointed to the boy's left hand, "I believe he died of sepsis—"

"I didn't notice that at the river!" Sadie interrupted.

I offered her a small smile. The poor sheriff looked horrified that she hadn't seen that the boy was missing his thumb and two fingers on his left hand.

"Don't feel too bad, Sheriff. The way his arm was positioned, bent back under his bloated side, you would have had to look closely. Most people—even law officers—don't allow their eyes to linger on the body of a dead child for too long. It's perfectly reasonable that you only visually skimmed the body, especially since you're a mother yourself. That's what your town pays me to do—the job that no one else wants to."

The sheriff stepped right up to the table and stared down at the boy's face. I watched her features relax as she pursed her lips.

I had misread Sheriff Mills. She was like me. Death fascinated her.

"Sadie," she said tightly. "Stop calling me sheriff. We work together in a small department, no sense in being overly formal." She dipped her chin at the boy's gray face. "Couldn't he have lost his fingers the way he'd gotten all those bruises—by hitting boulders in the river?"

I tilted my head. She was aggravated.

"All right, Sadie it is then." I slipped on a new glove and picked up the hand. Sadie leaned in for a closer look. "These phalanges were cut with a sharp instrument, probably a knife."

I met her gaze for a few long seconds, then returned my attention to the body. In life, the boy's face would have been flushed with color and his wavy blond hair would have fallen over his forehead, nearly covering his right eye. I imagined him flipping it back to see better. He had once been an attractive youth, full of energy and promise. Now, he was a corpse. And no one even missed him, it seemed.

"I'm heading over to Wilkins County this afternoon. I have a lead." She must have seen the disappointment on my face. "When will you be finished here?"

"An hour or so to sew him back up. I must send the samples off for toxicology testing. If you wait, I'd like to join you."

"I don't want to put this interview off, and I need you to take your time on this one. If you're right and it turns out that our John Doe is a victim of murder, we had better take care in building a strong evidential case from the get-go," she said.

I liked Sadie Mills very much. She attempted to stay one step ahead of everyone around her. My cell phone buzzed in my pocket and when I looked to see who it was, my mouth went dry. Trying to look like nothing was wrong, I smiled brightly back at Sadie. "I have to take this. It's the insurance company. A deer ran into my car in West Virginia when I was driving back."

I felt like I was a good liar, but with the way Sadie's eyes narrowed, I wasn't so sure I'd convinced her.

"I was going to ask you about that dent." She cocked her head and stared hard at me. "Almost every week since I became a cop, there's been at least one deer-automobile wreck. But I have to say, I never saw one on top of the truck before." She turned to go, then stopped and artfully raised her brows. "Careful, Russo. You might get away with a fib like that with other people, but not me. Now, I'm more curious than ever why you were gone so long."

After Sadie had left the room and the only sound was the constant rattling of my office window from the wind and rain, I let out a breath. I would have to be more careful with that woman. For a backwoods sheriff in rural Kentucky, she was on the ball.

Blowing out a sharp breath, I crossed the room and searched down the hallway. It was empty. After shutting the door, I pressed the phone to my ear.

"What do you want?" I asked.

As the voice started speaking on the other end of the line, I was too distracted to listen.

The last thing I needed was for Sadie to start snooping into my life. She had the tenacity to find out more than I wanted her to know.

I hoped that as long as the sheriff was knee deep in a murder investigation, she would leave me alone, which was safer for both of us.

6

LUCINDA

This time when I drove past the long gravel driveway, I felt braver. James sat next to me, and Martha had stayed back at the farm with the children. Sliding the window open, I searched through the branches that hung over the driveway like skeletal fingers. The wind and rain of the past few days took most of the leaves off the trees. Now, they covered the ground like a yellow, drenched blanket. The scent of pine needles and mud reached my nose, and I inhaled the earthiness of the cool air.

My heart stuttered when the cabin came into view. James had Goliath at an extended trot as we whisked over the pavement. The view of the cabin was fleeting—there was just enough time to see its brown boards and a raggedy-looking blanket hanging over the porch railing. The remaining dog didn't rush out to chase us. The forest around the cabin was quiet and the pickup truck wasn't in sight.

Craning my neck, I looked back until the driveway was swallowed by trees and darkness even as the sun climbed higher in the sky.

"Lucinda," James spoke my name softly, but my heart still skipped a beat.

"My word, James, don't scare me like that," I chastised, facing forward, and sitting back on the cushioned blue bench.

"All I did was say your name." He chuckled and reached for my hand. When he squeezed, his warm strength chased away the chill that seeing the cabin had caused. "All is peaceful. I did see the stain of blood on the road where the dog must have died."

I swiveled on the seat as my hand went to my heart. "I would have been well served not to hear about it. What are you thinking, James?"

My husband was still as handsome as the first time we courted. His brown beard was longer, thicker, and there were lines around his eyes that hadn't been there before. But his shoulders were also wider and his confidence surer than when he had been a lad.

James was not only my husband, but he was also my best friend. Not many women in the community could make such a statement. Unlike other couples, we were a team. James supported me and never questioned my thoughts or ideas. He encouraged me, like when I stood up to the bishop about allowing the neighborhood kids to go on a weekly horseback ride together or when the ladies from the quilting group wanted to visit an English quilting club at the Possum Gap Public Library to see their techniques and chat about a common love—quilts.

And the same went for supporting me when I worried over things that were probably nothing, such as following the same route from the previous evening. After I'd told James about my experiences—in rather dramatic fashion—he'd listened intently, then offered to take me back around the loop.

I had barely slept a wink and now, with the dawn breaking over the hills, I stifled a yawn with my hand.

"What do you expect to see?" James asked in his overly patient, relaxed way that sometimes made me raise my voice to him.

"The trailer, James. We're going to stop there and ask the residents if they've seen Albert. I told you this before."

James sighed as he scratched his chin with his free hand. The other hand casually grasped Goliath's long reins.

"No, we didn't discuss that at all. I would remember the conversation." He looked straight ahead, not meeting my gaze. "Especially since I think it's foolhardy."

We broke from the wild forest and the air left my lungs in relief. Open farmland where the sun shined down upon us was much more pleasant than the oppressive shade beneath the thick walls of trees at our backs.

"Foolhardy how?" I twisted the material of the hunter green dress I wore between my fingertips. "I saw the Peachy boy myself standing with an English teen in the very same driveway one time when we passed by over the summertime. If he ran away, surely those Englishers will know where he went." I snorted and pressed the wadded piece of material flat. "I wouldn't be surprised if the boy wasn't inside that trailer this very moment playing one of those video games and drinking soda pop."

James chuckled. "Since when are you so severe towards teens flexing their freedoms before joining the Church?"

I turned to him. "Albert is only fourteen."

James shrugged and eyed me cautiously. "We did the same thing. Ran around a bit at that age. You're not an elder, Lucinda, and we have no business or authority talking to Englishers about the boy. It's only been a few days."

"Vivian was missing for hours and look what became of her!" I sucked in my breath, regretting my outburst.

"Is that what's upset you so? You fear for Albert because of what happened to poor Vivian?"

My eyes misted and I quickly wiped them with the back of my hand. I looked away so my husband wouldn't see how raw my emotions were.

"Yah, that is some of it. Evil has descended on our community, dear James. We must be more vigilant."

James' hand moved to my shoulder and he rubbed it. I closed my eyes, enjoying the massaging strokes.

"Lucinda, I promise you, I'll never be lackadaisical again after the nightmare of this past summer. But you cannot live worrying so. Our young people have been running off for short periods of time since the beginning when our great grandparents staked their claim to this valley between the mountains. You'll go crazy if you replay what happened to Vivian on every other young person in the community. It was a freak event. For a troubled girl to hide among us will never happen again."

"Maybe not a girl. There are many faces of evil," I said forcefully, then dropped my voice when the trailer came into view. "There it is, James. Slow the buggy."

James did as I asked and when we came abreast of the tiny tan building, he stopped Goliath and faced me. "You won't let this go, will you?"

"Of course not. It's a simple conversation, nothing to get your beard in a wad." My words probably sounded more confident than I felt.

"I still believe it's a waste of time, although, I know how stubborn you are. If I don't accompany you, you'll come here alone and that is something I will not have."

I forced a tight smile. "Thank you, James."

James clucked to Goliath, navigating the horse to pull the buggy off the road into the grass where the ground was level.

Engaging the brake stick, he flung the door open

and stepped out of the buggy. I followed suit and walked around Goliath, giving him a pat on the neck as I passed by.

When I was next to my husband, he looked over. "What exactly are you going to say?"

"I haven't decided yet." I was being honest.

James shook his head slowly as he led the way. The wooden steps up to the stoop where the front door was were rickety and without a railing, I reached for James and he clasped my hand. We would never hold hands like this among our people, but there were times like this when something upset one or both of us and touching made us both feel better.

At the top of the steps, James looked at me and I nodded. He rapped on the flimsy looking door and stood back.

The glorious maple tree in the front yard hung over the stoop and the breeze rustled its brightly colored leaves. I was admiring the large girth of the tree and its splendid foliage when the door swung open. Turning quickly to the opening, I saw the boy I'd seen at the trailer before. The lad was close to Albert's age, with stringy brown hair and a wide, hooked nose. Pimples littered his face and there was still sleep in his eyes.

He rubbed them and glanced between James and me.

"I'm sorry to bother you at this early hour," James said, thrusting his hand out to the boy. "I'm James Coblentz and this is my wife, Lucinda."

It took the boy several seconds to grasp it and even though I wasn't on the receiving end of the handshake, I could see he had a weak grip.

The boy's face brightened considerably when he looked between our shoulders at Goliath.

"Your horse is a nice one," he said plainly. "Wish I had a horse."

James and I exchanged a glance. The boy was non-plussed about having an Amish couple he didn't know on his front stoop. His friendly tone and greedy eyes as he stared at Goliath put me at ease. I understood why Albert would strike up a friendship with this particular Englisher.

I spoke for James as he wasn't getting to the point quick enough. "Is Albert Peachy here? I've seen him hanging around and thought he might be spending some time with you."

The boy's eyes sharpened as they left the horse, fixating on me. "I haven't seen Albert for a couple of weeks." He suddenly stopped talking as he realized he'd given his buddy away.

I raised my palm and took a step forward. "No worries. What's your name?"

"Wade Blanchard," he answered politely. The way his gaze darted between James and me, I got the feeling he wanted to go back into the trailer and shut the door behind him.

"Well, now, Wade, you have nothing to worry about from us. We're fine with Albert being your friend and spending time with you—"

"That's not what Albert said." His voice held a twinge of whininess in it, and I worked hard not to frown. "He told me he'd get into an awful lot of trouble if you all found out. He said he'd be kicked out of his house and have to move some ninety miles away or something crazy like that."

The boy's agitation was troubling. Albert had given him a negative impression of our people. James remained silent and allowed me to do the talking. "No, that's an exaggeration. Our young people have opportunities to experience the outside world. But that's not a discussion we're here for. You seem like a nice young man and if Albert is your friend, I'm sure you understand why we're concerned. No one in the community has seen him for a few days. If he's been hanging around with you, he won't get into trouble." Wade's brow furrowed with doubt, and I added, "Promise. We only want to know he's safe."

From the corner of my eye, I caught the firm nod of James' head. He liked the way I'd handled the matter.

The boy exhaled, rolling his eyes. "I done told you, I haven't seen him all week. It's strange too. There's a show on TV he likes—a western set in Montana—there's cowboys and cattle, it has everything. He never misses an episode, but he missed this week."

I swallowed the knot that formed in my throat, and it hurt going down. I was about to ask another question when the boy began to back up. "Sorry, I got to go. If I see Albert, I'll tell him you all are looking for him."

He tried to close the door, but my hand stopped it. He looked up with wide eyes.

"Do you know the big fellow with the beard who lives up that way?"

"Cooter? When I nodded, he added, "Everyone around here knows him."

"What do you think of him?"

The boy licked his lips. "Ah, I don't know." He shrugged, then became brave while lowering his voice even though it was just us and him on the stoop and Cooter was nowhere in sight. "He's a jerk. Sometimes he pops his BB gun off at me when I ride my bike by his place. He laughs and waves like it's funny, but I don't like it."

"I wouldn't either," I admitted.

"We're sorry to bother you, young man," James was finished and stepped off the stoop while I lingered there.

"John Dover is your cousin, right?" I asked.

"Sure is." His face brightened. "How do you know Johnnie?"

"I met him the other day on the road. He helped stop my buggy horse when he got away from me."

The corner of Wade's mouth lifted. "That sounds like something Johnnie would do."

Here was my chance to learn more about the nice man who had come to my rescue. "He said he doesn't live in the hollow with the rest of the Dovers. Why is that?"

"Gosh, ma'am, you ask a lot of questions."

"Come on, Lucinda. We're done here." James' voice was not firm, it was pleading.

"I just wondered how that all worked. Someone once told me the Dovers all live in Jewelweed Hollow, but here you are on this side of the forest and from the sound of it, John—Johnnie—lives a little way from here."

"Oh yeah. Well, I'm not a Dover. My mama was. When she died, Mamaw wouldn't let us live over there 'cause she hates my daddy."

"That's unfortunate," I said, feeling instant regret that I'd asked the silly question. I wasn't normally a nosey or gossipy woman.

Wade shrugged. "Ah, it's not a big deal. She gave us this trailer to live in and the land it sits on. It belongs to me. Someday, when I'm old enough, I'll make daddy leave."

From the sounds of it, his grandmother was a practical woman. "Do you think it would be all right for me to visit her sometime and ask if she's seen Albert?" After the words slipped out of my mouth, I held my breath.

"Lucinda—" James said.

I didn't get the response I hoped for. Wade snorted out a harsh laughing noise, then wiped his face. "I wouldn't go up there if I were you, ma'am. My cousins ride ATVs and shoot off guns all the time. It will scare your horse."

Before I had a chance to say anything else, I found myself staring at the closed door with all of its dirty finger smudges. The place could use a woman's touch.

"Come on," James insisted, and I wasted no more time on the stoop. Once I stepped down, we walked side by side to the buggy.

"What was that all about?" James asked.

"James, I know you don't want to hear this, but if Albert doesn't show up soon, we'll have to make a trip down that lane to check with the people who live there."

"Why on earth would we do that?"

"They might know something. Albert probably passed through the same stretch of woods to reach his English friend's trailer." I grabbed his arm, keeping him from climbing into the buggy. "What if Cooter did something to him?"

James pushed his hat higher to wipe his brow. He looked at me with tired eyes. "That's better left to the lady sheriff to do."

My breaths came easier as if a great weight lifted from my shoulders. I threw my arms around James. He tightened and I could feel him looking around even though my face was buried in his chest. When he deemed it safe, he squeezed me back.

In a not-so-subtle way, James had just given me permission to speak to Sheriff Mills. If anyone knew how to find Albert, it would be her.

7

Chrissy Coleman was younger than I expected. Her glasses rested on the tip of her pert nose as she stared at her computer, poking at the keys with quick fingers. The layered blonde waves framing her face made her look like she'd stepped out of the 80s, but there were no wrinkles around her eyes. Instead of heels and skirt that would have been standard dress for this kind of job a handful of years ago, Chrissy's slim form was encased in a gray exercise outfit that managed to appear comfortable and stylish at the same time.

"I'm getting hot, almost there," she chirped.

Leaning back in the chair next to the reporter's desk, I glanced around the expansive room. A long line of windows let light in and offered an excellent view of Wilkins' Main Street and beyond the tree-lined street, the Puissant River. Partitions divided the cavernous space into about twelve workstations. All but two of the desks were empty, showing how hard hit the rise of social media and access to 24/7 news had affected old-school newspapers like the *Citizens Review*.

I could imagine the office buzzing with the sounds of telephones ringing and journalists chattering away as they prepared their stories in the bygone days when the paper's circulation was quadruple what it probably was now. The second floor of the red brick building was empty, except for a round-bodied redhead at the desk closest to the elevator—who Chrissy had already told me sold classified advertisements. I'd only spent a few minutes with the Chrissy, but I guessed the reporter's bubbly personality made up for the lack of employees.

When I introduced myself to Chrissy and explained why I was here, the reporter's mouth dropped open and her eyes bulged. Her excitement to delve back into a four-year-old case was promising and gave me hope that my trip to the neighboring town might not have been in vain.

"So, what is your Vic's description? How old is he for starters?" Chrissy glanced up and as hard as she tried to keep the corner of her quivering mouth from lifting, she failed.

The look of anticipation on her face bothered me but not because I thought it was inappropriate. She was a reporter after all. It wasn't surprising that she'd want a scoop on Possum Gap's floater. What made my stomach roll was that I felt the same way and it sickened me. The rush of adrenaline to find out who the kid was and why he ended up in the river made me ashamed. The boy wasn't much younger than Chloe. He was someone's child—and surely, somewhere, a mother, father, or grandparent missed him.

I drew in a breath and met Chrissy's gaze over the top of her computer. "He's a teenager. I have no idea who he is. There haven't been any hits in the database. He's blond, like Orville, but other than that and his age, I'm not sure why Adam thought my fresh case has to do with your cold one."

Chrissy's lips pursed, then she turned the computer around. I scooted closer and leaned in as the breath caught in my throat. "He *is* very similar," I mumbled while my eyes skimmed over the postmortem picture of Orville and the typed notes on the opposite side of the screen.

"I'm sure Adam told you that I disagreed with Billy's autopsy results." She paused and when I gave a nod, she went on, "I regret to talk ill of the dead, but Billy Denham was a drunk—a functioning drunk, but just barely. If it weren't for the fact that our mayor and coroner were best friends in high school, Billy would never have held onto the job." She gave a frustrated shake of her head. "Luckily, we don't get very many murders in Wilkins, so Billy's ineptness didn't cause too much trouble for the town, until Orville."

"Adam said you believed he didn't drown. What made you come to that conclusion?"

"Orville was a high school track star from a good family. He was dating a pretty girl, had a part-time job at the feed mill and a thirty-two score on his ACT." Chrissy's eyes shifted to the picture of his gray, lifeless body. "The world was his oyster…that was the first reason I didn't believe he'd be a jumper—"

"Billy's report stated a suicide or accidental fall."

"Yes, Orville's body was bruised as if it had fallen from the Turner Bridge just outside of town, but he didn't give any other scientific evidence that Orville was alive when he went into the water."

Letting out a breath, the hopefulness I'd felt a moment before diminished. "The file Adam sent me didn't have anything else in it that pointed to murder," I said.

Chrissy tilted her head. "He relied on the autopsy report. Once it came back with the findings of suicide or accidental drowning, our sheriff closed the case."

"And you still think he made a mistake?" I asked.

"I always have, which means Orville's killer is still out there. Trust me, I haven't slept well for years over this one."

Reporters often had sources of information that cops didn't. Chrissy probably networked through certain citizens that gave her news scoops—the type of people that wouldn't talk to the sheriff or a deputy but would spill their guts to an attractive young woman with a pen and pad.

I poised my own pen over the little notebook resting on my lap. "Okay, what do you have?"

The small, lopsided smile returned to Chrissy's lips. "Orville was missing for close to a month when his body was found in the Puissant. But the autopsy stated he'd only been in the water for a few days—that part of Billy's findings I don't dispute. In the heat of summertime, a body in the water for a month would show a lot more decomposition."

Chrissy paused for effect, and my muscles tensed uncomfortably. The reporter might be on to something.

"There was one finding that ol' Billy couldn't explain, although he tried to."

"What's that?"

"Orville was missing a couple of his fingers."

The rush of adrenaline to my head made it feel like my heart had stopped beating. "On the same hand?"

Chrissy nodded. "Billy said they broke off in the river. That doesn't make sense. Maybe if the entire body was decomposed greatly—sure—but that wasn't the case. Billy scribbled something about it in the report and later, when I asked him about it for the third time, he threatened my publisher with a slander lawsuit. It never would have held up in court." She stood up, glanced around, then sat back down. Even though she'd just checked for eavesdroppers, she still dropped her voice. "My boss is a coward and he didn't want to ruffle the coroner's or the sheriff's feathers. That may be why Sheriff Crawford is encouraging you to look into it. Now that Billy's dead, there's nothing holding him or the newspaper back."

I inhaled slowly, trying to control my eagerness. "The autopsy wasn't included in the paperwork Adam sent over—just his notes. Do you have a copy I can take with me?"

"Of course."

Chrissy dug through a dozen or more sheets until she came to the one she was looking for. After she walked to the copy machine across from her desk, she returned and handed me the copy. I skimmed the report while the reporter continued with her thoughts.

"When I questioned the family, Orville's mom— a single woman working three jobs to pay the bills— had no idea where her oldest son had disappeared to. She was adamant that he wouldn't have run off but with three younger children to care for by herself, she didn't know whether she was coming or going half the time, so I didn't get much of a lead there. Orville's father, who lived in Ohio at the time, was the person who mentioned something that opened the door to a nefarious ending for his son." She stopped talking just long enough to narrow her eyes and cock her head. "Orville told his father that he had made a new friend and who was spending a lot of time hunting with the teenager. But that's where my investigative work ended."

"You didn't interview Orville's friend?" My voice came out harsher than I'd intended.

"Oh, I tried, but I could not get access to the youth no matter what I did."

"Why not?" My curiosity meter went through the roof.

"Because he lived in Possum Gap." Chrissy sat back and folded her hands on her lap.

The jolt I experienced propelled me to the edge of my seat. "What's the kid's name?"

"Dover. Elwood Dover."

8

RUSSO

With its modern décor and Wi-Fi availability, the Possum Gap Café would have fit right into the cultural district in Newark. A few things would have raised brows, though. The approximately six-foot, seven-inch man in the flannel shirt sipping his coffee as he leaned over an outdated-looking computer with his spotted hound dog sprawled next to his giant muddy boots would have earned a second glance, no doubt. And the late afternoon sunbeams shining through the windows made the gun holstered on another patron's hip gleam. I'd gotten used to the exuberance to open carry in the town, but this was the first time I'd seen a lady sporting a gun. The woman's wrinkled face was at odds with her strong, slender body. But it was her bright red hair that caught my eye.

The gun-carrying lady strongly resembled one of the women who'd ridden up on Sadie, Buddy, and I in Jewelweed Hollow when we were investigating the trailer shootings.

Darcy hadn't stopped talking since we'd sat down. I took another sip of my overly sweet cappuccino and refocused on the beautiful yet chatty secretary. When our eyes met, I could tell she suddenly realized that I'd been a million miles away. She sighed heavily, grasped her cup in two hands and lifted it to her mouth. Then her eyes drifted to the windows overlooking Second Street and my gaze followed suit.

I could see rocky, tree-covered hills in the distance. Although there were only a few puffy white clouds dotting the deep blue sky, the weather forecast called for rain and possibly even storms later in the day. The limestone walls of the courthouse and its intricate clock tower stood out from the surrounding green landscape. The building impressed me. It was a pleasant surprise in a struggling town on the edge of the wilderness. It teased at the prosperity of a long-gone era when the people of Possum Gap had money to spend and cared about appearances. Those days were long gone. It was a bloody miracle to get a pothole filled in current times. Small towns across America were facing the same challenges—not enough work to keep their young people around, which caused population numbers to drop and subsequently tax revenue.

But it wasn't just about the money. Although the people here were friendly and genuinely trying to eke out an existence in the place they were born, the rise in drug use and alcoholism was destroying the inner fabric of the community. Broken homes, crime, and hopelessness were overtaking most of the good things the town could boast, like a winning high school football team and this quaint little establishment.

Darcy cleared her throat and my eyes focused on her. I inhaled the rich, nutty scent of the warm brew and smiled at her. She'd straightened her black, kinky curls and wore a pretty floral sundress. The orange clutch purse on the table matched the colors of the flowers on her dress. She could have instantly been teleported into any restaurant in Manhattan and no one would have batted an eye. Darcy Beaumont was a fish out of water in this rusty little town.

The young woman also had a crush on me. Since I was a decade older than her, I could only assume it was because I was someone new in town.

The lift of Darcy's brows made my smile grow. "Why are you so nice to me?" I asked.

Her eyes widened and her mouth dropped open, then snapped shut. I had never even kissed those luscious lips and yet, Darcy had sort of already claimed me.

"Um, because it's the right thing to do and I like you, Russo." She giggled nervously and sipped her latte. "You northerners are a strange lot."

I lost the smile. "How so?"

"You question everything—even when someone is friendly—like you're paranoid or something."

I cracked a smile again. *Oh, if she only knew.* "We aren't an unfriendly lot up north, but we sure aren't as open to conversations with strangers as your people are."

"They're your people now," she reminded me.

She gazed back out the window and a sunbeam landed on her face, causing her dark skin to glow. Darcy would have made it as a model if she'd escaped Possum Gap as a teen.

"Unless you're moving back to New Jersey." She blew out a breath, and in what seemed to be an act of courage on her part, our eyes finally locked. "Is that it, Russo? Have you put in your notice and Sadie hasn't told me yet?"

I'd been informed that the previous coroner, Johnny Clifton, owned the local funeral home and died at the beginning of summer. He worked straight up to the day a sudden heart attack took him out at the age of eighty-four. Since none of his children followed in their father's mortician footsteps, the Clifton family—the founders of this little town—were obsessed with finding just the right person to take over Johnny's business as the mayor and Sadie were in hiring a new coroner. Natural deaths counted for most of Possum Gap's deceased, but with the rise of drug ODs and the occasional backwoods clan killing, the town's officials didn't want to rely on the surrounding counties for resources. I'd interviewed for the job over a Zoom call nine months after graduating from school. I had worked as an assistant coroner in New Jersey for a grand total of six months before I'd picked up and moved across the country to the hills of Kentucky. It was an attempt to distance myself from my family, among other things.

Foolhardy, I learned. Nothing broke family ties—especially not miles.

I set my cup aside. "I plan to stay in Possum Gap for as long as the sheriff will have me."

Darcy sat up straighter. "What does that mean? Sadie thinks you're doing a great job. When you didn't return from your vacation, she wasn't a happy camper, you know. This town will always need you."

My heart experienced a tremor, and I didn't like the feeling one bit. "I can't make any promises because I don't know what the future holds, that's what I'm really saying."

She looked me in the eyes. "Have these trips for coffee and lunch been proper dates? I mean, we're both in agreement that they're dates, right?" Her jaw sagged and her mouth scrunched to the side. "Because Sadie seems to think you're just being polite and too cowardly to be honest about it."

The urge to reach over the table and place my hands over hers was strong, but I resisted. I didn't know where I'd be in a few weeks, let alone a year. It wasn't fair to Darcy to lead her on. But I'd always kept my private life, well, private. I never felt an inclination to explain anything to a woman before, especially not one I wasn't even sleeping with.

I'd never met a woman like Darcy though. She was the perfect combination of poise and self-doubt. She was a bookworm, like me, and possessed a genuinely upbeat nature that offset the sometimes doom and gloom of my profession.

Darcy Beaumont deserved honesty if nothing else.

"There were family matters I had to address back home. I hope those things have been resolved, but I might have to go back for good. I'm kind of in a holding pattern."

Darcy let out another breath, deflating even more. "Can you talk about it? I'm a good listener."

A shadow passed over Darcy's concerned face and I glanced back out the window. Gray clouds were gathering over the town. With the loss of the sun, a sinister vibe wrapped around me.

Damn. I only felt like this before something bad happened.

I finished off the last few drops of my cappuccino and worked to lighten my voice even though my mood had darkened considerably.

"Someday, I'll tell you everything. I promise."

The words slipped out of my mouth unexpectedly. I didn't usually make promises because I had a habit of keeping them. If Darcy knew the truth about me, she wouldn't be sitting there with puppy-dog-eyes right now. Maybe I should be frank and push her away like I did everyone else.

It would be better for her—safer too.

But instead of Darcy pouting or begging or the other usual behaviors, a smile lifted her mouth and her eyes twinkled.

"That's a start, Russo. It's a start." She picked up her clutch and nodded toward the door. "Looks like we might get some more rain. I have to get back to the office."

She began to rise and I swiveled my head. The armed lady with the red hair was gone and so was the lumberjack dude. The café was empty except for a grandmotherly-looking woman sitting at the table near the counter.

"Did you see the red-headed woman at the counter a moment ago?" When Darcy nodded, I asked, "Do you know who she was?"

Darcy made a snorting-chuckling noise. "I didn't think a Dover was your type, Russo."

I was at the same time impressed and not surprised that Darcy knew who the redhead was. I frowned back at her. "She's not. When I went with Sadie and Buddy into Jewelweed Hollow that time, I'm pretty sure she was one of the family members who came close to running us over with her ATV."

"Sounds about right. That's Lucy Dover. She's Geraldine Dover's—the matriarch of the clan's—youngest child. No one messes with Lucy. She can be bitchy but she's never done anything to me personally."

I liked Darcy's forgiving attitude. That would come in handy if anything more than friendship blossomed between us. "I studied a map and the Dover's compound isn't too far from the part of the river where the body washed up."

Darcy settled back into her seat, crossing her arms on the table. "Do you think the Dovers know who the boy is?"

Ah, Darcy was an optimistic type of person. If someone had mentioned the same thing to me, I would have assumed the Dovers were somehow involved with the suspicious death, but Darcy's mind went in a completely different direction.

"Perhaps. It's a large family. Someone might know something," I said.

A rolling clap of thunder sounded in the distance and we both turned our heads to the windows. The streak of lightning crisscrossed the clouds hanging over the mountains. I'd noticed that thunderstorms and rain were frequently in the Possum Gap's weather forecast.

"I'll go with you." Darcy jumped up. "If we hurry, we can get to my Jeep before it starts raining."

I followed her lead more slowly. "Ah, that's not what I meant." Darcy ignored me and kept on going, so I raised my voice. The words rushed out of my mouth.

"I don't think it's a good idea for us to visit the Dovers without Sadie or Buddy accompanying us."

Darcy slowed just enough to look back as she swatted the air with a flick of her wrist. "They'll all hush up if we bring the law. I grew up with Willow Dover. We haven't talked in a lot of years, but once we were close. I even spent the night with her back in the hollow a few of times when we were kids."

"Really?" The department's secretary was full of surprises. "I'm surprised your folks let you hang out with people like that." When Darcy's brows shot up and she stopped, planting her hands firmly on her hips, I quickly added, "They have a confederate flag the size of a house flying on their land."

"It's complicated, Russo. You can't judge the entire family by the ignorant actions of a few of them," she said in a chastising way.

"I'm sorry to be judgmental, but they pulled guns on me."

Darcy started for the door again. I followed her after tossing a twenty-dollar bill on the counter.

When Darcy opened the café's door, I was bombarded with a thick scent of water and vegetation.

Darcy slowed when she reached the sidewalk. The rain was almost upon us. I could see the sheets of it racing over the lower hills towards the town.

"If you have questions, I can help you get them answered."

"What will Sadie say if she hears about you and I

going to Jewelweed Hollow without her?" I could imagine her pinched face at the news.

"There's no law keeping us from visiting an old friend. Besides, Charity is doing paperwork in the office today. She can cover for me until I return."

"Sounds like you're looking for some excitement in your life," I said.

Darcy sped up and I lengthened my strides to keep up with her as she headed towards her yellow Jeep at a fast clip, which I agreed was a better vehicle for the rutted gravel road than my sportscar.

The wind caught her hair, whipping it across her face. "I could use a little time out of the office," she admitted.

This is a terrible idea! I shouted inside my head.

But my curiosity had been roused and things were moving too quickly to think hard about the consequences. I passed by Darcy. "I've got to get something out of my glove compartment."

Darcy held her hair out of her face with her hand. "I have a pistol, if that's what you're going to fetch."

Of course she was armed. Everyone in Possum Gap was. Darcy also worked in the sheriff's department and Sadie probably insisted she carried a weapon. Still, her matter of fact, calm-as-a-cucumber proclamation sent my mind spinning.

"Yeah, well, they didn't exactly throw out the welcome mat last time. It won't hurt to for both of us to be armed."

Darcy gave me the thumbs up and before any more doubts could creep in, I made a beeline to my car.

Leave it to the goings on in this small town to take my mind off the bigger matters at hand.

I was thankful for the diversion.

9

SADIE

"It's kind of like chasing a ghost, ain't it?" Buddy asked.

He leaned against the doorframe to my office and, because of his hulking size, took up most of the opening.

"Chrissy Coleman is convinced Orville Walker's killer is on the loose and our cases are connected." I leaned back and glanced out the window. Clouds hung low over the western hills. If I wanted to reach Jewelweed Hollow before dark, I had to head out soon. "I thought I was just going through the motions when I went to Wilkins to talk to the reporter, but now, I think she could be on to something."

"We don't even know who this kid is," Buddy said with a huff. "If he was from Possum Gap, Wilkins, or any of the surrounding towns, he'd be identified by now."

"I know, it's strange. That's why I have to talk to Elwood Dover."

"That's a bad idea, Sadie. Have you forgotten the last time we visited the hollow?" Buddy's frown was deep and his eyes worried.

"This is different. Elwood would be twenty now. He's no longer a minor and his grandmother can't hide him from me the way she did with Chrissy."

Buddy gave a firm shake of his head. "You're missing the entire point. Why would Geraldine Dover keep the boy quiet four years ago? If his friend simply drowned, it wouldn't be a big deal to answer a few questions."

My first deputy didn't say much but when he started talking, it was usually significant like right now. "I see where you're going, and I'll be careful. Four years is a long time. I'm betting Geraldine and the rest of her clan aren't concerned about a kid who drowned in the river that long ago." Buddy raised a single brow at me, evidently not buying a word I said. I lifted my chin. "Besides, I didn't break my promise about Dillon Cunningham. He'll be staring at cell bars until he's hunched over and bald. She owes me one."

"Um." He scratched his chin and continued to frown. "I think that made you even by my reckoning."

I pushed my chair away from the desk and stood up. "You worry too much. I'll see you in the morning."

"I'd like to come with you, Sheriff." Buddy crossed his arms over his barrel chest.

101

I lifted my jacket off the peg. "If I remember correctly, you're celebrating your fortieth wedding anniversary with Teresa tonight. Weren't you all planning to head over to the Cracker Barrel next to the interstate?"

Buddy's cheeks, which were usually ruddy, turned a darker crimson. "I can give her a rain check until tomorrow. She'll understand—"

I cut him off with a raised hand. "You will do no such thing. Teresa looks forward to your date nights and today is a special celebration. She'll beat you with a switch if you cancel."

"I'm not going to enjoy my food worrying about you in the hollow by yourself with those rednecks."

Buddy stepped aside while he let out a giant breath.

"It's not about you having a good time. Tonight, it's all about Teresa." I shooed him with my hands. "Get going before you're late."

"I'm keeping my radio on just in case you need me," he said firmly.

"Oh, that's romantic."

I was about to slip past the large man when he moved over, blocking my way. "Take Mendez or Wallace with you. Hell, even Russo is better than going alone. It's not a full moon or the first of the month. The town is quiet. We can spare a deputy or the coroner."

"I am not leaving us short-staffed for a neighborly visit to ask a few questions."

"They aren't your neighbors, and they won't talk to you. You're wasting your time."

Buddy was right about the first statement and probably the second too. But I had to give it a try. And by God, I wasn't going to be intimidated by residents in my jurisdiction. The Dovers might think they were above the law, but they weren't.

"Where is Russo anyway? I figured he would have stuck around until I got back from Wilkins out of shear curiosity as bummed out as he was earlier that he had to stay behind."

We walked side by side up the long hallway to the entrance of the building.

"Charity said he went out for a late lunch with Darcy, and they didn't come back to the office." When my eyes narrowed, he shrugged and quickly added, "Maybe they missed each other... a lot."

His low, suggestive chuckle made me grunt in reply.

"I'm sorry, but Darcy barely knows him, and he up and disappeared for six weeks. What is that fool woman thinking?"

"She's not thinking. That's the way it works. Surely you aren't so old and jaded that you've forgotten how physical attraction works." Buddy wiped his mouth with his hand, trying to hide a second round of chuckles.

"Darcy is too smart for recklessness." I didn't believe my own words. I wasn't sure why it bugged me so much that my best friend's little sister, a grown woman, might have hooked up with Russo—but it did.

"Excuse me, are you the sheriff?" Two men stood in the lobby. The shorter one spoke while the other one—who was as tall as Buddy and nearly as stocky—didn't look at us. He was too busy checking out the department, his eyes darting back and forth around the room.

Both men were completely out of place in their suit pants and starchy button-up shirts. They had sunglasses tipped up on their heads even though the sky outside threatened more rain. I also picked up from the simple question they weren't from around here. The speaker sounded like Russo and I would have bet money the pair was from the northeast.

Charity had already gone home for the day and our dispatcher worked the phone lines in a back room while Mendez and Wallace made the usual rounds.

Even though I was curious about the well-dressed men with their hawkish faces, I cracked a smile because the speaker was addressing Buddy instead of me.

"Get going," I ordered Buddy. "And don't forget the flowers."

I could sense that Buddy really didn't want to leave, especially with the sudden appearance of the newcomers, but he and I knew very well if he was one minute late to the country-cooking restaurant, he'd be in big trouble from the missus.

"Call me if things go sideways," Buddy said as he backed away.

I waited until my first deputy went through the front door before I turned my attention to the men. "I'm Sheriff Sadie Mills." I reached out and shook the shorter man's hand. The other guy didn't offer his hand, so I put my full attention on the one who was looking at me. He wasn't a short man—I'd guess five feet ten, but compared to his companion, he looked like a hobbit.

"Raymond never mentioned you were a woman." The man's fingers tapped his lips as if he was trying to figure something out. "How very interesting."

The man's voice was smooth and every word that left his mouth was enunciated and very proper. I didn't like the way his eyes roamed over me, but I was equally as distracted by the way the other man didn't look at me at all. The hairs went up on the back of my neck. Something was very off with these two.

"Do you mean Russo?" Noticing the similarities in bone structure and speech pattern, I knew what he was going to say before he opened his mouth.

"I'm Anthony Russo, Raymond's older brother." When my eyes shifted to the giant at his right, he followed my gaze. "This is Jimmy Conti, our cousin."

Jimmy still didn't glance my way.

"It's nice to finally meet some of Russo's family. Welcome to Possum Gap." For some reason I couldn't explain, the words were hollow. I didn't want these men in my town, let alone throw out the red carpet. But I was raised in the upper south and being polite under most circumstances was ingrained in me.

Anthony's smile seemed forced. "And what a nice little town it is. We lost GPS signal several times and began to worry we'd never find Possum Gap."

"You drove all the way from New Jersey?" I asked as my gaze shifted to the glass door. The clouds had thickened so I couldn't tell from the sky what time it was, but the clock on the wall behind the men's heads screamed loud and clear that I needed to get a move on.

"Oh no." He snorted and grimaced like I'd said the stupidest thing. "We flew into Lexington and rented a car. Should have picked the truck in hindsight." He cocked his head. "Do all your rental places have four-wheel drives on their lots?"

It was a random question that was not important, and I was impatient to leave, but something about the intensity in Russo's brother's face and the almost jittery way Jimmy continued to scan the room gave me pause.

What the hell were Russo's relatives doing here after the long visit he'd just had with them?

"Yeah, I guess so. People in these parts rent trucks to pull livestock trailers and pick up feed at the local mill when theirs are in the shop." I took a step to the side and thought about these two city folks walking in on Russo and Darcy doing God knows what. I thought quickly. "Russo isn't here right now. He's out on assignment. On the south side of town, you'll find Gordon's Motel. It's clean and cheap. They even serve pancakes for breakfast. Tell Mariel that Sheriff Mills sent you over. I'm sure you're both exhausted. I'll contact Russo and tell him where you are. You can meet up later this evening."

"That's not going to work. I must see my brother at once. We already stopped by his apartment, and he wasn't there. Why don't you tell us where he is and we'll get out of your hair." Anthony's façade of nonchalance had slipped away and was quickly replaced with irritation.

"Sorry, I can't do that. Be patient and I'm sure he'll get back to you in a little while." I started to leave, and Anthony grabbed my arm which I immediately jerked from his grasp. "I don't care if you're Russo's bother. I've told you everything I can, so you better leave before the length of your stay here becomes out of your control."

Anthony smirked while he raised both of his hands in a surrender motion. "Hey, hey. No need to get snappy, Sheriff. We'll be on our way, but I wouldn't be surprised if we see you again real soon."

Jimmy led the way and Anthony fell in behind him at a leisurely pace, right out the front door. I stared through the glass until they disappeared into the parking lot.

"What the hell," I mumbled to myself. The encounter had been unsettling, and I experienced a warning jolt of adrenaline surge through my veins.

If I wasn't in such a hurry to get to Jewelweed Hollow before dark, I would have followed the men. We all had relatives who were jerks, but Russo's brother was in contention for winning grand prize for rudeness.

When I went through the door, the breeze was cool and misting. I zipped up my jacket and walked quickly to my car. If I didn't get behind a tractor, I would arrive in the hollow with some daylight to spare.

I had no idea the reception I'd receive, but figured it had to better than the last time I was there.

10

RUSSO

The winding gravel driveway hadn't changed at all in the last couple of months. It was still full of giant ruts and puddles that I would have worked hard to avoid if I'd been driving. Darcy didn't have a problem with the terrain. In her Jeep, we were rocked up and down like we were trapped in a saltshaker. The drizzle had increased to a steady rain and the windshield wipers swung back and forth noisily.

As I held onto the grip above my seat, I grunted with each bump. "This isn't a race. Why don't you slow down?" I bit the edge of my tongue when we dipped sideways.

"Not used to country driving, huh?" Darcy said with a flash of white teeth.

The department's gregarious secretary was having

too much fun at my expense. I fixed a smile on my face and held on tighter.

We cleared the forested part of the trip quickly, breaking into the meadow sooner than I thought possible. I braced my hand on the dashboard when Darcy hit the brakes. Heavy fog hung over the tall grass and partially obscured the singlewide trailers and doublewides from view at this distance. Weighted down by the rain, the enormous confederate flag was flat against the pole. We passed a few horses and a dozen cows grazing together. The livestock didn't raise their heads, too intent on munching the grass. A fluffy black and white collie jogged ahead of us like it was ushering us to its masters. The dog appeared to be eerily intelligent.

"I'll do the talking," Darcy said when she eyed me.

Now that we were going slower and the gravel was grated nicely, I was finally able to speak to her without biting off my tongue. "You sound like the sheriff. She has a habit of saying the same thing to me."

Darcy giggled. "It's because the minute you open your mouth, everyone knows you're an outsider." She dipped her head. "Well, your khaki's probably give them a clue even before you open your mouth."

"You know, in most places, it doesn't matter where you were born and raised. Having a conversation doesn't require a birth certificate."

"We're not most places, if you haven't noticed." Darcy's voice was pert and when she shot me a sideways glance, her large brown eyes were laughing. She was a striking woman when she smiled.

"Yes, I figured that out a while ago. I just want to make sure you know how"—I paused, searching for a word that wouldn't sound rude—"unusual it is."

"I know, Russo. That's why I like you. I'm all for leaving this town and experiencing some normalcy for a change."

"Then why haven't you moved away?"

We drove by several kids playing on a ramshackle porch that was attached to a mold-stained trailer. I couldn't help pressing my hand against the bulge in my pocket where the handgun was hidden. I really hoped these people would be reasonable this time, and that Darcy and I wouldn't end up being fed to the huge pigs that lifted their heads from a long black trough when the Jeep pulled up alongside their enclosure. "You keep saying you don't like it here, and you're educated and savvy. How come you haven't left already?"

Darcy scrunched her face and sighed. "Russo, you're clueless. Somedays I hate living in the hills, but it's not so easy as all that. My sister and aunt, and all my cousins are here. And what would Sadie do without me?"

I rubbed my eyes, wondering how this woman could contradict herself in the same sentence and I was the clueless one.

"I'm sure she'd miss you, but you have to think about yourself and what's best for you," I said.

"Trying to get rid of me, huh?" When I shook my head and searched for something to say, she grunted. "I get it, I do. For all the pimples, the hills grow on you. The longer you're here, the more you'll understand." Darcy glanced my way. "That is, if you're planning to stay."

Before I could answer the same burley, redheaded man with the beard who had approached the cruiser when I was a passenger in the back seat with Sadie and Buddy walked out of the mist. Darcy rolled to a stop.

"Hey, Summit. Is Willow around?" Darcy asked pleasantly. She sounded perfectly comfortable talking to the large man who had a pistol holstered to his belt like it was the 1800s and we were in the Wild West.

A bunch of kids gathered around the Jeep. Most of them were redheads and they all had a lot of tangled hair. The boys and girls were similarly skinny and dirty looking. A little girl—maybe seven—waved at me and I returned the gesture without much thought. On closer inspection, the kids looked athletic and sported tanned faces and arms even with the first frost nearly upon us.

"Darcy, it's been a long time. How come you haven't come over to get spearmint for your mamaw's tea lately?"

This smiling, soft spoken man was the same one who had basically growled at Sadie when we came looking for answers. Sure, she was law enforcement and that made a difference, but Summit's demeanor oozed niceness towards Darcy. I leaned closer to her and tried to make eye contact with the Dover's main guard. He only had eyes for Darcy.

"She died last winter," Darcy's voice lowered as she dipped her chin.

Damn. I heard the sadness in her voice, and it bothered me immensely. I had no idea she'd lost her grandmother recently, proving how little we knew about each other.

"I'm sorry to hear that. She was always good to me." A nostalgic smile tugged at the corner of his mouth. "I remember that time the school bus quit right in front of her house on Main Street. All the other kids got picked up by their folks quickly, but we couldn't get ahold of mine, so she fed me dinner—meatloaf and fixings—then we watched the *Golden Girls* together until Mamaw Gerrie finally figured out where I was."

"My grannie was like that. She'd feed anyone, anytime. I miss her."

Summit left it at that with a few nods and a great sigh. "Willow is up on the hill. She'll be excited to see ya."

"Thanks, Summit," Darcy drawled. Her southern accent sounded stronger than usual. Almost as if was adjusting to her surroundings and the person she spoke to.

"Sure. Don't be such a stranger. I still got a few bundles of this year's spearmint crop left. You should make some tea to honor Mamaw Beaumont." Summit finally looked my way. His brow knitted and his mouth dipped into a frown. The gregarious man didn't seem to like me.

"Sounds good to me," Darcy said as the Jeep rolled forward. She stuck her hand out the window and the kids waved, then dispersed, running off in every direction.

I caught a strong, tangy whiff of hickory smoke. The meadow was a drenched, colorful landscape. Thick milky mist rose off the barely contained river on the left that paralleled the gravel road. If it didn't stop raining soon, it might flood the road. The raging sound of water was loud, but my attention was on the hills surrounding the hollow. It was a stunning location, marred by junk trucks, plastic toys, and overgrown yards. The dogs that weren't directly playing with the kids skulked around the buildings, looking like they wanted an excuse to bite someone.

But for all the negatives, the vibe inside the hollow was relaxed. Kids played in the rain and their parents hung around on their porches, smoking cigarettes while they watched us drive by. We weren't greeted by a gang of hillbillies with rifles the way we were last time.

"Is Summit your age?" I continued to look out the window at the rundown structures that we drove past. It was hard to believe people lived inside some of them.

"Two years older. When Willow and I were sophomores, a couple of football players started pestering us and Summit took care of them."

I glanced over. "All by himself?"

"That's right," Darcy said, then giggled. "He's a good friend to have."

"I've had a couple of friends like that myself." When her eyes lit up, I added, "Protective ones."

"Summit is misunderstood. He's a good guy. Spends most of his time growing herbs and selling them for some extra cash."

"I bet he has quite the green thumb, and herbs aren't the only plants Summit grows." From what Sadie had said, Emmitt's growing endeavors included marijuana.

Darcy's face became serious. "It's the twenty-first century, Russo, and a free country. As long as no one gets hurt, who cares."

I didn't really care except that people who dabbled in illegal commodities tended to be dangerous. The sound of the river lessened as the road curved away and we began to climb the hill.

A couple walked by sporting a large red umbrella. They were probably in their fifties judging by the swaths of gray at their temples. Unlike most everyone else in the hollow, these two had brown hair. They smiled and waved, and Darcy called out the window, greeting them by name.

I began to breathe easier. "Everyone is being so nice," I said.

"What did you think was going to happen? The Dovers would come out with guns blazing?" She threw her head back.

"Pretty much."

Darcy grunted. "That's just because Jax Dover died in that trailer and Christine—who's just a teen—was peddled for sex by that Cunningham guy. The family was on edge. Can hardly blame them."

I turned away and smiled. Sadie must not have enlightened Darcy on how close we all came to dying that day. Darcy parked the Jeep beneath a tall tree whose leaves were still mostly green. The rain was just spitting at the moment, and I didn't bother grabbing Darcy's umbrella. She didn't seem to care either as quick as she was out the door and walking up the front porch steps.

Unlike the other homes, this one's yard was immaculate. Late blooming white roses circled the doublewide, and a line of wildflowers decorated each side of the pavers leading to the house.

Darcy waited for me at the top of the stairs. When I reached her, she moved in close and I leaned back, wondering what she was up to. Her fingers worked deftly on my buttons, undoing the first couple ones. "Sorry, but you look like a cop."

"That's the first time anyone's said that to me." I grinned back at her.

Darcy's chest swelled before she let out a breath. "You're in the hollow. Casual is better. Don't forget, I'll do the talking."

I nodded, perfectly happy to observe the conversation and be able to keep a lookout at the same time. I was paranoid that an ambush wasn't out of the question.

The door opened after one rap.

A tall, slender redhead burst through the doorway and grabbed Darcy into a tight hug. This must be Willow. I stood back, not wanting to interrupt the reunion.

"Summit just called me! Oh my God, Darcy, where the hell have you been?" Willow's voice was sharp, and her words ran together.

Darcy pulled back a little. "Just doing the same ol' thing. Working at the department and hanging out with Tanya most of my free time."

"How is your sister? I see her pretty face up on those billboards for selling properties." Willow still hadn't released Darcy, gripping her shoulders and giving an occasional shake while she talked.

"Oh, you know her. Busy, busy, busy. Her and Joey are getting divorced."

"No kidding!" Willow's head turned and she looked me over thoroughly. "I never liked him. He wasn't good enough for the likes of Tanya Beaumont."

When Darcy saw Willow staring at me, she quickly explained, "This is Russo, my...uh...partner." Darcy's brown cheeks flushed darker as she became flustered. "He's the new coroner."

Willow released Darcy and walked straight up into my personal space. "You were with the sheriff that day when she came looking for that douchebag, Dillon Cunningham."

I swallowed. "Yes, I was. And your family didn't leave a very good impression on me."

I saw Darcy's eyes widen past Willow's shoulder. Willow cocked her head and stared a few more long seconds before she suddenly erupted in laughter.

She slapped my arm. "You're a funny one, and not from around here, are ya?"

Before I could respond, Darcy spoke up. "He's from New Jersey."

"A Yankee, huh." Willow's gaze skimmed me again. "But a cute one."

Darcy sucked in a breath. "Come on, girl, you're making him squirm."

Then the young women laughed together until a voice called out from inside the house. "Don't be a ninny! Bring 'em in, Willow!"

I remembered that scratchy voice. Geraldine Dover, the matriarch of the family.

Willow and Darcy sobered quickly. Darcy grabbed my hand, tugging me through the doorway just as a rumble of thunder cracked over the countryside.

The living room was well-lit and full of knick-knack-covered shelves. The pine board walls were jammed with photos. Every frame was a different size and style. Literally every inch was taken up with Dover faces.

My mind registered the cluttered room as my gaze shifted from Geraldine sitting in her burgundy recliner with her feet up to the enormous, black-bearded man sitting on the edge of a folding chair in front of her.

"Time to be on your way, Cooter," Geraldine said firmly.

"But—" Cooter began to argue and when Geraldine raised her hand, he snapped his mouth shut and stood abruptly.

"Say hello to your ma for me. I haven't seen Lita in a long while. Tell her she needs to stop by for a sip of shine sometime—and to bring Kaine along. I'm sure Jessie would enjoy catching up with your pa."

Cooter barely paused long enough to nod his head in Geraldine's direction.

I caught a whiff of body odor that made me wrinkle my nose when the giant walked by. I couldn't understand why Cooter glared at me. If I'd ever seen the smelly, bare-chested, suspender-wearing man, I would have remembered.

"Tell your mama I'll call her tomorrow," Geraldine said.

She was answered with a grunt and the lifting of his hand before he went outside.

Geraldine's gaze passed quickly over Darcy and landed on me. "I'm sorry to hear about your mamaw's passing, Darcy. She was a good woman."

"Thank you, Miss Gerrie. She always enjoyed teatime with you."

The way Geraldine's eyes bore into me made me uneasy. So did the dead, staring eyes of the buck on the wall above her head.

"What brings you and Sadie's man into the hollow

on a rainy day, Darcy?" The pleasantness had left the old woman's voice. She was all business now.

I spoke before Darcy could respond. "I'm not Sadie's man. I'm the coroner and work for Possum Gap's citizens."

Geraldine burst out laughing, then recovered just a quickly. "Are you claiming to work for me, young man?"

"Of course." I ignored Darcy's wide eyes and plowed on. "We have an unidentified body that we pulled from the river the other day. Darcy accompanied me here to ask if you or any of your relatives might know his identity. He's a teenager, blond hair, blue eyes. One hundred and twenty pounds."

Geraldine's lips curled as she listened.

"I'm sorry for his forwardness, Miss Gerrie. He's a northerner," Darcy said.

I chuckled. I couldn't help it. There was literally less than eight hundred miles from New Jersey to southern Kentucky and I was being treated like I was a foreigner from a faraway country.

"His ways are not our ways," Geraldine said quietly.

"I mean no disrespect, ma'am. But there's a dead kid and we're trying to figure out who he is so we can inform the family and figure out why he ended up in the river," I said.

Geraldine's brows knitted. "That boy is like an unwanted dog who broke off its leash and ends up in an animal shelter three counties over. No one will retrieve it because it wasn't wanted in the first place."

"That's a cold thing to say."

The lightning beyond the window drew my attention. Leafy branches swayed and their leaves flipped up, signaling another round of storms rolling in.

"It's the damn truth. If that boy had a family that cared, you would know his identity and wouldn't have to bother old ladies for clues." She grunted and shook her head. "I have no idea who that boy is. But I guarantee he's not a Dover and has nothing to do with my family. Does that suit you, Raymond Russo?"

"You know my name?"

The twisted smile on Geraldine's face made the breath catch silently in my throat.

"I make it my business to know everyone in this county and what they're up to. Don't forget that."

I licked my lips and gave a nod of my head.

Darcy touched my arm. "We'll be going, Miss Gerrie. You have a fine afternoon."

"Stop by sometime for a proper visit—without the outsider," Geraldine instructed.

Darcy nodded and backed up, tugging me with her.

"Call me, Darcy. I'd like to catch up," Willow said, but she didn't leave her grandmother's side.

The scene as we left the house reminded me of my own grandfather sitting in his study. There were always one or two sons or grandsons at his side. Here in the Kentucky wilderness, it seemed the women were in charge, which was fascinating.

The door had barely shut when Darcy started talk-ing. "I told you to keep your mouth shut. Now you've gone and made her mad."

"That's not surprising," a woman's voice said from behind us.

We turned to find the sheriff standing at the bot-tom of the steps with her hands on her hips. She didn't look happy to see us either.

11

SADIE

"This is the last place I expected to find the two of you," I said.

Darcy looked guilty as hell. She dropped her wild-eyed gaze to her booted toe that she scuffed back and forth over the wide planked floorboard. Russo gave me a small, mischievous smile and shrugged.

Darcy wasn't brave enough to speak. Russo was overly confident when he tried to explain. "Darcy and I were following a lead and—"

"What lead?"

Darcy peeked over her shoulder at the house, then jogged down the steps. She whispered when she could have been talking normally. "Russo and I were at the café when we saw Lucy Dover. It got us thinking that the Dovers might know who our floater is."

"So, you decided to play detective and come to the hollow by yourselves to poke around?"

Russo and I were close in age and Darcy wasn't a kid, yet the disapproving sound of my voice and the way I scowled at them made me feel like I was talking to Chloe after finding our she'd skipped school.

Russo inhaled deeply, defiantly. "We're both professionals and Darcy has friends here. It just made sense." He crossed his arms over his chest. "I'm surprised you didn't show up earlier."

They were in good health and obviously fine. Illegal shenanigans went on in this hollow all the time, but this didn't appear to be one of those moments.

"I would have been here sooner, but I was delayed by your brother and cousin Jimmy." I paused, letting it sink in. "Well, Anthony did all the talking and Jimmy just stood there like a creepy nincompoop."

I imprinted the look on Russo's face to memory, not being able to say for sure whether his slack jaw and bulging eyes were from shock or fear.

"Anthony and Jimmy are here—now?"

The breathless way he asked made me take a step forward. "Are you okay, Russo? Having relatives stop by for a visit shouldn't cause as much stress as you appear to be experiencing."

Russo's face paled and he tried to smile but failed. "Anthony said he'd never come down here. He's not much on rural living, if you know what I mean. Besides,

I just saw him a few days ago." He hesitated. "Did he say if everything was all right back home?"

My muscles loosened and I relaxed a little bit. I hadn't even thought about the possibility of illness, or worse, a death in the family.

"He didn't mention anything like that, just that he wanted to see you immediately."

I watched the emotions flit over Russo's face. Worry, anxiety…curiosity, in quick succession. Darcy cocked her hip and stared at him as intently as I did.

"If it was my mom or dad, he would have said something. He's dramatic though and likes the attention a sudden appearance brings."

He brushed by Darcy.

She gave me a quick shrug and hurried to catch up with him.

"I better get back to town and see what they want, in case it's important," Russo said, sounding more like his steady self.

"How come you weren't answering your cell phone?" I asked.

He didn't slow down, sparing me a sideways glance. "There's no reception and my battery is dead."

His answer was too smooth. And although reception was sketchy this far into the hollow, my phone had vibrated in my pocket a moment ago, confirming that there was a pocket of reception right here.

"Hey, Russo."

He stopped at the passenger door of the Jeep and finally looked up.

"Did you learn anything about the kid's identity?"

"No, Sheriff. Sure didn't."

Russo jumped into the Jeep and Darcy followed suit only after she looked questioningly at me, and I gave her a nod of my head. I'd rather they were out of the hollow anyway. Things were calm so far, but you never knew what to expect with the Dovers.

"Sheriff, I already told your man that I don't know anything about that poor dead boy, and no one else here does either." Geraldine leaned over the porch railing looking down on me. She was alone for a change, which I found odd.

"Where's Elwood? I need to talk to him," I said flatly.

Geraldine laced her fingers together. She was trying to not show emotion, but I noticed the slight intake of breath and the shifting of her feet. A border collie trotted up the steps with a stick in his mouth without acknowledging my presence. Geraldine dropped her hand and began stroking the dog's head.

"Why do you want to speak to that young'un?"

Geraldine would lie, steal, and cheat to protect her family. Now that I stood here after rehearsing in my head what I would say to her, I decided to just go with complete transparency. The old matriarch would see right through any sweet talking I did anyway.

"Elwood was friends with that Wilkins County teenager that drowned in the river four years ago. I thought that case might be related to this new one."

Geraldine made a humming noise. "Orville Walker."

A boom of thunder bellowed overhead, and the clap of lightning quickly followed. I glanced up at the threatening rain clouds. The wind was charged with energy. The storm moved northeasterly over the mountains. If it drifted a few miles in this direction, we'd get drenched.

"That's right." I spoke up to be heard over the rustling branches above my head. Showers of leaves fell on the lawn—the only mowed yard in the hollow.

"You're tenacious, Sadie Mills. After all these years, I reckoned that boy would never get justice. And here you are, asking about him."

"Chrissy Coleman tried to interview you—"

Geraldine snorted loudly, cutting me off. "That young reporter didn't know what she was getting herself into. I done her favor."

My heart dropped into my stomach. The sky darkened even more. It must be twilight, but it was difficult to tell with the swiftly moving gray clouds above. A chill raced up my spine. Could the Dovers be involved with Orville's death? My head swam with questions.

"What do you know about his death?" I hated the hopeful sound of my voice.

"Nothing at all. But perhaps if you ask the right

people the right questions, you'll figure it out on your own."

Geraldine's pinched lips told me she wasn't going to elaborate. Life and death, good and bad—it was all just a game to her. She enjoyed sitting on her hilltop, pulling the strings, and watching what happened next. I was sure she knew more than she was saying, but it would be useless to beg. Geraldine had just given me her blessing to speak to her grandson, and that's what I came for.

"Where can I find Elwood?"

"He's hunting for morels in the woods out yonder, behind the barn."

"Elwood is looking for mushrooms in the rain?"

"Best time to find them if you ask me." Her hair was gray at the roots but still fiery red on the ends and the brightly colored locks whipped around her face. "We're in a lull. If you hurry, you might find him before the next storm breaks. She lifted her face to the wind and closed her eyes for a few seconds. I reckon you have an hour."

I was glad I wore boots. Zipping up my jacket, I started for the packed dirt path that led around the cluster of weathered-looking barns behind the double-wide. I took a few steps and stopped. When I turned around, Geraldine was still there, petting her stoic dog and watching me go.

Since we'd come to a sort of truce since I'd locked her son's killer up for a very long time, I thought I could ask her one more question. "What did you think would happen to Chrissy if she pursued the story?"

"That she'd end up floating face down in the river like Orville."

Ah, her honesty was both refreshing and disturbing. I didn't linger any longer. Geraldine Dover was a dangerous woman, but I respected her knowledge of the ever-changing weather conditions in the mountains.

The dirt path led between two large tobacco barns and past a crooked shed. Searching through the windows, I saw a stack of hay in the one barn and a tractor and other farm equipment in the other. Three long-eared goats stood in the doorway of the shed. One of the goats bleated, then disappeared into the dark opening. My own grandparents had a small herd of goats to clear their hillside of weeds and kudzu vines. One thing I remember was how they hated to get wet in the rain.

The fast walk through the Dover's wooded land was very different than when I followed Christine Dover at a run through the trees. This time, I had been given permission to be here. I was sure I was being watched as I glanced around, seeing nothing but tree trunks and boulders. There were a million places to hide and if you knew the forest as well as any Dover did, it wouldn't be difficult to sneak up on me.

I reached inside my jacket and touched the handle of my 9 MM that was holstered around my chest. Neither Summit nor Geraldine seemed to care that I was armed. They probably figured that if it came to a shootout, I was greatly outnumbered. But my heart was steady as my breathing became more labored walking uphill. For whatever reason, Geraldine wanted me to solve Orville's case although she didn't want to come right out and tell me what she knew. I wasn't sure what to make of her behavior. Was she pointing me in the direction of my own doom or was she helping me? And I still didn't know if the Wilkins cold case was related to my current river victim. If Russo was right, and there was no reason to doubt his expertise, our young John Doe had been dead when he went into the river...and that was exactly what Chrissy believed about Orville. The boys were similar sizes, ages, and complexion. Found along the same river in neighboring counties.

Could all that be a coincidence?

I stopped in my tracks. The wind whistling through the trees drowned out other noises, but thought I heard a branch snap.

Still as a statue, I waited and listened, suddenly very aware of how lonely this mountain was.

"Sheriff, what in the world are you doing out here?"

My gun was in my hand when I whirled around.

John Dover stood there, burlap bag in one hand and the other raised, fingers splayed.

"Whoa, don't shoot me." The only emotion in his voice was amusement. He wasn't worried about his life, making me wonder if he'd been following me for some time.

I didn't immediately lower my gun. John wore blue jeans and an orange and white flannel shirt that was equally faded. His brown hair was pulled back and there was even more stubble on his face than when I'd seen him at the Apple Festival. The tall, rubber boots he wore were sensible on a day like this.

He broke into a smile before I lowered the gun. I glanced around the ever-darkening woods and not seeing anyone else, I finally holstered the gun. "Are you really searching for mushrooms in a storm?"

John draped the bag over his shoulder. He moved in such a loose, unconcerned way, you'd never know he'd just had a gun pointed at him.

"It's not storming…yet." His grin disappeared and he stared back at me. "Seriously, why are you in the hollow?"

An emotion flicked across his face and if I didn't know better, I would describe it as concern. I swallowed and squirmed a little under his intense look.

"I'm looking for Elwood Dover. Is he with you?"

"He's over yonder." John pointed at a rise where several boulders rested on top of each other like perfectly stacked children's blocks.

I exhaled, my shoulders slumping. More uphill.

"You shouldn't be up here, you know."

The wind howled through the trees, and I could see the clouds full of rain descend on the hollow below us with pouring rain. Geraldine had been off by about thirty minutes.

John saw the wall of rain when I did. "Come on!"

I felt the stubborn urge to ignore his shouting demand, but he seemed to have a plan and when he pivoted and ran, I followed him.

We jumped over scattered fallen logs and went around a bend, ending up behind the boulders. Raindrops struck just when I saw the fissure between two of the huge rocks. John went through the opening first. With one last look at the deluge coming straight at me, I ducked inside.

Enveloped in darkness, I pulled the flashlight from the loop on my belt. John already had his turned on. The space was cramped but dry. I took a couple more steps to stay clear of the opening where rain sprayed inside. John sat a few feet away with his back against a stone wall.

The musky smell was unmistakable. "Is this a bear den?"

John set his flashlight on the ground and aimed it at the opposite wall. When the storm passed, enough light should shine through the crack to get by without a flashlight, but by then, I'd be out of there anyway.

He shrugged. "It's been a few years since one claimed this cave. I think we're okay to wait out the storm."

Rain poured beyond the opening. It didn't look like it was letting up soon, so I joined John on the dirt floor, sitting down next to him. I didn't have patience for any of this.

"By the time the deluge stops it will be dark," I complained, staring past the fissure at the water world.

John chuckled and I glanced his way.

"Do you have a date to get to?"

He asked it without sarcasm, and I was at a loss for words for a moment. When I found my voice, I was still not sure how to respond. "I'm investigating a possible murder. That's why I'm in a hurry to get out of this stupid cave and talk to Elwood." It suddenly occurred to me that the person I climbed the mountain to talk to was out in this terrible weather. "Where do you think he is?"

"Eh, don't worry about my little cousin. I'm sure he jumped into another crack in the hill like we did."

John leaned back and folded his hands behind his head like being holed up in a cave during a rainstorm was no big deal at all.

We sat in silence. His use of the word "date" was annoying. Did he mean an appointment or a real date? And why did I care? John Dover was definitely not my type...well, it had been so long since Ted and I split and I'd been so alone that I didn't really know what exactly my type was anymore, except that it wasn't a Dover.

Still, when I'd turned around and found him gawking at me in the woods, I immediately experienced a flood of relief that it was him and not one of his fiery-haired relatives. And maybe even a little bit of a thrill—and that bugged me the most.

"How come you don't live in the compound with the rest of your kin?"

He looked sideways with a raised brow. "You're awfully interested in my life, Sheriff. Are you sure it's not personal?"

I leaned back and grimaced. The man was driving me crazy. I quickly formulated an answer. "It's my job to ask questions."

"If you say so," he said with a soft snort that indicated he didn't believe me. He paused for long enough that I thought he wouldn't answer when he finally did. "My ma and dad wanted better for me." He glanced away. "I went to college, did you know that?"

I did, but I didn't want to him to know I performed a full background check on him weeks ago. "I guess that didn't work out for you."

"Ouch." John winced in a teasing way. "I felt obliged to follow through for my folks' sake and became the first-generation college graduate in the family. I wanted to become a lawyer at one time."

I was surprised but didn't let it show. "What changed your mind?"

We barely knew each other but he sounded like we were old friends chatting. I liked his laidback conversational tone and wondered if everyone got the same familiar treatment with him.

"Dad got sick, and Mom needed me around the house to help with the farm chores. He passed away eight months after I graduated. Then she was diagnosed with cancer. It was another five years before I buried her next to my dad. By the time I was free to do as I pleased, too much time had gone by. I knew I would never pass the bar after that long."

I drew my knees to my chest, feeling terrible. "It's never too late, you know," I said quietly.

John chuckled softly. "I'll remember you said that."

When I met his gaze, I thought I saw the flicker of something, and the air pulsed between us. Hating the sensation, I returned attention to the rain falling beyond the cave's opening. "What do you do anyway?"

Since I was a cop and he was a Dover, I didn't expect an honest answer, but anything to break the tension swirling around us was fine with me.

"I have an apiary," he said.

"You raise bees?" I found the idea fascinating and his tattoo on his upper left arm finally made sense.

He laughed and the hearty sound of it sucked the chill right out of the air. "I guess you can say that. Mostly I collect honey. My apiary is called Sunrise Promise. I also make candles and lip balms from the wax, any by-product related to the bees."

I had bought jars with the same name on them at the Farmer's Market and even snatched one up at the Apple Festival.

"I've had your honey! It's good. But I've never seen you at the honey stands before." I twisted to fully face him.

"Because I'm a Dover, and I thought my last name would keep some people from buying my products. I have a few people who peddle my wares for a small commission on each sale. It keeps me in the shadows where I'd rather be."

I digested what he said. He had done a damn good job of keeping his connection to the honey a secret. I had no idea. "Do you make decent money in that business?"

"Ah, it's about the money to you, huh?" He grinned and I noticed the dimple beneath his stubble.

"Isn't money important? I mean, that's why we work, isn't it?"

Out of the corner of my eye, I saw him shrug. "Is that why you're the sheriff of Possum Gap? I find it hard to believe the county pays you enough to make the job worth it, but you still put your life on the line every day to do your job."

Couldn't argue with that. "Still, you have to earn a living, don't you?"

"I sell at the festivals and online and make more than enough to survive."

"I heard you were a survivalist."

"If growing my own food and storing it for the winter makes me one, then yes, I am. Oh, and the arsenal in my closet counts too, right?"

The corner of his mouth twitched, and I could tell he was trying not to smile. John Dover was more pleasant to talk with than I ever imagined he would be.

"You never explained exactly why you don't live with your kin in the hollow," I reminded him.

He inhaled deeply before speaking. "Things go on here in the hollow that I don't always approve of. That doesn't mean I don't love my family, because I do. I just don't want to be too tight with them, you know what I mean?"

Oh yeah, I sure did. The rain lessened to a thick drizzle and the flailing branches on the trees settled. "Do you come up here very often to hunt mushrooms with Elwood?"

"Several times a year. Sometimes Summit or Willow tag along. This time, it was Elwood. The best mushrooms are found in the wooded hills around Jewelweed Hollow."

"What's he like—Elwood?"

"Why don't you ask him yourself?"

I followed the lift of his chin. Elwood jogged through the opening. He was tall, lanky, and dripping wet. After he shook out his red hair, he said, "Shoot, John, I 'bout made it back here before it poured."

"Where did you take shelter?" John asked. In a fluid movement he stood, and I followed suit.

"I hunkered down under that giant fallen poplar trunk on the east trail head." Elwood shifted his gaze to me, looking a little suspicious. "Howdy, sheriff. Are you here to arrest me or John?"

The kid had a sense of humor at least.

"Neither. I just wanted to ask you some questions."

"Must be mighty important to hike up here on an evening like this." Elwood shook his head again and he was close enough that he sprayed me.

I wiped the drops off my cheek with my wrist. "It is. What can you tell me about Orville Walker?"

Elwood's eyes widened and before I knew what was happening, he ran back outside at lightning speed.

I turned to John. "Really?"

"I'll catch him."

Then John was gone too.

I wasn't prepared to make a sprint thought the wet forest, but I wasn't about to let John do all the work and took off after him.

12

LUCINDA

The rain poured down, streaming off the schoolhouse roof where the gutter was bent like a crooked hose. I waited on the balls of my feet, watching Martha from across the yard. She stood in the shed where a dozen horses were tied inside to the long hitching rail. In her arms was cradled a pot which I knew from our earlier conversation was full of beef taco filling.

Every Wednesday evening the youth gathered at the schoolhouse for some social time. Volleyball was a girls' favorite and boys usually played baseball on the bottom field. After the games ended, the youth met in the schoolhouse for a light dinner. Then they'd be on their way home by nine o'clock in the summertime and seven during the winter months.

This evening's onslaught of rain had changed

plans. The boys played a friendly game of basketball while the girls lined the wall of the dual cafeteria-gymnasium, chatting and smiling.

"I'll get the pot from Mrs. Mast, Lucinda. No worries." Marvin Miller had somehow snuck up behind me. Before I could stop him, he sprinted out into the storm.

Without much thought, I tightened my black bonnet that covered my white cap, popped the umbrella, and dashed after him.

The sounds of the young people were obliterated by pounding rain as I splashed through puddles to reach the shed quicker. By the time I made it to cover, my feet were soaked straight through my boots to my socks and the umbrella was flipped up and barely useful.

Martha handed me a handkerchief and I dabbed my eyes, then wiped my face. Her laughter made me look up.

"My oh my, Lucinda, why are you so impatient? I can understand the lad doing something so silly as galloping through a downpour like a runaway horse, but you should know better," she chastised while grinning broadly.

Marvin pulled a towel from his saddle bag and dried his face off as well.

"I thought you'd want the umbrella." I blinked, staring back at my older friend. "Are you saying you want to trek back over there and become drenched?"

Martha swatted the air. "Of course not. I'll wait ten minutes and there will be a lull." She pointed at the western sky. "See there, a break in the clouds."

I followed her finger and sighed. From the schoolhouse doorway, I didn't have this same view of the sky. I felt a little bit ignorant and my cheeks warmed. Martha was always right.

"Ma'am, I'll run it on over if you like, that way you don't have to hurry or anything," Marvin said, offering his hands to take the pot.

Martha cocked her hip and stared back at Marvin, whom I could swear had grown an inch or two more since the fateful summer month when he'd instantly become smitten with Charlie Baker. He's lost her and his friend, Vivian, in one fell swoop. Yet for all that, the boy still had bright eyes and a cheerful manner. The extra twinkle might be because of the new family who had moved in next door to the Millers. Well, not so much the entire family, but the eldest daughter who was a slim brunette with warm brown eyes whose friendly ways matched his jolly personality perfectly.

"You must be extremely hungry for my famous tacos, eh, Marvin?"

Marvin grinned back at her. "Yes, ma'am. I'll run it over to the schoolhouse unless you want my help to make the crossing?"

Martha waved him away. "Tell your mother we'll be over when the rain slacks off. Now, off you go."

The Amish teen wasted no time. His lanky legs carried him through the puddles and straight into the schoolhouse in just a few long strides. The metal-sided building, which most Englishers said looked more like a barn than a school, was large enough to hold the entire congregation which consisted of twenty-six families and over three hundred men, women, and children.

Martha touched my arm, and I turned away from the rainy scene to face her.

"Tell me what happened to upset you so, Lucinda," Martha said.

I reached out to pat the closest horse that just so happened to be Martha's dapple gray gelding. "I had an encounter with a horrible Englisher on Dark Hollow Road the other day." The memory rose, clouding my vision. "Two huge dogs chased Goliath and you know how he is."

Martha's face became still. "It didn't end well for the dogs, eh?"

I shook my head. "He kicked out, seriously injuring one of them. If that wasn't bad enough, a foul man ran out to the road." I swallowed hard. The sound of the rain pelting the tin roof made me talk louder. "He shot his own dog, right then and there."

Martha patted my shoulder. "Perhaps he was doing it a kindness. The dog might have been suffering and unrepairable."

"It wasn't just shooting his dog that upset me. He said the most horrible things." I sucked in a breath as my stomach constricted. "That entire stretch of road is ominous, don't you think?"

Martha leaned back against the post. "You know how some Englishers are—alcohol, drugs—it's no wonder he behaved the way he did. Isn't that where the Dover family lives?"

I nodded. "Back in the hollow I've been told."

Martha made a *tsk, tsk* noise between her clenched teeth. "You shouldn't go that way. I never do."

Martha sounded like James. "True, but it shaves three miles off the trip to the other side of the community."

"Sounds like it's not worth the loss of time." The lull of rain Martha spoke of took place and she stepped away from the post, ready to head back to the schoolhouse.

I fell in step with her. "Wait, there's something else."

Martha slowed and frowned. "Oh dear. Go on and say it."

"James and I went to the trailer that's just outside of the wooded part of the road—"

"Where you suspected Albert might be?"

"That's the one. We talked to the teenager who lives there. And I was right, Albert is friends with the boy."

Martha stopped short of leaving the shed. With the slowing of the rain, our people began filing out of the schoolhouse. Before long, others would approach us. We didn't have much time to talk.

"Does he know where Albert is?" Martha asked in a hushed voice.

"No, he said he hadn't seen him in a couple of weeks, and that it was unusual." I let out a ragged breath. "Albert has been going there to watch Westerns on the television set."

As if talking to herself, Martha muttered, "That's what many of our boys do, and if it's the worst of their rebellion, their parents are lucky."

I became annoyed that my bright friend hadn't caught on yet. "Don't you see, Martha. If Albert isn't there and his English friend doesn't know his where-abouts, something awful might have happened to him."

"It might have, true. But teenagers lie easily. Maybe the boy did not tell you the truth. He could know ex-actly where Albert has been and is covering for his friend."

Martha had more common sense than most peo-ple, but her lack of urgency upset me. "Aren't you worried?"

"Of course, but you could be overreacting because of Vivian. That type of thing doesn't happen here, and surely not more than once. I'd say Albert is spending time with another Englisher and will come back when he's good and ready."

"He's fourteen."

"Some start early." She nodded toward my children, Sarah and Josh, who raced around the gravel parking lot with roughly ten other children jumping puddles. "Lucinda, I'm telling you this as a good friend, focus on your own children. You have enough on your plate and shouldn't spend so much time worrying about everyone else's."

"What if he's in trouble?" My stomach churned at the thought.

Martha threw up her hands. "You are not responsible for Albert, even if something dreadful happened to him."

"James and I are leaving early tonight. I'm calling the sheriff when we arrive home."

"That's about the wisest thing you've said in a while, Lucinda. And no worries, I've made a phone call myself—one that I pray will lead to even more assistance if Albert has encountered something unsavory."

As we dodged the dripping eaves and found ourselves under the brightening sky, I felt a sense of peace for the first time in several days. Martha's actions showed that she agreed with my suspicions; she had reached out for help.

But time was of the essence and our lady sheriff would know what to do.

13

SADIE

My heart pounded in my chest as I rounded the boulders and nearly smashed into John's back. He had Elwood by the shoulders but didn't have to hold on tight. The young man appeared to have already given up.

"Dang, Elwood. What has gotten into you?" John huffed the words out.

Elwood pointed at me. "She's the sheriff!"

"So? Do you run off every time you see an officer of the law?" John didn't wait for Elwood to answer. "Because that's pretty dumb if you do."

"And dangerous," I chimed in. "Are you going to stand still and talk to me, or do I have to cuff you?"

Elwood shrugged out of John's grip, dropping his head to the forest floor. Luckily, the rain had quit. Drops still fell from the leaves above splattering my nose.

"Naw, I'm done running." He wiped his nose with the back of his hand. "What do you want?"

John smacked the back of Elwood's head. "Be polite!"

Elwood let out a harsh sigh. "What do you want, Miss Sheriff?"

I almost laughed and John turned to me. "I promise, Grannie did teach him manners."

Elwood jerked his head to flick his red locks out of his face.

"I'm told you and Orville Walker were friends. Is that true?"

"Yeah, what of it? He's been dead for four years."

Elwood had a buffalo-sized chip on his shoulder like most of the Dovers.

I believed what John said about Geraldine teaching Elwood and the rest of the clan's kids manners. But she also taught them lawlessness and rebellion against any kind of authority and that's why this skinny redneck young man thought he could be rude to me.

"I've reopened his investigation."

"I thought he drowned," Elwood challenged with a raised brow.

"New information has come to light that it might not have been an accident."

John stood next to his cousin, staring at me. I tried not to look at him though.

"Do you think it's some kind of serial killer?" John blurted out. "Because if the boy who was found the other day also ended up in the river already dead, a killer who preys on boys might be on the loose?"

My head jerked John's way. Dammit. He just said out loud what I'd been worried about all along. His blue eyes pierced mine. I wasn't sure if he was worried or more intrigued with his own notion.

"Let's not get ahead of ourselves," I told John, then turned back to Elwood. "Is there anything you can tell me about Orville's disappearance?"

Elwood's shoulders sagged. "I don't want no one else hurt if what Johnny says is true." His chest deflated. "I tried to tell the sheriff over there in Wilkins that I thought something bad happened to Orville when he up and vanished."

"You went to Wilkins County and spoke to Adam Crawford?"

"Yeah. Grannie Gerrie took me. Jessie came too, but he sat in the car the entire time."

"What did you have to tell them?"

Elwood stared at his booted toe as he pushed leaves around in the dirt. "Orville was starting to use meth."

"But he was a soccer player—"

Elwood laughed. "Do you think that makes him perfect or something?"

"Are you using?" John asked when he gripped his younger cousin's shoulder and forced Elwood to face him.

"No, I ain't dumb. That stuff is gross."

"Then why would Orville get into it?" I asked, quickly reassessing the dead teen in my mind.

Elwood shrugged. "I don't know. Probably because Molly was doing it and he liked her."

"Molly Davis?" John blurted out loudly. "Are you being honest, Elwood?"

"I wouldn't lie about that," Elwood said.

John rubbed his face with his hand.

"Who's Molly Davis? Is she related to Cooter Calhoun?" I knew a lot of people in the county but not everyone. Although, the name sounded familiar.

Elwood looked away. It was John who answered me.

"The Calhouns are distant kin to the Dovers. I'm surprised you didn't know that, Sheriff."

I guess I never thought about it. "I haven't had any trouble from the family, but my predecessor sure did."

I remembered Jimson Calhoun and his girlfriend, Shauna, accidentally blowing up their trailer while they were cooking up meth. The couple and their two-year-old baby girl perished in the explosion, and three hundred acres burned on Bushy Mountain before the blaze was contained. That was around seven years ago.

John said what I was thinking. "I thought all the drug-dealing Calhouns were long gone."

Elwood turned his head away and John walked around the young man to look him in the eye. "Are you saying Molly is following in her uncle's footsteps?"

"I don't know where he got it, I just know Orville was smoking the stuff and he liked Molly Calhoun."

John and I looked at each other. "Molly's name isn't mentioned anywhere in the file."

"It wouldn't be. I'm like the only one who knew."

"And you told this to Sheriff Crawford?" I asked.

Elwood shook his head. "No, I just told him that Orville had been smoking it and that it might have had something to do with him being in the river."

"Like he was drugged out and had an accident?"

"More like he probably pissed off the dealer because he had no money."

"How did Molly get into the picture?" John asked. His narrowed gaze and crossed arms indicated that he was just as curious as I was.

"I knew they were hanging out and she was into the stuff. I kind of put it all together. I asked her about him later and she wouldn't talk to me about it. Just up and walked away. Well, she flipped me off first."

"Is Molly your age?"

"Yeah, maybe a year older." Elwood took a harsh breath. "Can I go now? I don't know anything else."

I held up my finger as he pivoted to leave. "Wait. When was the last time you saw Orville?"

Elwood stopped and scrunched his mouth. His eyes lifted. He was trying to remember. "Like two weeks before he up and vanished. That's all I know, I promise."

Elwood's promise meant nothing to me, but his slack jaw and round eyes made an impression. He wasn't lying. That didn't mean he didn't know something important without realizing it, and I wouldn't rule out a follow-up visit in the future.

"Go on. That's enough for now."

Elwood didn't waste time. He took off at a jog and quickly disappeared at the dip in the trail.

John and I followed at a walk.

"Do you know this Molly girl?" I asked, looking sideways at John, who stayed in step with me.

"Way back when I was a teenager myself, I dated her mama. Jewel was around ten years older than me, and the relationship only lasted a few months, but her daughter made an impression on me."

"So that would make Molly?" I was quickly doing the math in my head.

He nodded. "She was only four at the time and I was sixteen, but I felt protective over her even after I stopped seeing Jewel."

"You dated a twenty-six-year-old mother when you were only sixteen?" I hated that my voice came out sharp.

John smirked back at me. "What boy wouldn't if given the chance?"

I rolled my eyes and let out a breath. I didn't know why it bothered me so much. Maybe it was that my Chloe was just sixteen and I would never allow her to date a guy ten years older. Which shot my mind in another direction altogether. I hardly knew John. He was more educated than I'd originally assumed and his outdoorsy, survivalist personality wasn't exactly out of the norm around here. But he was intelligent and could have become a lawyer if his family situation had been different.

"Have you kept up with the kid all these years?"

"Naw. I lost track of Molly when she turned five and her mama hooked up with a scary-looking biker dude. After that, there was a long line of bad relationships for Jewel and a lot of chaos for Molly. I'm not surprised she's into crap now after the way she grew up." He eyed me as we started the descent. "It's better to be raised by folks who ignore you than ones that drag you into their drama."

After the way my thoughts had wandered, his statement took me aback. I was about to respond when I stepped in a muddy patch and my foot went right out from under me. John's reflexes were quick. He grabbed my arm before I hit the mud and pulled me up against him.

"Shoot!" I exclaimed.

John used both his hands to brace me, then hoisted me into a standing position again. He didn't immediately let go and our eyes met. My stomach did a somersault and I wriggled away from him as fast as I could. When I looked back, he was just walking along as if nothing had happened.

"Sorry to touch you," he said with a sarcastic tone. "I didn't want to see you end up covered in mud."

I started forward. "That's all right. Thanks for catching me."

"My pleasure."

I did not look his way. I had more important things to think about than how a Dover's quick save had affected me. He simply caught me before I hit the mud. That's all.

"You say you lost track of Molly, but have you heard anything at all about her since then?"

"The last I heard, she moved to Lexington."

I couldn't stop myself from grunting. The distance to travel to the Kentucky's bluegrass region to interview the young woman would slow down the progress of the investigation.

"I'll have Darcy locate her address. I want to talk to her, John."

"I would be disappointed if you didn't."

I swallowed and looked straight ahead. "Any chance you'd want to tag along? It might help to have someone she knows with me."

"It's been a long time. She might hardly recognize me, but sure, it's worth a try." He grinned and reached out when I slid a few feet down the wet slope.

This time, I righted myself and ignored his outstretch hand.

He cracked a smile that made me smile in return. John's good mood was contagious. Here I was, investigating a possible double homicide, and I was enjoying it way too much. I shook my head to clear my thoughts. I had to get back to business.

"Let me give Darcy a call. She should be back to the department by now. I'd like to head out this evening, if that's okay with you."

"Sounds good to me."

Water dripped from the branches above our heads and my boots were packed with mud. The air had turned chilly and even as the clouds lifted, the sky was the buttery color of dusk. Hickory smoke trailed across the meadow, and I inhaled the sweet, charred scent. One of the Dovers had a fire going in their chimney and I could hear children's laughter on the breeze.

The hollow could be a pleasant place when you were invited to be there. If you weren't, it was downright frightening.

My cell phone rang, suddenly breaking the woodsy silence. I quickly pulled it from my pocket, startled that I had reception. The noisy sound was out of place in the deep forest.

It was a local number that wasn't saved to my phone. "This is Sheriff Mills."

"Sheriff, Lucinda Miller here. Do you remember me?"

I stopped in my tracks, and John waited beside me. A face immediately clicked in my mind with the feminine voice. How could I ever forget the Amish woman who I'd shared a horse with on the mad gallop through the cornfield to save her family from a crazed teenager? The time I'd spent with the Amish woman had been incredibly intense, so hearing her on the phone was a bit of a jolt.

"Yes, I do. How is your family?"

"We're very well, thank you." Silence. I was about

to ask why she'd called me when she found her voice again. "Can you come to our farm?"

"Is something wrong?" My heart started pounding.

"Oh, no. Probably not. But I'd like to talk with you in person if you have the time."

I glanced at the ever-darkening sky. No, I didn't have time, but a woman like Lucinda wouldn't have called and asked me to stop by unless there was a problem—and more than likely a serious one.

"Sure. I'm just a few miles away. Give me fifteen minutes."

"Thank you, Sheriff. You are very kind…and prompt."

I hung up and glanced at John. The way his brows shot up, I knew my face gave me away.

"Change of plans. I'm not sure if we'll have the chance to drive to Lexington today. I have to speak with an Amish woman and I'm not sure how long it will take."

"Lucinda Miller?"

Now, I was intrigued. "Yes, how did you know that?"

"Just a lucky guess, I reckon." He ran his hand through his hair. "I'd like to go with you if you don't mind. Mrs. Miller owes me a pie."

I pursed my lips, wondering how John Dover knew Lucinda Miller, but figured I'd interrogate him on the car ride over. We needed to get off the mountain in a hurry.

I lengthened my strides, watching where I stepped

and speaking loudly enough for John to hear me without having to turn my head. "You're full of surprises."

"If that impresses you, I'll try to keep them coming."

I didn't look back, but I didn't need to. I could hear John's breathing close behind and knew that if I suddenly stopped, he'd bump into me.

Perhaps if whatever Lucinda wanted to say didn't take long, we could still see Molly.

And the opportunity to spend more time with John Dover had nothing to do with my train of thought.

14

RUSSO

Darcy pulled up in front of my apartment and put the Jeep into park. While the rain poured down, we sat in silence. Running into Sadie at Geraldine Dover's house was a bit unnerving, yet also satisfying. She was a good cop and followed leads even after business hours. I liked that about her, but at the same time, her persistence bothered me. She was too perceptive of a woman not to read right through whatever charm Anthony might have tried to flatter her with.

The fact that they'd met—and Jimmy too—was a worst-case scenario. Anthony had promised me he'd never come to Possum Gap. Whatever the reason he did, worried me even more.

"Do you think Sadie is mad at us?" Darcy's voice cut through the rain pounding the jeep's metal roof.

"Why would she be?" I tried to focus, but probably sounded distracted. "I don't normally investigate supposed murders."

The inside of the cab was warm, and the windows steamed up as the rush of rainwater made trails down the glass. "Sadie is different than any other sheriff or chief I've met. She thinks out of the box and goes with the flow to solve mysteries. Since we ended up at the same place, she was probably impressed."

A faint smile crept up Darcy's lips. "That would be something." She suddenly turned sharply, facing me. "Do not tell my sister. She'd kill me if she found out."

"Since I don't even know her, the secret is safe with me. But isn't she the sheriff's best friend?"

Darcy slumped. "Yeah. Hopefully, Sadie is impressed as you said. Then maybe she'll word it in a way that takes the heat off me, you know?"

I nodded. "It's been fun, Darcy. Thank you for accompanying me on my mission."

"It feels like we wasted our time. I mean, we didn't find out anything important."

I winked at her. "Just the fact that we were exactly where Sadie went tells me we were on the right track. That's enough for now."

When I clutched the door handle, a bunch of words tumbled from Darcy's mouth.

"Do you want to grab a bite to eat later? Your family can join us. I'll give Anthony and Jimmy a tour of the town. I'm sure the rain will stop soon."

Darcy's brown eyes were bright, and she leaned forward, wide-eyed, and hopeful looking. I hated to burst her bubble, but it had to be done…for me and for her own safety.

"Let's do a rain check." I gestured out the window. "My brother won't be in the mood for socializing."

Before Darcy could try to change my mind, I opened the door and jumped out into the rain. As I jogged up to the front door, I didn't look back, but I heard the Jeep pull away. The place I rented was a first-floor apartment in a square brownstone that had been built in the 1950s and probably hadn't changed much over the past seventy years. The green awning over the doorway kept the rain off me, but just barely as I pulled the keys from my pocket. When I turned the key, I realized the door was already unlocked.

I closed my eyes and inhaled deeply before opening the door.

"It's about time, Ray." Tony sat on the sofa and Jimmy at the small round kitchen table.

The efficiency made it easy to see almost the entire eight-hundred-square-foot apartment at a glance. Jimmy held one of the bottles of beer from my fridge in his hand and Tony sipped from the only wine glass I had. From the way Tony winced after he swallowed, I guessed he wasn't impressed with the cheap Bargain Store brand I'd picked up months ago.

"I see you've both made yourselves at home." I shook the excess water from my hair, then removed my jacket and draped it over the nearest chair. Drops immediately began pooling on the vinyl floor below it. I eased into the recliner, ready for the lecture.

"My God, Ray. This place is a dump. It's bad enough you moved to the land of the hillbillies, but couldn't you find a house to rent that didn't have a neon billboard shouting: Calling all serial killers, rapists, pill heads and pedophiles! This place is a shit-hole."

Tony paused when Jimmy laughed. He set the glass down on the end table and leaned forward, clasping his hands. Tony was six years older than me, and Jimmy was that much older than him. I had a younger brother studying at the University of New York who was a lot more fun to hang out with than either Tony or Jimmy.

I ran my fingers through my damp hair. "Months ago, you told me to find someplace faraway and unexpected to lay low for a while." I spread my hands wide. "Isn't this the perfect place to disappear?"

Anthony barked out a laugh. "I said to go where you'd blend in. Dammit, Ray, you wouldn't stick out any more here if you had an orange construction cone on your head."

Jimmy laughed again. I didn't bother to talk to my cousin. He was Tony's man. If Tony told him to help me, he'd do it. If Tony ordered him to hurt me, he wouldn't blink an eye.

"I like it here. It's different. I told you last week, small-town living is peaceful."

Tony threw his hands up in the air. "Yeah, yeah. You like the fresh air, nice people, and pretty scenery."

"That's right." I sat back and folded my hands on my lap. "What's going on that you'd leave your hot new wife, the four kids on the weekends, and the family business to visit me in this dump, Tony?"

Tony filled his cheeks with air, then blew out loudly. "I wish I was anywhere than here, bro. I do. But we've got a problem."

My palms started to sweat. I chose to remain calm. Panicking never helped anyway. "What kind of problem?"

"The last shipment didn't make it to Chicago." Anthony's face was stony.

"Okay. What happened to it?"

"The best I can figure, we got hustled by the Flores boys."

I rubbed my forehead. "That's not good."

"No, it's not, bro."

"You could have called." I stood up and walked toward my brother. "Does this mean they know about me?"

Tony nodded. "They might. Ma was frantic. She insisted Jimmy and I come down her personally to talk to you—"

"I'm not changing my story. We've been through this a hundred times. Nothing has changed."

Tony jumped to his feet. "Dammit, Ray. If they know you're the one who narced on them, they will come for you."

I paced across the floor towards Jimmy, then turned. "It was the right thing to do."

"That woman was a whore! Who the fuck cares what happened to her!" Tony's temper flared. His face turned red and he puffed out his chest.

"She was a twenty-year-old college student selling sex to pay her bills. She had a mother and a father and a little sister. Her name *was* Frederica, Tony. And it was my job to figure out who bludgeoned her to death. And I did just that. I did my job."

I was tired. I'd explained this so many times, it was engraved in my mind. So was the image of the petite brunette's mashed, bloody face.

Anthony threw his head back and groaned. "Oh, my God, Ray. Where the hell did you get your unreasonable sense of morals? It certainly wasn't from our parents or grandparents."

"Aunt Dorothy," Jimmy said. When Tony and I swiveled simultaneously to look at him, Jimmy took another swig of his beer before adding, "When Ray was a kid, he followed that crazy, cat-collecting old bat around like a puppy dog. She was a non-conformist. Grandpa couldn't stand her. I remember when she got old Mario put behind bars for running over one of those damn cats. He was grandpa's right-hand man, and he ended up in the joint for three years."

"He purposely swerved to hit her pet. Mario was a sick douchebag. He deserved what he got," I argued.

"You've always been one of those nutty PETA anarchists," Jimmy said.

"Because I don't think grown men should purposely run over old lady's cats?" This was precisely one of the reasons I dreaded the holiday season. "Aunt Dorothy was an educated, well-traveled, and kind person. I'm proud if I inherited any of her genes. It's better than taking after Uncle Luca, who smelled like a pound of goat cheese that was set on fire by a cigar."

Tony laughed while shaking his head and wagging his finger at me like ma usually did. "That's funny, but let's get back on subject. Your high morals put away one of the Flores boys and you know the family isn't happy about it." He snorted, his face getting redder. "I don't care about their damn feelings, but I do care about you, bro. If they've figured out that you're here, they'll come for you."

"They aren't going to locate me," I assured him. My gut wasn't as confident of the statement.

Tony flicked his finger between Jimmy and himself. "If we found you, they can."

I inhaled deeply, then smiled at my big brother. "You're underestimating yourself, Tony. *But* you being here does put me in danger, don't you think?"

Tony pointed at me again. "You weren't answering you phone or emails. And Ma wouldn't leave me alone about it."

"What about Dad?"

"He's not happy, Ray. This could blow up into a falling out between the families, which hurts business."

Yes, our father would be thinking about the bottom line. He was laser-focused, cautious, and didn't make mistakes. That's why our family was wealthy, and he wasn't sitting in a prison cell.

"Okay, Tony. Where do you want me to settle that I'll be safer than here? Tell me that and I'll go."

Tony stepped closer. "That's the entire point! You shouldn't settle anywhere. Move around, don't put down roots. You've stayed in this hick town too long. And you weren't supposed to come back here to begin with."

"I like my job. Possum Gap and Sheriff Mills need me."

Tony tilted his head and his cheeks darkened another shade. "Do you like breathing, Ray? Because I guarantee if you stick around one place too long, you won't have the luxury anymore." I straightened up and frowned back at him and his face loosened a little. When he spoke, his voice had lost some of its edge. "Look, I get it. I do. You're different than me and Jimmy. And Ma and Dad don't mind you doing your own thing outside of the business. But Ray, you brought this on yourself and it's up to you to make sure Ma doesn't have to bury a son."

Anthony spoke in a smooth, coaxing way. There was a hint of pleading to his voice, but mostly he sounded like his practical self. He wasn't wrong and deep down

I knew this impromptu trip to the Kentucky backwoods was from his concern over my well-being. It also annoyed the crap out of him that he couldn't control me.

I paced to the only window in the room and looked out. The rain had stopped and the clouds lifted, brightening the sky even though it was nearly dusk. Lush green mountains loomed over the town and mist rose from the dark creases in the places where the ground dipped sharply. It was breathtaking and yet creepy at the same time. The oppressive hills provided a barrier to the outside world that I liked. But they also isolated us. We were captives to nature here, and surprisingly, for a city boy, that appealed to me greatly.

"Okay, Tony, you win." I turned around. "Give me a week or two to help the sheriff solve our latest case. A floater washed up from the river—a boy—I think he was murdered before he went into the water. Another boy was found in a similar fashion around twenty miles downriver four years ago." When Tony rolled his eyes, I quickly added, "Sadie needs me, Tony. Come on, a week isn't going to make a difference."

Tony licked his lips, then exhaled for a long time and very loudly. "You're full of yourself, Ray. A case like that might take months or even years to solve"—I began to speak and he raised his palm to shut me up—"but I'll give you a week. You pick the place, I don't care where; just as long as it's far from here." Tony's eyes narrowed. "Do you understand me?"

"I do."

Tony picked up his coat from the back of the chair and Jimmy stood up after chugging down the rest of his beer, set it on the table, and went to the door.

"You guys are welcome to stay here. There's the couch and I have a cot in the closet."

Tony snickered and Jimmy rolled his eyes as he opened the door.

"We're getting out of here, Ray, as fast as we can." He grabbed me into a bear hug. I stood limply in his grasp. "Watch your back, bro. The Sheriff and her deputy seem to have their act together, but they wouldn't stand a chance against the Flores family if they find you."

The corner of my mouth lifted as I thought about the Dover clan. "You might be surprised," I said.

"For your sake, I hope you're right." Tony made eye contact and held my gaze for a few long seconds before he followed Jimmy outside.

When the door closed behind them, I walked to the refrigerator and pulled out a water bottle. I wanted to get back to the department to research the Wilken's drowning victim and study the Puissant River area maps.

If I only had a week to help Sadie crack the case, there was no time to spare.

15

LUCINDA

"**C**an't I ride my pony?" Sarah asked in a whiny voice that made me clench my teeth.

I turned away from the kitchen sink and crossed my arms. Sarah sat on James' lap. He was finishing up his last bite of peanut butter pie and not looking in my direction. Phoebe had fallen asleep in her highchair again and her chubby cheek rested in the mashed potatoes on her plate that she hadn't eaten. Josh sat on the chair in the corner of the room, completely focused on whittling a chunk of cedar wood into the shape of a horse. I gasped when his hand slipped from the wood and the knife nicked him. He was a ten-year-old boy and more than old enough to work with the small knife, but if he cut himself deeply, I would be the one doctoring his wound and cleaning up the blood he spilled.

"Ack, Sarah. Look out the window, will you? The rain may have stopped for the moment, but it could start again at any time." The sides of Sarah's mouth dipped and she crossed her arms, mimicking me. "Besides, it's almost dark. Go on and get your pajamas on. I'll be in to read you a book once I've put Phoebe in her crib."

James lifted Sarah from his lap. "Go on, girl. Do as your mama tells you. There will be time a plenty for riding in the morning—unless you have so much energy that you want to sweep the kitchen floor?"

Sarah squealed, then took off into the hallway. I hid a smile as I dried the last dish and placed it in the cupboard. "Josh, finish that up. If I'm not mistaken, you have a reading assignment to complete for school."

Josh was less dramatic as he set the partially finished statue on the shelf and closed his pocketknife. "I don't see why Miss Rosetta sends work home every night. She doesn't like us kids very much."

"To the contrary, Josh. Rosetta challenges you all more than previous teachers have, and I for one am glad for the push." I wiped down the counter, then hung the cloth over the curved faucet.

"I wish my teachers had made me read more," James chimed in. He was carefully disengaging Phoebe from her spoon. "You know more words than me and I'm an old man." James winked at me.

"Yeah, I do know a lot of English words and what they mean," Josh agreed. After he wiped his hands on the sides of his pants, he jogged out of the room, leaving James, Phoebe, and me alone.

"I'll clean her up," James said as he picked the stocky twenty-month-old up.

I nodded, grateful for the break. It took a minute more to clean the highchair and push it back against the wall. As the sun dipped below the hills to the west and the windows darkened, the kitchen seemed to brighten even more. I glanced at the baby blanket that I was knitting where I had tossed it on the couch. It was for Bethany Mast and her first born child. The babe wasn't due until December, but at the rate I was going, I might not finish the project in time for the birth.

Sighing, I picked it up and sat down. I would rather read a few chapters of the newest book I'd borrowed from the library. It was a story about a woman who travels in time back to Scotland in the 1700s. *It will have to wait.* It had already kept me from chores too often this past week. In the beginning, the romantic scenes made me uncomfortable, then I started reading them to James and we would laugh and blush together.

I crossed my legs, tucking my feet under my green dress and picking up the long needles. When a flash of light traveled across the wall, I rose and padded on bare feet to the window. Looking out, I inhaled sharply. A police car was parked in front of the hitching rail. I ran back to the counter and quickly coiled my hair into a bun and put the cap back on. I didn't have time to insert all the pins, but a few would be sufficient inside and without the wind blowing. Next, I slipped on the black crocs, then there was a knock on the door.

After smoothing out the front of my dress and taking a deep breath, I crossed the room and opened the door. Sheriff Mills smiled at me and I smiled back.

"Hel—" My mouth snapped shut when I saw the kind Englisher who had stopped Goliath from running away with his pickup truck. Mr. Dover's hair was still tied back in a ponytail and although he wasn't wearing the same shirt, he looked very similar in faded trousers and a denim jacket.

John stepped around the sheriff and extended his hand. "Good evening. I thought this was as good a time as any to collect my pie."

As we shook hands, he winked. I glanced at the sheriff and discovered she was looking at him with a raised brow.

"I'm surprised you two know each other," Sheriff Mills said.

"Mr. Dover assisted me in slowing my horse down the other day." I smiled at the English man who had his head tilted just enough to spy on the sheriff's reaction.

I worked to keep my face neutral, but I inwardly smiled. Being quite perceptive about such things, I sensed the tension between these two. Later, I would tell James that the sheriff liked Mr. Dover, but didn't realize it yet. Mr. Dover already knew.

"Why of course!" I hurried over to the hutch and opened the doors. "Will it be peanut butter, cherry or pumpkin?"

The sheriff made a huffing noise, but Mr. Dover moved forward. "My oh my, that's a difficult choice." He made a show of sniffing each one, then he cupped his chin with his fingertips. "I do declare, your pumpkin reminds me of my grannies on mama's side of the family. I've missed her pies, so let's go with the pumpkin."

I took the pie over to the counter and began wrapping it in foil. "This time of year, I always have pies on hand. Don't be shy if you're hungry for one like your grannie made." When the sheriff leaned over the counter to see the pie better, I returned to the hutch. "Please, Sheriff, you'll take one as well, won't you?"

"I couldn't—"

"I insist. What's your favorite?"

The sheriff came reluctantly forward. "My daughter likes peanut butter a lot, if it's really no trouble."

"It's no trouble at all, especially after everything you did for us last summer," I said, busying myself with the wrapping of the pie. It wasn't a subject I liked to remind myself of.

"Thank you very much. Chloe will be thrilled. I don't bake."

"No! That surprises me," Mr. Dover said.

When I glanced his way, I saw the twinkle in his eye, then the sheriff shook her head, amused by the banter.

"It's great that John and I get pies and all, but exactly why are we here? You sounded more urgent on the phone than you appear now."

I wiped my hands on the cloth and set the pies aside. "Come sit with me at the table."

My pulse picked up as the sheriff sat across from me and Mr. Dover took the seat next to her.

"Sheriff, I'm sorry to drag you out on a rainy night."

"Please, call me Sadie. And we were just a few miles away."

I leaned over the table. "Oh...on Dark Hollow Road?"

"Yeah, that's right. How did you know?" The sheriff's—or Sadie's—brow knitted.

"That's where I was when I met Mr. Dover. Has he not told you about my calamity?"

Sadie swiveled in her seat to look at Mr. Dover. "No, he didn't."

Mr. Dover shrugged. "Guess I didn't get around to it. We have been preoccupied this afternoon." The corners of his mouth lifted.

"Mrs. Miller, what happened?" Sadie pulled out a notebook and pen, ready to take notes.

"If I'm to call you Sadie, then you must call me Lucinda." When Sadie nodded, I continued, "I was taking a short cut to my friend's home and normally don't pass that way."

"Nor will she again," James said from the hallway. When he arrived at the table, he shook their hands.

"I've heard much about you, Mr. Dover. Thank you for coming to Lucinda's aid."

"Glad to help." Mr. Dover leaned back in the chair. He seemed uncomfortable with the attention and content to let Sadie do the talking.

James pulled up the chair next to me. "It's good to see you, Sheriff, in a less urgent situation."

"I agree," Sadie said.

"Go on, Lucinda. Finish what you were saying before I came in." James reached over and patted my hand. Being around Englishers, he wasn't as reserved as he would have been if we were sitting around the table with our people.

"James is right. I will no longer go that way if I'm alone or with the children. There's a brute of a man who frightened me and my horse."

Mr. Dover leaned forward and nudged Sadie with his elbow. "Cooter Calhoun."

Sadie's eyes grew larger, and she inclined her head. "Did Cooter threaten you?"

"Goliath accidently ran over his dog." I stopped myself and let out a breath. "That wouldn't be truthful. The large horse was aggravated with the dogs and kicked out on purpose. I felt terrible about it"—I glanced at James—"and was going to offer to pay for veterinarian fees, but he shot the dog before I had a chance to say anything."

James jumped in. "He called my wife horrible names and frightened her. The gunshot and yelling

173

caused the horse to run off. Lucinda and Goliath could have been seriously injured if Mr. Dover hadn't shown up in the nick of time."

Sadie glanced at her watch. "Don't let Cooter get to you. He's a big jerk and likes to run his mouth, but he's probably already gone to the pound for another dog and forgotten all about you by now."

Seeing Sadie begin to rise, I blurted out, "Wait! There's something else more sinister."

The sheriff sat back down. "Go on."

"There's a boy from our community who's been missing for a few days."

Sadie opened her mouth to speak, but James interrupted her. "Well, we don't really know if he's truly missing. Lucinda is concerned that he may be."

"You're either missing or you're not missing." Sadie shot James a frown and a disapproving gaze. "What's the kid's name?"

I answered. "Albert Peachy."

"How old is he?"

I noticed how Mr. Dover sat forward.

"Fourteen. But the boy has been acting out—rebelling, I guess you'd say," I said.

"Is he doing that Rumspringa thing?" Mr. Dover asked.

"That doesn't usually happen until children reach seventeen, but our community doesn't even recognize the practice," James said.

"But you said he was rebelling. Isn't that kind of what it's all about?" Sadie asked.

"Well, sort of. It's a time when youth in some communities are allowed to experience the outside world. Children like Albert are impatient," I pointed out.

"Okay, I can fill out a missing person report and we'll go from there. What are his parents' names?"

"Oh, they don't want to do that right now." I glanced at James. He quickly looked down at the table. "It's something that worries me, and I wanted to talk to you about it."

Sadie lowered the pen. "A fourteen-year-old has been gone for a few days and the parents don't want me to investigate?" The tone of her voice was judgmental.

James straightened. "It is not unusual for our children to run away to a friend on the outside or a relative who went English."

"Do you think he might be off playing Xbox with some English kids?" Sadie puckered her lips. Mr. Dover's brows rose high.

"Perhaps...I hoped you could take the information down and keep a look out for him. Maybe talk to some people without it being official." I held my breath and my heart pattered in my chest.

Sadie exchanged a glance with Mr. Dover. They were both English and might see things the same way.

"Okay, sure. Who do you think he was hanging out with?" Sadie asked.

I shifted my gaze to Mr. Dover. His eyes flared. He knew.

"There's a tan trailer just a mile south of where Mr. Calhoun's dogs attacked my horse. A teenage boy lives there. His name is Wade Blanchard. I went to talk to him. He wasn't much help, and yet he was also wondering where Albert was. I know it's not much to go on and Albert could very well be staying with another friend or even one of his cousins who went English."

James spoke up. "Most of his cousins have left us, which is probably a reason why his folks aren't more concerned about his whereabouts."

Sadie got a faraway look on her face, like she was thinking deeply about something else. "What does Albert look like?"

"He's a lanky boy and short for his age. His full head of curly blond hair is what most people notice about him."

"Do you have a picture of him?"

"No, of course not." When I saw her brows crinkle, I added, "Our people aren't allowed to take photographs."

16

SADIE

Once the car doors were shut and I'd started the engine, I finally turned to John. "Are you still up for a drive to talk to Molly?" The pink blush of the sky that wasn't obscured by clouds indicated we didn't have much daylight left.

"Of course. I don't have anything else to do tonight." He cocked his head and grinned. "On one condition."

"I don't like conditions." I slowly pulled onto the roadway, aware that buggies, kids, bicyclists, and pedestrians were everywhere in the Amish settlement.

"Wow. You are so uptight. I'm hungry, that's all. I would dig into the pie, but I think if we're going to drive all the way to Lexington, I need some real food in my belly."

I suddenly realized that I hadn't eaten since

breakfast and was starved myself. "We'll stop at the burger place off the highway at exit 86," I told John without looking his way. The road was still slick, and I slowed when a couple of girls whizzed by on bikes without reflectors.

"Sounds like a plan." John lowered the seat back and shut his eyes.

It wasn't until we pulled back onto the highway and he was eating his burger that he started talking again.

"Are you thinking what I'm thinking?"

A nearly full moon hung between the break in the clouds. Streetlights flicked on and the rhythmic drumming of the car speeding along relaxed me. After I took a sip of my milkshake, I said, "There are tons of blond kids around. Just because Albert is similar in coloring and size to our young John Doe, doesn't mean he's in danger."

"Sounds like you're trying to convince yourself that."

I barely knew John, but he'd read me quite well that time. "If we're going by patterns, Orville and our unidentified body met their ends four years apart. Albert went missing a few of days ago."

"It could all be random coincidence, right?"

I let out a breath and watched the dilapidated buildings of an old, shutdown factory flash by. "I don't usually believe in random anything. My gut tells me they're connected and without anything else to go on, it's all I have at the moment. But the autopsy Russo conducted says our floater died approximately a week ago, so at least we know that the body isn't Albert."

"How did you end up as a cop, Sadie?"

When he said my name, a shiver raced through me. "I got pregnant with Chloe the end of my senior year. Ted—my ex—and I married because it seemed like the best thing to do at the time. While he was in law school, I quizzed him a lot. I knew I couldn't stand a desk job, but I was fascinated by law and order. Law enforcement seemed like a good fit. I never really dreamt of becoming sheriff though. That sort of just happened after Sheriff Buckley dropped dead of a heart attack and Buddy wouldn't fill in for him."

"But you ran when the term ended and got elected. You must have liked the job enough to go to the trouble."

My thoughts drifted back to a couple years ago when I ran against Daly Clifton—one of the old trolls of the county. Sure, he had money and the votes of everyone over seventy, but I had Tanya.

"Tanya got me elected. She's a great campaign manager."

"You two were inseparable in high school."

My head snapped sideways. "Did you attend Possum Gap High School while I was there?"

John swallowed his last bite of burger, then took a large sip of cola. He'd insisted on buying both our orders and I was in such a hurry to be on our way, I didn't argue with him.

"I was a sophomore when you were a senior," he said quietly. "I'm not surprised you never noticed me. I was kind of scrawny back then. All of my flame-haired cousins stole the show," he added with a chuckle.

I searched my memories for John Dover's younger self. Nowadays, he was tall, well-muscled, and had a playful charisma that the ladies loved. It was hard to imagine him not sticking out in the high school crowd.

John could tell I was wracking my mind to remember him. "I played soccer with your hubby, but I sat on the bench my entire sophomore year. It wasn't until I was a junior that it kind of clicked with me."

A trickling of a memory flicked in my mind. I was in the bleachers with friends and Ted walked toward me with a couple of his buddies. Another kid followed behind with his head down. When the group reached us, there was barely enough space on the seats for us. The skinny kid turned around headed back down a couple of rows, sitting by himself. I had felt sorry for him even though I didn't know his name at the time.

"I had no idea you were a Dover back then." I eyed him. "You've changed a lot."

His smile broadened. "You look the same."

I barked out a laugh.

"No, really, you do. Compared to all the other women from school, you're completely natural. No makeup or jewelry. Your hair is the same rich brown color from back then."

I let out the sigh carefully and quietly. If he wasn't

a Dover and I wasn't the sheriff, I would think that he was flirting with me.

"Girls mature faster than guys. I guess I had hit my stride and you were still working on yours."

"Something like that," John muttered.

Our conversations were easy and that bugged me, so I got back on topic. "It's this exit. How are you going to handle seeing Molly after all these years?"

"Eh, she was just a little kid back then. Like I said, I doubt she'll remember me and besides giving you some company on the trip, my presence probably won't matter much at all."

I pulled off the highway and our conversation stayed light, talking about cooler weather in the forecast and how his bees hibernated over the winter. The apartment complex I parked in front of was more upscale than I expected. Amenities included a swimming pool, dog park, and a large sign pointed to the gym.

"Looks like Molly has done okay for herself," I said before we exited the vehicle.

I still wore the uniform and worried that Molly might clam up when she saw it, but when she opened the door, her eyes were only for John.

"Oh my God, you're John, Mamma's x-boyfriend!" She flung open the door and hopped out on the covered walkway, staring at him.

Molly's long blonde hair was braided. She wore sweatpants and a comfy looking tie-dye sweater. A vanilla scent wafted from her apartment into the night air.

"How are you, Molly?" John asked.

"I graduated from nursing school six months ago and I've been working nights at the hospital. Today is my day off."

"Wow, that's good to hear. I'm sorry I never visited—"

Molly shook her head and her braid bounced from side to side. "Oh, Mamma wouldn't have wanted to see you and you know how she gets. It was rough for a lot of years, but a few years ago, I got out of Possum Gap and my life changed."

The young woman's gaze finally settled on me. Well, first it skimmed over my jacket. "You came all the way here from Possum Gap? What did Mamma do?"

"I'm not here about your mother, Molly. I'm Sheriff Mills and I'm working on an investigation. I have a few questions for you, if you can spare a minute."

Molly nodded and gestured for us to enter her apartment. "Do you all want a cola or water or something?"

"Nothing for me, thanks." The apartment was sparsely decorated and very tidy. With only one painting on the cream-colored walls and a small sofa and a rectangular kitchen table with benches, I guessed she'd recently moved in. A new job in a new town equaled a new apartment.

Molly pulled out two bottles of cola and handed one to John. He took it and sat on a stool at the island. I remained standing and she sat on the other stool.

"What's going on?" Her legs were crossed but the

way she bounced her foot, I knew she was suddenly nervous about my visit. Who wouldn't be if a sheriff from their hometown showed up on their doorstep unannounced?

"I want to talk to you about Orville Walker."

"Oh, wow." She turned to John. "Are you dating this woman?"

"Not yet," he replied.

My cheeks burned and I ignored him. I didn't get flustered—ever.

Clearing my throat, I leaned on the island. "A body of a teenager was found in the river the other day. There are enough similarities to Orville. It's my understanding you were one of the last people to see Orville before he disappeared. You didn't want to talk back then. Are you willing to open up now?"

Molly popped her neck before focusing her attention on John. "Well, this isn't the reunion I was expecting."

"Sorry, Molly." John shrugged. "If you can help us get to the bottom of Orville's death, it might help with the new kid's case. He hasn't even been ID'd yet."

Molly closed her eyes. I was about to speak when she began.

"I met Orville at the Possum Gap Fair when we were sixteen. I thought we might start dating, but it turned out he didn't like me that way."

"Was Orville gay?" I asked.

"Yeah, but he didn't want to be. And he hid it from

his parents and everyone else. I was the only person in the world who knew."

"Okay. Did that have something to do with his disappearance?"

"Maybe. He got all depressed and started to hang around with Elwood Dover. I didn't like him very much. He was obnoxious, and I think he's the one that introduced Orville to drugs. It got so bad that I told him I didn't want to hang out anymore. I had enough of that kind of shit—" She stopped and scrunched her face. "Sorry about that. You know, with my mama and all her boyfriends."

"When did you cut ties?" I asked.

"A few days before he went missing." She sniffed and dabbed at her eye. Her shaking foot was vibrating the counter. "For a while I thought it was my fault, but my psych classes made me realize that he was on a collision course with trouble and nothing I did or didn't do was going to stop him."

"The coroner thought it was an accidental drowning. His toxicology report was clean, so he wasn't using at the time of his death. Sheriff Adam Crawford and Chrissy Coleman weren't so sure. What do you think?"

"I think his friend got him killed."

I glanced at John and he was staring past Molly.

"Elwood?" I asked.

"No, his other friend. Jeremiah Calhoun."

"Tell me more about the Calhouns," I said as we pulled out of the apartment's parking lot.

John was ready. "Kaine and Lita rarely leave their property. It's even worse since Jeremiah died. I reckon I haven't seen either of them in person in few years."

I navigated the traffic, wondering where all these people were going at this late hour. The streets were lit up like it was daytime and parking lots were full and businesses thrived. Back in Possum Gap, the roads would be clear, with only a few evening stragglers that did their shopping later than usual because the high school football team had an away game. Now, they were hurrying home. The only businesses that would be open were the gas stations—and the café which stayed open until ten o'clock on the weekends. In Possum Gap, pretty much everything closed when the sun set.

"Cancer, right?"

"Yeah. Jeremiah had leukemia. He struggled with it for years. I often wondered if he'd been living in a better place, with better people, he'd still be around today."

I glanced over. John was looking straight ahead as he slowly rubbed his jaw. His stubble was more prominent than it had been than when he'd snuck up on me hours ago in the woods.

"Are you saying poverty gave him cancer?"

John gave a shake of his head. He lifted his chin. "They're dirt poor and uneducated, Sadie. Maybe if Jeremiah had gotten medical help earlier or if he'd been taken care of in the first place, things would have been different."

"How old was he when he passed?"

"Around seventeen years old, I think," John said.

"And when did he die?" Thoughts shot through my mind like stray bullets.

"I believe it was four and a half years ago." After he said it, John made a grunting noise. "Molly said Orville hung around with Jeremiah and Elwood. Perhaps Jeremiah's death affected Orville and he really did commit suicide."

"Anything is possible at this point."

And it was. But the missing digits kept me returning to murder. How could Orville and the boy in the river this week both have fingers missing? I refused to believe it was coincidence.

The sign for the highway came into view when my cell phone rang. It was Russo.

"Hey, what's up?"

"Are you still in Lexington?"

We were almost to the intersection leading onto the highway when I hit the brakes and pulled into a Fast Chicken parking lot. "Yes, why?"

"I have an ID for our body."

Russo paused and I urged, "Go on."

"Liam McCoy. He's been missing for nearly four years."

"So, he was around thirteen at the time?"

"Yeah. And get this, I only got a hit on him after

I expanded my search to all fifty states, Canada and Mexico. Guess where I found him?"

"Just tell me, Russo."

"Ontario, Canada. The boy's a Canuck."

"Then how the hell did he end up in Possum Gap?"

"Darcy and I asked the same question and with a little more digging, we uncovered Liam's grandmother is a Kentuckian and currently living in Lexington. Her name is Paula Simmons. I have her address for you."

After I wrote down the address and Russo gave me a few more details, I hung up. John faced me, waiting.

"You're stuck with me a little longer," I told him. "We're heading back into the city."

"And to think, my plans for this evening were to finish reading a fishing book and go to bed before midnight. Sadie Mills, you certainly have livened up my life in a very short time."

It was strange having John Dover ride along with me, and yet also familiar in a way. For all our differences, we grew up in the same town and knew the same people. It was a connection that formed a bond of sorts. Here in a different city—a larger one—we were kindred spirits, sharing the colorful Possum Gap History.

And the way this case quickly expanded into unfamiliar territory, I was glad for the company.

17

RUSSO

O nly darkness was beyond my office window, although I could see the outlines of a tree's branches swaying in the moonlight.

The aroma of coffee was strong, and I inhaled before taking a sip. "The office brew master is okay in a pinch but thank God the café stays open late on Fridays. And of course, thanks to you, Darcy, for running over there at this hour."

Darcy stretched out her legs in front of her as she clutched her own cup across the desk from me. She had on a pair of dark, high-waisted jeans and a yellow blouse. Her large hoop earrings kept drawing my attention.

"It's getting late. Did Sadie say when she'd be back?"

"It depends on whether or not she can locate the

grandmother. I already alerted Canadian officials that the boy's body was recovered here in Possum Gap, but it's doubtful anyone contacted next of kin this soon. Sadie could have waited until the morning and made another trip, but I guess she didn't want to."

"Sadie has many virtues; patience isn't one of them." Darcy's gaze went to the window. "Does it scare you to think someone might be out there right now who murdered a couple of teenagers?"

I took another sip and thought about her question before answering. Her wording made me smile a little. "Crimes are being committed every minute of the day across this country—from theft to homicide. Knowing what's happening out there makes me feel better. That's the only way to protect yourself."

"You're awfully gloomy, Russo. How did you ever get so paranoid?" Darcy tilted her head, narrowing her eyes. The intensity of her stare made me squirm in my seat. She had online access to files through the sheriff's department that could reveal who my family was. As long as she—and Sadie—didn't suspect anything, and begin digging deeper, my secret was safe.

"I work with dead people, and I've seen nearly every kind of death possible. This line of work makes all of us paranoid."

A deep voice cut into our conversation. "When's Sadie getting back?"

I looked up to find Buddy striding in. His great size and booming voice startled me enough to make my coffee go down the wrong pipe. The big man waited while I coughed.

Darcy stood up. "Are you alright? I have first aid emergency training."

I waved her away and cleared my throat a couple of times before I could talk. "I'm fine." Then I answered Buddy. "We have an ID for our floater and there's a family tie in Kentucky she's following up on."

"Is he a Lexington boy?" Buddy asked. His snow-white hair contrasted greatly with his tanned, rough skin.

"Canadian," I said.

Buddy snorted. "Nothing surprises me anymore. We have an accident on Second Street with several injured. Looks like alcohol played a part." When I stood, Buddy elaborated, "No fatalities. But since it's in the city limits, we're working with the police department. They're short staffed this weekend between Chief Tanner's daughter's wedding and three officers being out sick."

"What do you need, Buddy?" Darcy was ready for action.

"A boy out on Dark Hollow Road wants to talk to someone. He wouldn't give dispatch any information. It doesn't sound urgent, so it'll have to wait until morning." Buddy handed Darcy a piece of paper. "Can you call the kid back and tell him we'll be out there tomorrow?"

"Sure, Buddy. I'll get right on it."

I grabbed my jacket. "I'll come with you. Maybe I can help."

Buddy shook his head and kept walking. "This is pretty straightforward and since we don't have any bodies, you might as well head home and rest up. You did a good job tracking down the boy's identity. I reckon tomorrow is going to be a busy day."

Darcy lingered until we couldn't hear Buddy's heavy footsteps any longer.

"I'll go make that call." She glanced at the floor and inhaled. "Well, I'll see you in morning."

As she pivoted, I took a step forward. "Wait. What's the name on the paper?"

Darcy held it up. "Wade Blanchard."

"Wait, I saw that surname on a plat map of the southeast side of the county. Isn't that close to Jewelweed Hollow?"

"Just up the road, *why*?" Darcy's brow knitted. She was concerned and rightfully so.

"I wonder if this Blanchard kid has something important to say and by morning, he could change his mind or one of his relatives might make sure he keeps his mouth shut."

"Okay. What are you saying?"

"We can go out there and interview him—"

"I don't think that's a good idea, Russo. I'm guessing Sadie is still upset about us going to the compound to snoop around. We need to leave the investigating to the professionals."

Darcy sounded sure of herself, but I saw the flicker of doubt in her eyes. "It might be important. How would you feel if tomorrow something terrible happened to the kid?"

"Buddy's a pretty good at sorting out the real problems with the matters that can wait."

I had mixed feelings about bringing Darcy along anyway. She knew everyone by name, it seemed, and spoke their language. I was just an outsider. But after witnessing firsthand how quickly tensions rose among the Dovers over the summer, having her join me might not be the safe.

"I'll stay in touch with dispatch. It's probably nothing, but I'll sleep better if I at least see what the kid has to say." I was almost through the door when Darcy picked up her cup of coffee from the top of my desk.

"I'm coming with you."

"You don't have to—"

"We're a team." When I raised a brow, she chuckled and swatted me on the shoulder. "No one's going to talk to you with that accent anyway."

"I'm not the one with the accent."

As we left the office, my mind drifted back to Liam McCoy.

How did a Canadian kid end up floating in a river in this strange part of the world?

18

SADIE

I was just about to turn away from the door when a light flicked on in the window. John leaned sideways to look inside but I stayed planted where I was. The tree-lined street was still and quiet. It was a tidy neighborhood mostly made up of older, two-story Victorian style houses. Paula Simmons' house was brick, with three large oaks in the front yard. A narrow slab of wood with the word *welcome* written in cursive on it sat near the front door. The home felt cheerful with the decorative pillows on the porch swing.

The door opened a few inches. "Hello, I'm looking for Paula Simmons."

The woman had gray hair and an abundance of wrinkles on her face. Yet for the age her face showed, her body was slim and her movements loose. The pants and flowery top gave me the impression she'd changed before answering the door.

"I'm Paula. Is there something wrong?" She cracked the door a little more and looked me up and down before switching her gaze to John who stood off to the side.

I was glad I was in uniform. Otherwise, she might not have opened the door. "I'm sorry to bother at this hour. It couldn't wait until morning."

"Oh dear. What is it?" She stepped onto the porch, leaving the door ajar behind her.

This part of the job was always hard. I took a deep breath and looked at the woman. A spray of moonlight lit up her face and I could see the worry in her bluish eyes.

"Maybe we should talk inside. You might want to sit down."

"No, no. My house is a mess. You can do your talking right here."

There, I heard it—a little Appalachian twang. "I'm the Sheriff from Possum Gap. Are you from there?"

She shook her head. "Tennessee, in the Smokey Mountains, though I've lived here in Lexington for a third of my long life."

The woman was old but not frail. "I have bad news I'm afraid. The body of your grandson, Liam, has been found in my town."

When Paula wobbled a little, John took her arm and guided her to the porch swing. She sat down while John and I took the wicker chairs.

"I never thought that boy would be found. At least he can be laid to rest next to his granddaddy." She blew out a long, shaky breath. Her eyes were moist, but she was handling the news better than I thought she would. "How did you identify him? Was it his teeth?"

John's eyes flared and I ran the question through my head a second time. "Paula, your grandson died about a week ago."

"That's impossible. He's been gone for three years." Paula patted her chest as she caught her breath.

I left the chair and joined her on the swing. When I put my arm around her shoulders, she was shaking.

"Do you want to me call anyone for you? Maybe another relative or a friend?"

Paula shook her head vigorously. "There's only me. I have a couple of girlfriends that I play cards with on Sunday afternoons, but I'll ring them tomorrow." She shrugged away from my touch and I sat back. "Tell me everything, please, everything."

It took a few minutes to recount finding Liam's body in the Puissant and what Russo's examination revealed. When I finished, we sat in silence. I'd forgotten John was even there until he sniffed, and I looked up.

He was staring at me and when I raised a brow, he quickly looked away.

"Liam was a troubled boy, but it's no wonder. His mother was a piece of work. She was never content to stay in one place very long." Paula paused, her eyes darting upwards, and she silently counted on her fingers. "She and the boy stayed here with me for two years, which I believe to be a record for her."

I hesitated. "Where is she now?"

"Joy died of a drug overdose last year. She had problems before Liam disappeared, and afterwards, she was a complete mess."

"Do you have any idea how Liam ended up in Possum Gap?" John spoke up in a quiet voice.

Paula took a deep breath. "His mother dated a fellow from their for a short time, that's all I know."

I sat forward on the swing, my feet firmly planted to keep it from moving. Here's the connection I was looking for. "When was this?"

"It must have been four years ago. Joy lived with him for a while before they had a falling out. From the sounds of it, he wasn't as into the drugs as she was. Her addiction put a strain on the relationship. She moved back here when they split, but Liam liked that fellow and begged her to take him back to visit him."

"Liam returned to Possum Gap, then?"

"Not that I ever knew. Now, with the news you bring, I guess he did."

"So, it would have been around a year after the breakup, is that right?" I had my notebook out and jotted down dates. If what Paula said was accurate, somehow, Liam went back to Possum Gap and never left.

But he was alive until a week ago...

Paula nodded. The creases on her face deepened as she frowned. She was thinking the same thing.

I said a prayer my head that Paula could answer the next question. "Do you remember the name of the man Joy was dating in Possum Gap?"

"I never forget a name, and his was unusual, so even easier to remember."

I exchanged a glance with John. He too was frowning, his brow knitted tightly.

I held my breath. "Go on."

"Summit Dover. Joy showed me a picture of him one time. He had red hair and a beard the same color."

19

RUSSO

The only redeeming thing about the place was the huge oak tree draping most of the front yard with its branches full of golden leaves. Even in the moonlight, the tree practically glowed. The damp grass made my shoes and the bottom of my pants wet. A sideways glance at Darcy confirmed that she didn't seem to care as she marched up to the front door of the single-wide trailer. I slipped my hand into my jacket and fondled the revolver in my pocket. It only held five rounds, but it would do in a pinch. Dad always said if a person was a good shot, a big gun wasn't necessary. I might not live a violent life like Tony and Jimmy, but we did have things in common. The same as them, I'd spent too many hours to count at the range as a kid with Dad, Grandpa and my uncles. I knew how to shoot.

While Darcy knocked, I looked around the front of the house, then at the dark, desolate roadway. There weren't any houses in sight and no vehicles had passed since we pulled up. It looked like the perfect place for an ambush. Now that we were here, a cold pinch of uncertainty gripped me. Maybe we should have let Buddy and Sadie handle the call in the morning.

"Looks like no one's home," I said in a voice barely louder than a whisper. The only other sound was the wind through the branches. Long shadows came and went with the quickly moving clouds passing over the full moon.

"There's a light on," Darcy said, standing back with her hands on her hips. She didn't look like she was going anywhere.

A yowling sound pierced the night and my heart froze. Then another joined in, and another, growing louder until the primitive cacophony sounded like it was coming from right behind the trailer.

Darcy grinned at me. It was nice that my terror amused her.

"It's only a den of coyotes, Russo. Chill. They probably just made a kill."

Predatorial animals were out of my realm of experience. I didn't care if Darcy thought I was an idiot for being cautious about a hungry pack of sixty plus pound canines on the loose nearby.

I started down the steps. "Come on. We'll come back in the morning."

The scraping sound of the door opening turned me back around. The teenager who stepped out was a scrawny kid with messy, shoulder length hair. He closed the door behind him and shook Darcy's hand.

"I've seen you at the café, haven't I?" the boy asked.

"I practically live there," she said with a laugh and a smile. "I'm Darcy and this is Russo. Deputy Gallenstien told us about your call."

He nodded slowly. "Are you cops?"

I continued to look around. The coyotes had stopped yipping but that might be because they were sneaking up on us. My head and gut shouted simultaneously at me to get the hell out of there.

"No, but Russo is the town's coroner and I work at the Sheriff's Department. We wanted to check in on you and make sure everything is okay." Darcy's voice was soft, friendly, and soothing.

The boy relaxed, tucking his hands deep into his pockets. "An Amish lady and her husband came by the other day asking about my friend Albert Peachy. I should have just said something when they were here..." He trailed off, glancing past us.

"You can tell us. We're here to help," Darcy said in her coaxing voice.

My focus on survival was momentarily suspended as what he said registered in my mind. "You're friends with an Amish kid?"

"Yeah. Have been for over a year."

"Is that a thing?" I directed the question at Darcy

at first and when she shrugged, I spoke to Wade. "How did you two meet?"

The boy leaned back against the metal siding. "Sometimes, I work at the mill, carrying feed bags and stuff for customers. His family is there all the time. We started talking and one day, he just showed up at my house." The corner of his mouth lifted. "I saw his horse tied to the electric pole and I couldn't believe it. Albert asked if I had a television set and of course I do."

The Amish were full of surprises. "Why did they come to see you?"

"Albert's been missing for several days. Somehow, they knew about me and how we hang out together sometimes. They thought I knew where he was."

I stepped up beside Darcy. The lurking coyotes still worried me, but suddenly, I had a lot of questions that needed to be answered.

"Were they relatives?"

"No, some neighbors, I guess."

I only knew one Amish family and surely, it wasn't them. "What were their names?"

"I think Miller...Lucinda, and I can't remember her husband's name."

I swallowed hard. What were the odds?

Darcy spoke up. "Has anyone filed a missing person report?"

Wade shook his head. "I don't think so."

Darcy took out her phone and began typing notes on it. "Albert Peachy you said?"

"Yeah."

Another missing boy? Could just be a runaway… or…something much more sinister. The fact that a body of a teenager just showed up in the river and another male, about the same age, had suffered the same fate a few years ago made the missing Amish boy a real concern. "Did you remember something about Albert that would help his community and us find him?"

He nodded and took a couple steps to reach the edge of the stoop, not looking at us. "Albert started doing meth. I don't know why. It was stupid."

I remained quiet as his words sank in and Darcy inhaled sharply.

It took a few seconds to recover from the kid's statement. "How old is Albert?"

"Same as me—fourteen."

"Why would he do such a thing?" I asked.

"I dunno. He was kind of wild and liked to try things. I tried to stop him but he wouldn't listen."

"How long was he using before he went missing?" Darcy asked. Her frown said it all. She was disappointed.

"Only a few times, maybe for a month or so. I don't know if it has anything to do with him going missing, but I think it might be important."

I opened my mouth to ask another question, and Darcy raised her hand. "Wade, where are your parents? They should be here for this."

"My mom is dead, and Dad stays at his girlfriend's apartment in town on the weekends. He says it's closer to work." He licked his lips. "I don't really care. I do just fine."

How depressing. Poor kid was raising himself. My family with their criminal dealings certainly weren't the ideal way to raise children, but at least my brothers and I had parents who were involved in our lives—maybe too much so. They loved us and made sure we had great childhoods. We were never alone. Kids like Wade were forced to grow up way too early. That he was talking to us by himself said it all—he was on his own.

"Who sold him the drugs?" I asked.

Wade shook his head vigorously. "I don't know for sure. But he was beginning to spend a lot of time in the hollow."

Darcy inhaled sharply. "Jewelweed?"

"Yeah. Albert's been doing some odd jobs up there for my grandma."

Darcy and I looked at each other. I recovered first. "Do you think Albert was getting the meth from the Dovers?"

Before the kid could answer, Darcy cut in. "The Dovers grow weed. They don't cook up that crap."

I tilted my head, shooting her an are-you-serious frown. "Haven't you ever heard of criminal activities escalating over time?"

"Geraldine wouldn't allow that kind of drug operation to go on in her hollow." Darcy sounded pretty sure of herself. I wasn't buying it though.

"Did Albert play handyman for anyone else around here?" I asked.

"I don't think so," Wade said. "Look, I hope you find Albert. I wasn't too worried about him until that other boy turned up in the river." His hand clutched the trailer's door, but he paused, leaning back. "Is Albert dead?" His gaze flashed between me and Darcy.

I didn't answer because it wouldn't surprise me if the Amish kid had met a terrible fate. Being missing and on drugs wasn't a healthy combination.

"Of course not!" Darcy exclaimed, grasping Wade's shoulder. "He's probably out having a good time and isn't ready to return to the strict lifestyle just yet. When we find him, I'll personally swing by and let you know."

Wade gave a small, shaky smile before he slipped into the trailer and shut the door behind him.

I took the porch steps two at a time and when I touched solid ground, I glanced at Darcy who was in step with me. "I know it's past your bedtime—"

"Oh, shut up, Russo. I'm all in, but I think you're wrong about the Dovers having anything to do with this Amish kid's disappearance."

I didn't say anything. Darcy was an optimist, and she hadn't seen the crazy shit in the hollow with the family that I had. I hoped she was right but was mentally preparing for the worst.

And if Darcy's rosy picture of the Dover clan was wrong, we might be in real danger—and I was preparing for that too.

20

SADIE

I threw the car keys onto my desk and went straight to the coffee maker. It was pushing midnight and the department was empty. Moonlight shined through the window and my office was a tad cold, so I didn't take off my jacket. John sat in the chair. He hadn't looked at his phone in hours. It made me wonder if he had anyone in his life at all that was wondering where he was at this hour.

"You can head home, John. I appreciate your help"—I grunted softly—"and frankly, the company. But the day is over and after I touch base with by first deputy, I'm heading home. My daughter needs to see her mama in the morning before she goes on a weekend trip with her dad and step-mother."

John swiveled in his seat. "I bet she's not looking forward to that."

After I poured myself a cup, I sat down across from him. I was used to all-nighters. Wasn't he tired?

How he knew how my daughter felt about spending the weekend with Ted and Sandra was beyond me, but he'd hit the nail on the head. If we hadn't found a body and all the chaos that ensued, she'd be spending the weekend home with me. Ted's invite had been well-timed and I would have been a rotten parent not to insist she went. Between a few quick text messages, we hadn't discussed the forced trip and I half expected to find Chloe at the bottom of the staircase with her arms crossed, ready for a fight.

"Well, she didn't really have a choice this time. I'm going to have my hands full for the next few days." He didn't budge and after taking a sip of coffee, I set the cup down and crossed my arms on the desk. "Don't you have anything to do at home?"

He shrugged. "Sure, I do. I'm hesitant to leave, though."

"Why is that?"

"Because you might need me and my ride is back in the hollow." When my brows shot upwards, he quickly added, "If you're fixing to talk to Summit, I have to be there. He's my cousin."

Before today, I'd only met this man—that I remembered—on one occasion, yet it felt like he'd been around much longer. Sometimes that happened, where you met someone who you instantly had a connection with. I wouldn't say it out loud, but that's what seemed to be going on with John Dover. We'd passed each other in the high school halls without me noticing him, but I'd certainly made an impression on him. Here I was, up to my eyeballs in a probable murder investigation, spanning years and possibly multiple victims—I didn't want any distractions.

"Look, you've been helpful, but I'll take it from here. Head on home to your bees and whoever else you need to take care of."

"There's no one else." He grinned. "Except Dixie. I'm sure she's missing me."

The inside of my mouth felt chalky. "I'm sorry that I kept you from her all day. Better get going."

John stood up and moved to the back of the chair, loosely gripping the top of it. "I think the two of you would get along just fine. She's a lot like you—independent and a little grumpy."

Grumpy? I quickly searched the day's events, trying to figure out why he'd say such a thing.

"She also has brown hair, a lot like the color of yours." His grin widened. "Although, I think she's better on the trail than you. She never gets lost." When I didn't say anything, because what could I say, he started for the door and stopped before he went through. "Call me if you need anything, Sheriff. Just don't go to the hollow by yourself. If you don't want me tagging along, bring a couple of your men—just some friendly advice from a Dover."

Then he was gone. I sat back. Was it a warning or a

threat? With a Dover, it was hard to tell. I could say that he was unlike any other Dover I'd met though.

"Was that John Dover?" Buddy stepped into the office and his booming voice broke the sweet silence of my rambling thoughts.

"Yep." I figured it was better to be upfront with Buddy rather than have him learn about the joint mission on his own. "He helped me out today when I went to Jewelweed Hollow. His presence made it possible for me to talk to Elwood."

Buddy snorted loudly. "At least you came back in one piece. If a Dover made that happen, then I guess it was a good thing he was there."

I rubbed my eyes. Buddy had already filled me in on the details of the accident and I was sore and exhausted. The hike up and down the mountain had taken its toll on my body. I was proud to say that I rarely got lost. What kind of woman was Dixie if all John could say about her was that she had brown hair and a good sense of direction, and why did I even care?

"I'm going to head home and get some rest. Once I drop Chloe off at Ted's in the morning, I'll be in. We have a lot to go over." I didn't mention an early morning trip to visit Summit Dover. We would be shorthanded until Monday and I wasn't waiting that long to interview him. Buddy would have to cover in town and if I had to go alone, so be it. One thing was for sure, I would ask John Dover to accompany me.

Could Summit Dover be the one to connect the

dots from Liam back to Possum Gap? I would know more in the morning. Downing the rest of the coffee, I grabbed a few file folders and stood up.

"Anything else before I go?" I asked Buddy, whose blue eyes were bright and alert even though he'd been going just as long as I had.

"Oh, just a kid who wanted to talk to someone. Said it wasn't an emergency, so we'll send someone out in the morning."

"Did he say what it was about?" I suddenly felt more awake.

"No, he wouldn't say anything on the phone. It's probably something with a parent, you know how teens are when they don't get their way."

I stood there thinking. "Where does he live?"

"Out by the Amish settlement." Buddy saw me hesitate. "Sadie, I'm sure he's asleep. You can't go out there at this late hour. If it was important, he would have said something."

I didn't like being conflicted. Buddy was probably right...and I had to get home to my own child.

"Send me the name and address and I'll check in on the kid first thing in the morning." I patted Buddy's huge bicep as I passed him.

Damn. I hated when I ran out of hours in the day.

21

RUSSO

The drive over the rutted, potholed gravel road was far more terrifying by moonlight than it had been earlier in the rain. As I searched the inky darkness between the tree trunks, I regretted my decision to allow Darcy to drag me back to this forlorn place hidden deep in the woods. The draping branches over the roadway seemed to be saying, "Go away, you're not welcome here" or "Stay away, outsiders." Let's just say the vibe was far from pleasant.

I sniffed in the scent of pine needles and mud through the open windows. Normally, I liked the earthy smells. Right now, it only reminded me how far away from civilization we were.

When the headlights caught the yellow shine of eyes in the trees, I leaned forward. "There, did you see that?"

Darcy chuckled. But the sound was a little jerky, like the wind whispering through the trees was getting to her too. "It was just a coyote. Nothing to worry about."

As soon as she'd said it, a shrill scream pierced the night air, causing me to suck in a breath. I couldn't speak and felt paralyzed as the wailing continued.

Darcy touched my arm and I nearly jumped out of my skin. "Relax, Russo. It's just a bobcat. They sound that way."

"Like an infant being decapitated?" Seeing how calm Darcy was made me question her sanity.

"Yeah, it's looking for a mate or it just killed something."

"Oh, I guess those two things sometimes go together."

"Ha ha, you're so funny," Darcy said, swatting me on the upper arm.

Her warm, vibrant tone chased away some of my ill feelings.

"Maybe we should have left this to the professionals," I suggested, already knowing what her response would be.

"Russo, you can't be that much of a scaredy-cat."

"I like to think of it as more of a strong self-preservation personality disorder." I did not look her way. More shining eyes appeared in the darkness and my hand curled around the revolver in my pocket.

"If there's a kid in trouble, we have to do everything in our power to help him, don't you think?"

"Sure, I guess." I finally pulled my gaze from the dark forest. "Isn't that what Sadie and Buddy should be doing?"

"I already told you. We're understaffed this weekend. Nearly the entire police department is at the wedding, and we only have a handful of deputies on a good day. Besides, if there's anything going on with the Dovers, I'm more likely to get it out of Willow or Summit than Sadie is."

"They might all be asleep, like a normal person at this hour. Have you thought about that?"

Darcy made a swishing sound. "There's always some Dovers awake, that I promise you."

"Do they have nightly guards?"

"Something like that." Darcy looked ahead and hit the brakes.

The seatbelt ripped into my chest. "Geez, do you have to brake like that?"

"Shh," she ordered.

I followed her gaze. We hadn't even arrived at the meadow yet and two people stepped out from the trees. *Speak of the devils.* They were dressed similarly in faded jeans, black boots, and sleeveless shirts. Summit's was gray with a confederate flag blazing across the front. Willow, a few inches shorter, wore a black shirt. The picture was so faded, I couldn't tell what it used to be. The camouflage bandana across Summit's forehead went with the redneck Rambo look, and Willow's long straight hair billowing out behind her as the wind picked up made her resemble a witch—but the temptress kind.

I pulled out my gun and held it close to my hip.

"Put that away," Darcy said. "I texted Willow. She knew we were coming."

"Why didn't you say something?" I slipped the gun back into my pocket.

"I enjoy watching you squirm." She swatted my arm again and laughed. "The look on your face, Russo. Did you think we were going to get into a gunfight?" When I just stared back at her, bristling at her chiding, she went on, "Oh, come on. You act like we're going to die. These are my friends. We're going to have a conversation, then go home. That's it."

Darcy didn't wait for me to answer. She jumped out of the Jeep and slammed the door behind her. I got out more slowly. The moon peeked over the dark tree line. The only sounds were the rush of water from the swollen river to our right and the occasional screech owl in the branches above.

Summit had a rifle strung over his shoulder. A knife was strapped to Willow's belt—a hunting one from the looks of it—that hung loosely on her slender hip.

Yeah, nothing to worry about here.

Darcy looked completely out of place in her fashionable olive colored goloshes and matching short rain jacket. Her hoop earrings shined in the low light. Compared to Summit and Willow's faded attire, she was a beacon of light in the creepy forest.

"Thanks for coming out here to talk to us this late at night," Darcy said in her usually upbeat tone.

Summit lifted his chin towards me. "What's he doing here?"

By the snarl of his lip, I understood. Summit had feelings for Darcy, even though she was clueless. Of course, she might be ignoring his interest in her on purpose. One never knew with beautiful women.

"Russo and I are partners at the department. We're working a case together," Darcy answered without hesitation.

I swung my head in her direction. The secretary was taking our nosing around a little too seriously.

Holding up my hands, I said. "Look, have you seen Albert Peachy in the last few days?"

Summit's narrowed eyes found me, and he took several steps forward to stop right in front of me. "You have some damn nerve showing up here and demanding answers from me—"

"Asking and demanding are two different things—" I interrupted, but Darcy cut me off just as fast as I had Summit.

"Whoa, Summit. We're concerned about the boy, that's all." She glanced around, and from my vantage point, she only saw trees and darkness like me. "Especially with the other kid that was pulled from the river and what happened to Orville. We were hoping you could help us out."

Darcy's cheerful voice was light in the thick,

nighttime air. It did the trick and Summit's shoulders dropped.

He leaned towards Darcy. "I haven't seen the kid since last week. Grandma Gerrie hired him because she thinks the Amish work harder than her grandsons." He snorted out a sharp chuckle. "Well, that may be true, but damn, she doesn't know the half of it with that kid."

"What are you talking about?" Darcy asked, her gaze passing between Summit and Willow.

"He put the moves on me," Willow said, smirking. "Of course, it was a big fat strikeout."

I chimed in. "Hitting on an attractive woman isn't a big deal."

Darcy turned so fast, I swayed back expecting a finger in my face.

Willow's smile took up her entire face. "You think I'm pretty?"

I swallowed hard. The young woman suddenly looked predatorial with her flared eyes and pursed lips.

"Seriously, Russo?" Darcy belted out, her pleasant voice biting into the cool breeze.

One woman looked like she wanted to stick her tongue down my throat and the other appeared to want to rip it out. Summit was grinning now, but strangely, he came to my aid.

"That's not important, Willow." Summit became serious. "My point was, Albert isn't the strait-laced, religious kid that Grannie thinks he is."

"We heard he's been doing meth. Is that true?" I asked Summit, trying to ignore the women.

Summit shrugged. "Seems to be the case," he said.

The entire scene was surreal. Here we were chatting on a ridiculously long gravel drive at midnight with the wilderness pressing in on both sides. I knew firsthand these Dover people were lunatics, but like flipping a switch, something changed in my perception of the red-headed clan. The relationship normalized at that moment, and I suddenly felt like I was talking to one of the boys from another family back in the city. Sure, we were all up to no good, and we could turn on each other at any moment, but we were also on the same criminal boat. The Dovers weren't much different from the Russos. They made a living from illegal activities, just like my family did. They were secretive and wary of strangers, the same as my people. And they were loyal to their own, which was the core my family's value system.

Summit talked with a thick southern accent that I had to concentrate half the time to understand, yet I read his tone immediately. He was also worried about the kid.

"Did you give him the shit?" I asked. Darcy sucked in a breath and her head swiveled to see Summit's reaction.

His lips turned down in a tight frown. "No, man. We don't do that stuff in the hollow."

It would probably be foolish to believe this man who I hardly knew, but for some strange reason I did.

"Where would Albert have gotten a hold of it around here?" I asked.

The wind gusted and it was damp and cool.

The Dovers looked at each other. Their eyes said it all. They knew exactly where the drugs came from.

Willow gave a jerk of her head towards me and Summit sighed loudly.

"Do you really want to know, city boy?" Summit asked.

I held in a snort. *Boy?* I was older than him. "Yes, I do."

The shadow of confliction passed over Summit's face, then Willow blurted out, "Calhoun. Talk to the Calhouns."

22

SADIE

Putting on my sunglasses, I raised my face to the sunshine before I stepped through the doorway into the department. It seemed like forever since the sky wasn't clouded and gloomy. Reluctant to leave the pleasant warmth, I pushed the door open and went in.

Normally, Darcy would greet me with a cup of coffee at the door. Since she was a morning person, she would fill me in on everything happening at warp speed. I looked around. The front office was quiet. Deputy Johnson sat in Darcy's seat with the phone pressed to his ear. He raised his finger to stop me from walking past the desk and I waited.

It had been a difficult morning. Arguing with Chloe was never fun. Unbeknownst to me, she'd made plans to hang out with her best friend this afternoon and going on an impromptu trip with her dad and Sandra to Gatlinburg ruined them.

I rubbed my eyes. My daughter should follow in Ted's footsteps and become a lawyer. The girl sure was persistent when it came to making her point. Glancing back out the glass doorway, I tried to push my daughter out of my mind. She might be annoyed, but she was safe and on her way. I needed to focus on what happened to Liam and the investigation, and Chloe being out of town for a few days made that a lot easier.

When Johnson hung up, he immediately stood. "Buddy is out on Highway 36. Mayford's cows were out again and one of them got hit by a car."

"Any injuries?" Better Buddy than me for a herding operation.

"The SUV is totaled, but the driver's airbag deployed and she's fine. Went to the hospital to make sure, you know how that goes." Johnson looked down, then up, grinning. "The cow appears to be fine. At least that's what Buddy said with a slew of obscenities after she nearly ran him over and he had the radio on."

I nodded. "Where's Darcy?"

"She's not here. I thought you'd be able to tell me where she is." He scratched his buzzed head. "I really don't want to man the phones again."

I searched my mind for a conversation with Darcy about if she had an appointment this morning and came up empty. "Did you check her calendar book over there?" I pointed to the corner of the desk where the book was already opened. Darcy's desk was always obsessively organized and today was no different.

"Nothing written on it. Well, except an appointment at the nail salon at three."

The young deputy was skinny and still had a few pimples on his ruddy cheeks. He started to step backwards from the desk, ready to escape when I stopped him.

"You're on the phones until I figure out where Darcy is." I didn't wait for his response, heading to my office at a fast clip. "It's not like Darcy to be late," I muttered to myself as I turned into my office and went straight to the desk. It was the same as I'd left it the night before. And there weren't any little notes that Darcy was so fond of taped around the telephone.

My heart started banging in my chest as I pulled the cell phone from my purse. I had just hit dial when I heard the cat meowing ring tone and Tanya came through the doorway.

"Good timing." I hung up. "I was just calling you."

"Where's Darcy?" Tanya didn't bother to say hello. Her eyes were wild, and her mouth hung open. She had on a nice, cream-colored blouse and a pair of brown pants. The suede boots matched the top. From the head down, she was put together and ready for a busy day selling houses but seeing her bushy hair and a face lacking any makeup at all, I knew she'd left the house in a hurry.

The muscles through my shoulders tensed. "She hasn't come in this morning—"

"She never made it home last night—at least that's what Buella said, and you know how she gets up at the crack of dawn to sweep the sidewalk." Tanya paused to catch her breath and run her hand through her messy hair. "What about the coroner? Is he here?" Tanya was savvy. She must have been working every angle on her way over. "His car is parked in the lot."

"How do you know which car is his?" I asked, picking up the phone and dialing Russo's office.

"Only one with New Jersey plates." She walked to the window and looked out. "Darcy was supposed to meet me at the café this morning at seven-thirty. She never texted that she wasn't coming and you know how she is about staying in touch."

Tanya's voice shook as the phone call to Russo rang for an amount of time that I knew he would already have answered if he was anywhere near his office. After I hung up, I called his cell number. That went immediately to voicemail.

"Have you called her?" I knew she had, probably a dozen times, but I had to ask.

"All morning and she's not picking up," she practically growled the words out.

"Maybe she's with Russo?" I said quietly as I waited for Buddy to answer his phone.

"Dammit, Sadie, you know if she hooked up with him last night, she still would return my text messages.

No man wouldn't keep her from answering the phone!" Tanya shook her head vigorously and immediately apologized. "I'm sorry, girl. I'm a mess and that's my fear talking."

I squeezed her arm as she stopped her pacing to stand next to me.

Buddy finally answered.

"Boss, I'm up to my knees in mud out here. Didn't Johnson tell you I'm trying to get this damn herd off the road?" Buddy was huffing and his voice cracked when the reception was interrupted.

"Buddy, listen to me. Do you know where Darcy and Russo are? Darcy never showed for work and Russo is missing too."

"What? Who's missing? Shit, Darren, move to the left or that black one is getting by you!"

Buddy's attention was not on me. Aggravation twisted my stomach and I shouted into the phone, "Darcy and Russo! I can't find them!"

"Hold on, Darren—dammit, let 'em go. I'm trying to talk to Sadie!" Buddy coughed, then sucked in a breath. "The two of them were at the department late last night."

"Whatever for?" I asked. Tanya brought her head next to mine to listen to the conversation.

"I don't know, guess they'd been on a date or something."

Tanya closed her eyes and nodded slowly. Maybe for the first time in Darcy's life, a man had kept her from checking her phone.

"Tell me everything, Buddy," I ordered. "Tanya's here and she's worried sick."

Buddy explained in between raspy breaths—indicating that he was still walking—the conversation he had with Darcy and Russo the night before. When he mentioned the Dover boy who had called in, I interrupted. "Do you think they went over to talk to him themselves for some reason?"

"Your guess is as good as mine. Sounds like you need me. Darren can figure out how to get these damn cows back into their field and I'll head back," Buddy said.

"No, you better stay out there until the cattle are put up or we'll have another wreck on our hands. I'll take care of things here." I hung up before Buddy could argue and turned to Tanya. "Looks like your little sister and my coroner might have been playing detective."

"Whatever for?" Tanya's voice was sharp with confusion.

"Darcy mentioned an interest in joining the force, and especially investigative work several times in the last month."

"But she loves running the office," Tanya argued.

"Yeah, well maybe she's growing bored with the position. I don't know." I picked up my car keys and thrust the cell phone back into my purse. "I think I know where they went." When Tanya started walking with me, I stopped her. "Can you stay here and help

Johnson? We're woefully understaffed as it is and without Darcy or Charity, we don't have anyone to man the phones."

Tanya tilted her head and pointed a long finger at me. "You're going to bring my little sissy home safe and sound, right, Sadie?"

"Yes, ma'am. But the odds are better if I'm not worried about your safety and what's going on here in the department." I stared at Tanya until she dropped her gaze and gave a nod of her head.

"You better keep me posted. I can't stand not knowing what's going on," Tanya said firmly.

"Yeah, you and me both," I muttered as I hurried out of the office.

The roads were dry, but the leaves of the late-season corn glistened in the sunlight, still wet from last night's rain. My drive towards the hollow had been full of phone calls, some trying to locate Darcy and Russo and a few others that were non-related. Darcy was a smart young woman, but way too trusting and lacking in any real experience in law enforcement. Russo had impressed me numerous times, and something about his cool demeanor made me think he had his fair share of run-ins with the law. After meeting his brother and cousin, I wasn't so sure that he would have been on the right side, though.

Deep down, I still held out hope that Darcy had worked her charm and the two were off together someplace having a good time. But the sensible part of my brain screamed that it was out of character for both of them to avoid calls from the workplace. Russo and Darcy were both obsessive professionals.

I found the boy who had called in the day before tightening a rusted chain on a bicycle. After the introductions were made and being informed he was alone, I asked, "Did anyone from my department come by last night? It would have been late." I held up my phone with a picture of Darcy for him to look at. It was an older photo—maybe two years old and taken at our annual office picnic at the pavilion by the lake. I didn't have one of Russo quickly accessible, but I didn't need it.

"Yeah, that's her. There was a tall guy with dark hair with her."

Sunshine dappled the ground beneath the large tree next to the trailer. The bright day was deceiving. Something bad had happened. I could feel it in my bones. "Do you know where they went after they left here?"

The kid's gaze drifted to the thick tree line a few hundred yards from the trailer and my heart froze. I knew what he was going to say before the words slipped from his mouth.

"I don't know for sure, but they asked questions about Albert Peachy. When I mentioned he had been doing some work for my kin in the hollow, they seemed really interested."

Would Darcy and Russo been crazy enough to visit the hollow in the middle of the night searching for answers? Possibly Darcy, but not Russo. He wouldn't have forgotten his last encounter on Dover lands. The Yankee had witnessed firsthand how dangerous the family was.

But the pair hadn't been seen since last night and neither were answering their phones.

I left the boy with his bike and jogged to my car, pressing my fingers into the side of my forehead. Worry pinched my heart. Why did Darcy have to pick now to pursue an interest in detective work?

As I climbed inside and started the engine, my mind shot in a dozen directions. I had gone from a supposed drowning victim and a cold case to three missing people—two of them coworkers—right quick.

The day was starting off worse than even I could have ever predicted.

23

LUCINDA

With clothes pins clenched between my teeth, I hung the last pair of James' pants on the line. The sun on my face felt good.

"Lucinda, should I put Phoebe down for a nap?"

I turned to the voice and found my niece, Mira, standing on the porch with my plump youngest child balanced on her thin hip. Mira had recently turned fourteen and her parents had brought her, along with her three older brothers, to Possum Gap for a quick visit on their way south for a vacation. While my brother and sister-in-law chose to stay with her parents four miles away, Mira had requested to spend the night with us. The girl was a lot like her mother at that age— a little mama hen who enjoyed babysitting. It wasn't until I had my own children that I found tiny people to be that interesting. But her enthusiasm for children was a blessing for me.

"Oh, how I wish you lived closer than Ohio, Mira. I could sure use a good babysitter like you to help with the kids."

Mira beamed as she struggled to hold Phoebe. I wasn't sure how my youngest had become such a lazy child. I could hardly keep Josh or Sarah confined to my arms when they were the same age.

"I would love that. Perhaps Ma and Da will leave me here while they go on to Florida. They can pick me up on the way back."

I pushed the basket aside and approached the porch. The front of my maroon dress was damp from the wet clothes, but the snappy October air was satisfying. "Ack, you shouldn't trade the beach for a week chasing a toddler around. I wouldn't allow you to do it even if your folks were agreeable."

Mira giggled as Phoebe planted a kiss on the teenager's cheek. A strong wind would blow the slender girl right off the porch, so I added, "Please put her down in her crib. She can do with some rest while we make sandwiches for our lunch."

Mira was such an agreeable child. She went straight inside and I looked over my shoulder, searching for the buggy that was making the *clip clop* sounds on the pavement. It was Martha's dapple gray mare and sure enough, the horse and buggy swung into the driveway. I shielded my eyes from the sun with my hand as Martha traveled with speed over the gravel stones.

The buggy came to an abrupt stop with the horse throwing its head and taking a step backward as a plume of dust rose around her.

"My, Martha, what's the big hurry. I'd think the devil himself were chasing you up the driveway with the speed you're going," I chastised.

Martha set the brake and climbed out of the buggy with quick movements, mimicking her horse. "Did you know that Ezra Peachy came to town with your brother?"

I sucked in a breath. Just hearing the name made goosebumps rise on my arms. "No, I did not. No one mentioned it to me."

"I heard he's traveling with Timothy, Grace, and their children to Florida. There's an Amish center there for our people to recover from problems like his," Martha said in between gulping breaths.

My friend wouldn't say it out loud. Ezra was addicted to drugs. My brother's close friend had been for as long as I could remember, and he'd paid the price for his foolishness.

"The last I heard he was in prison somewhere in Indiana for thievery. Did they release him?"

Martha's breathing calmed enough to talk properly as she braced a hand on her sweaty horse. Steam rose from the animal's back.

"Frannie told me the man was let out around a

week ago because of good behavior. He's been staying with the Peachys all this time." Martha's eyes glistened as if she waited from me to say something specific.

"But my brother only arrived last night, so they could not have traveled here together." I stopped and thought about what Martha had said but Martha didn't give me any time to think.

"Ezra must have found a way to spirit himself here on his own, and in a week's time, he talked to your brother and arranged to go on the trip with Timothy and Grace." I didn't miss the angst in Martha's eyes.

When I was small, I remembered Ezra's pale face and greasy blond hair. Even as a teenager, he'd gotten into things he shouldn't have. My brother protected his friend, shielding him all the way into adulthood when Ezra had been caught red-handed by the English authorities, stealing a chainsaw out of one of the townspeople's garages in the town of Blood Rock. Stealing might not have put him behind bars for very long. It was the box full of heroin in his back seat and his previous arrests that landed him in jail for three years.

"Ezra went English nearly fifteen years ago. Why does my brother keep the friendship up? Even if Ezra wasn't a criminal, their friendship supposedly ended a long time ago. And to take him to Florida with the family is completely unacceptable."

I glanced at the house and my mind instantly went to Mira. I was decided. It was better for her to stay here with us than to go on with her folks if Ezra was tagging along. I crossed my arms and shivered, remembering all too well the feel of Ezra's breath on my face when he'd touched my thigh, leaned in, and tried to kiss me. I was only twelve at the time and had been alone with him in the loft of the barn after my father and brothers finished stacking hay. No one else saw and the only person I ever told was Martha and that was only after a decade had passed and I'd born two of my children. Because of my strong little fist and fast legs, Ezra wasn't successful in his attempt to molest me. I'd slipped out of his grasp and made it down the ladder before he could catch me. But the memory was strong after all these years, and I still detested the man.

Martha leaned forward. "I understand this is difficult, will you come with me to speak to Ezra?"

I stood up tall and spoke louder than intended. "Why ever would I do something like that?"

Martha visibly swallowed. "Come one, Lucinda, you're smarter than that. Think," she urged. When I looked blankly at her, she said, "Ezra showed up right around the time that Albert went missing."

My hand went to my mouth. Martha was too clever by half. "Thank goodness Mira is here to watch the children. I'll tell her I'm leaving with you for a quick trip."

"Hurry! There's no time to waste," Martha shouted at my back.

I didn't need the urging. After what happened to Vivian, James, and the little ones, I understood the meaning of haste. I prayed that Martha and I were both wrong and that Ezra wasn't involved in Albert's disappearance.

24

SADIE

Geraldine Dover sat on the porch swing, rocking gently as she sipped her coffee. The way her long gray and red locks were coiled on top of her head didn't match her red and black flannel shirt and rubber, knee-high boots. I ignored the fierce looks on the faces of her family members gathered on the lawn in front of the doublewide. It was a little harder with Jessie. He leaned back against the railing, scowling.

I didn't have time for Dover shenanigans. It was bad enough I had to be here in the first place, and they weren't going to intimidate me with numbers. We had an agreement, just like all my predecessors. I would leave them alone as long as whatever they were doing in the hollow, stayed in the hollow, and no one got hurt. With my secretary and coroner missing, the niceties ended.

"They came here last night, I'm sure of it," I said to Geraldine.

"Watch your tone!" Jessie warned. "You ain't in town—you're in our hollow."

I was armed and had alerted Johnson to where I was going, although I'd ordered him not to inform Buddy right away. For all I knew, my first deputy was still chasing cows. If he'd known about this impromptu trip to Jewelweed Hollow, he'd have abandoned the herding mission and headed straight over here. I might regret my decision to keep him out it, but this time, my gut told me I'd get further by myself than with a team of law enforcement at my back.

I was too agitated to let Jessie's threat affect me. Running on pure adrenaline made a person brave—and stupid.

I returned my gaze to the Dover matriarch and after taking a deep breath, softened my voice. "You know I'd rather be anywhere than here right now. If you help me in any way, I'm asking nicely for you to do so."

"What do we get out of talking to you, Sheriff?"

I rolled my eyes. Why did this woman have to be so difficult? "Nothing, Geraldine. You're going to tell me what you know because it's the right thing to do." When the older woman's face remained rigid, I added, "And it makes you all look guilty. If I have to come back up here with an army to find my people, I will."

Jessie snorted, but that's when Geraldine cracked a smile. "You have a stronger spine than the last sheriff.

Your mama would be proud of you." She cocked her head and gave a curt wave to the rest of her family. They began to disperse, except for Jessie. He stayed rooted in place against the porch railing.

Instead of walking away with everyone else, Summit Dover came forward, along with a younger woman, who I assumed by the bright red hair was one of Geraldine's granddaughters.

"Not you, Willow. Go on back home." When Willow opened her mouth to protest, Geraldine made a grunting noise and gave the waifish-looking woman a frown that stopped her in her tracks. Willow dropped her head and joined the rest of her retreating kin.

Jessie lost the angry face when he joined his wife on the swing. Geraldine humming a tune I remembered but couldn't name would have been annoying any other time. But the guessing gave me something to do while I waited.

Once the yard was empty, Geraldine abruptly stopped humming the melody and nodded to Summit. "Tell the sheriff what you told me."

"Everything?" he asked.

"Just the parts that pertain to Darcy Beaumont and the swarthy one." Geraldine winked at me.

I felt sick to my stomach.

It was bad enough that this family had the run of more than a thousand acres of hill county; they also controlled the flow of news in Possum Gap. People were afraid to talk which made my job very difficult, forcing a situation where I had to trust the Dovers and what they said.

Summit cleared his voice as he ran his hand through his long hair. Usually when I saw him, it was tied back in a ponytail, but this morning it was free, and the wavy locks looked clean for a change.

"Darcy wanted information about the Amish kid."

Summit confirmed what Wade Blanchard had said earlier. "What time were they here?"

Summit's eyes lifted as he thought about it, giving me the indication that he searched his memories. "I reckon it was close to midnight. We talked only about fifteen minutes and they went on their way."

"Where did they go?" I had my fingers looped thorough my belt as I watched him glance at his grandmother. She nodded and he started talking again.

"That Russo fellow was interested in where Albert got his dope and I told him."

Dammit. My heart fell into my stomach. If the detective-wanna-be duo had gone snooping around a drug dealer's home, things could have gone terribly wrong for Darcy and Russo.

"Give me the name, Summit. You and your kin won't be in trouble for simply knowing someone is cooking something up. But if Darcy or Russo—or hell, this Albert kid—are hurt because you didn't tell me what I need to know to save them, you will be so screwed." I paused and let my gaze fasten on Geraldine. "And since they both work for the Sheriff's Department, the state will get involved. If that happens, anything and everything you might be doing up here is fair game."

Jessie smirked and Geraldine shook her head slowly, looking very much like my own grandmother when she was irritated about something. The wrinkles at the corners of her eyes deepened when she smiled. "Don't threaten me, Sadie." By not using my title, she was talking to me as a person, not as the sheriff of this town. "I'll let Summit answer your question, not because you're demanding, but because I like that Amish boy. He did good work for us when most of my lazy grandkids don't know how to hit a nail with a hammer. Her gaze flashed to Summit. "Not you, dear. You're one of the ambitious ones. Go ahead and tell her. She's likely to find out on her own anyway, but it will probably be too late." Geraldine lifted her chin and our eyes met. "It wasn't until Darcy and your coroner stopped by last night that we all put it together."

I turned back to Summit, and he said quietly. "I'll go over there with you, Sheriff—"

"You will do no such thing!" Geraldine rose from the swing and Jessie followed suit. "This is none of our concern. The sheriff can figure it out on her own."

I nodded at Summit. Having the burly Dover along could be beneficial or a hindrance depending on where I was going.

"Just give me a name and I'll take care of it."

Summit took a step closer. He licked his lips and stared at his booted foot as he dug it into the porch board. His reluctance to say the words made me hold my breath.

When he finally spoke, it was nothing more than a husky whisper. "Calhoun. Albert got the meth from the Calhouns."

25

RUSSO

I felt a throbbing pain at the back of my head at the same time a dank smell flooded my nose. Overwhelming thirst was the next discomfort. The side of my face was pressed against something rough and brittle, and my eyes were so damn dry they hurt. It took several seconds before I managed to open one of them.

Only a few shards of light sliced through the dust particles in the air.

The sound of boots scraping the floor above my head caused a trickling of more dust to dribble down on my face. The fuzzy-headed feeling lifted a little and the fog began to clear. I began to open my mouth but my lips wouldn't part. I suddenly felt the tight, abrasive thing stuck over my mouth—tape. When I tried to sit up, I couldn't. My wrists were bound behind my back and tied to something—maybe a post? I wriggled my feet and discovered they were also bound.

When I inhaled through my nose, I smelled death and my stomach rolled.

Fuck. This is bad—really bad.

Aches and pains flooded in. I shifted my weight and attempted to look around. It smelled musty, like a basement. But the floor was dirt. No windows. The space wasn't large, at least that was my impression, but I couldn't see very far. A conversation—muffled voices—came from upstairs.

My head became heavy. I dropped it back onto the dirt and closed my eyes.

What happened? What is the last thing you remember, Russo—think, dammit, focus!

Pictures crashed inside my mind...and then settled, moving slower.

I'm walking down a dirt path. Moonlight slices through the branches over my head. One of those obnoxious birds keeps calling out and the beating of my heart is unsteady.

The shick, shick sound of a shotgun being cocked splits the night air and I stop.

"What the hell do you think you're doing here?" a voice shouts from the darkness of the trees.

"We want to talk. Is this the Calhoun's residence?" I ask politely.

"Are you cops?" the hidden man asks. By the deep sound of the voice, I guess he's rather large.

"No, no. We're just looking for a teenager. He has blond hair—"

The sudden pain in the back of my head makes my vision blur and I wobble. Hands grip my arm, then there's a scream.

Darcy...

I blinked and I'm back in the basement room.

Darcy.

It takes all my effort to rock sideways. Stabbing pain shoots up my shoulders, but I ignore the feeling.

Once on my back, I turn my head and squinted, trying to see better. Five feet away is a lump on the dirt floor—no, it's a body. I recognize the yellow rain jacket.

Darcy.

26

SADIE

The clouds had moved off to the east and the entire sky was a deep blue, only marred by a couple of jet trails. When I usually see them, I wonder where the travelers are going—is it business or vacation? Within the state, across the country or even over an ocean? Now, the thoughts come and go quickly as I stayed close to the tree line, using the trunks as cover.

I'd left my car off to the side of the gravel road through Jewelweed Hollow and hiked this far, crossing Dark Hollow Road and jogging along it until coming to the winding driveway that I knew lead to the Calhoun's cabin. My heart had pounded in my chest until I reached the other side of the road, then it calmed, and my breathing returned to normal. The bright sunshine, blue skies, and chirping birds settled my nerves. I gambled that I had the advantage of surprise, but I still was fearful of what I'd find.

People usually didn't just go missing by themselves—especially healthy young ones who were probably armed. The fact that neither had returned my calls or text messages worried me greatly. Darcy and Russo were always connected to their cell phones. Everything within me fought against the conclusion that I knew was the most likely: that they were either incapacitated, or worse—that they were already dead.

If a body hadn't been pulled from the river that week and the Amish boy wasn't missing, I wouldn't be panicking. Add on Orville's cold case and the odds were against me finding my coroner and secretary safe and sound. A small portion of me bristled at their stupidity and recklessness, but another larger part admired their tenacity. One kid was dead and another missing. Time was of the essence. I just wished they'd called me instead of embarking on their own investigation.

My cell phone vibrated in my pocket and I pulled it out, checking who the incoming call was from. Dashing behind a large-trunked poplar, I swiped the screen and brought the phone to my ear.

"Hey, I can't talk now," I whispered, looking around and over my shoulders.

Chrissy's scratchy voice sounded like she was jacked up on coffee. "Sheriff, I have some news for you." I didn't interrupt and she continued. "I dug a little deeper into Orville's file and found a name—Calhoun. Does it mean anything to you?"

My breaths came in quick, shallow inhalations as I looked around. "Thanks, Chrissy. It sure does." I was about to hang up, then stopped. "Hey, I appreciate your help. There's more going on right now than you know. I'll make sure to keep you in the scoop first."

I barely heard her perky "thank you" when I hung up and continued my way, passing several NO TRESPASSING signs and moving deeper into the trees. I welcomed the cover. I'd called Buddy and he would be on his way soon. First, he had to get his arm in a cast and sling from the fractured humerus he'd suffered when a large heifer knocked him onto the pavement during the round up. Chief Tanner had cut his trip short and several of his officers were returning to Possum Gap with him. Of course, none of that helped me now. I'd ignored Buddy's pleas to stand down until backup arrived. Minutes may count here, and I wasn't taking any chances with Darcy's life. I'd promised my best friend I'd bring her home safely and that's what I aimed to do.

I would have done the same for Russo, but Darcy was like my kid sister. When Tanya and I had been teens, Darcy was still in the single digits and she thought it was her job to pester us to death. We'd spent so much time avoiding her that when she came to work for me as an adult, I didn't know her as well as I thought. Then, after a few years of spending more time by her side than

Tanya's, we'd really connected. All those memories of running as fast as I could to get away from the kid who wanted to be just like me came rushing back, and the realization struck me like a physical punch. Darcy had always copied me and going off on her own detective mission was part of a familiar pattern.

But this time, her shenanigans might have gotten her hurt...or worse.

When I finally had a full view of the cabin, I stopped in my tracks, peeking around a tree and listening for any noises that indicated people were around. Cooter Calhoun's pickup wasn't parked in the driveway, but two other trucks and three cars littered the side yard. They were all full of dents, faded paint jobs, and older than dirt. Weeds grew tall around the blue pickup with its hood popped open and a red Trans Am that had seen better days. The three remaining vehicles could be drivable, making me hesitant to leave the cover of the trees too soon.

Laundry hung on the line behind the cabin, mostly ripped pants and t-shirts. One of Lita's housedresses hung there, as well as a few of her balloon panties. A large, scary-looking black dog was chained to a tractor tire next to an overturned refrigerator with its door flung open. The dog chewed on something with its back to me. I quickly eyed the chain, measuring the distance the dog could go.

The sound of voices reached my ears and I dropped to the ground. I'd been holding my 9 MM ever since

I'd hung up with Chrissy, and with my back to the tree and the gun level with my chest, I listened to the murmurs of conversation, not able to decipher any of it.

I rose slowly and swiveled sideways to watch the house, keeping an eye on the dog. Several windows were open and a couple pairs of men's boots were scattered on the front porch around the front door. The wood was so aged, it looked almost black and most of the metal roof was rusted, making it shine bronze in the sunlight. It sagged in the middle and the trees closed in around it, their branches reaching for the cabin like the forest wanted to devour it. The place had to be a hundred years old, if not older, and when the breeze picked up, I shivered; not because I was cold, but from the thought of how many hill people had lived within its walls in this isolated part of the county.

As I deliberated whether to go straight to the front door or sneak around the back of the house to check out the old tobacco barn first, I leaned into the bark of the tree, trying to figure out where the Calhouns were.

Lita and Kaine were even more redneck than the Dovers. Rumors of incest and child abuse had hung over generations of family members, but nothing had ever been proven as far as I knew. They were dirt poor, lived off the land, and didn't like visitors. Buddy said they were distantly related to the Dovers, but even the Jewelweed Hollow clan kept their distance. Like all hill people though, they wouldn't completely shun others like them. It was an unspoken oath of loyalty or something that I never understood. Even when the hill people didn't get along, they'd team up against those they considered "townsfolk." They were outsiders, the people they'd never completely trust.

I was the sheriff of Possum Gap but knew my limitations where the hills began. Law officers were slim pickings this week, but on any day, there were not nearly enough of us as there were them. These people lived like they were part of a compound and none of them—the kids and elderly included—would think twice about attacking a sheriff to protect their own— or to cover up a crime that would put them behind bars if the staties arrived.

The sharp scent of pine needles overpowered my senses as the rays of sun caught the golden leaves in all their brilliance. It's just a forest in autumn, I told myself as the hair rose on the back of my neck and I heard the rustle of the leaves on the forest floor. Another scent trickled in—sweat.

I whirled around with my gun raised. John stood there, his hands up, and he was grinning.

"Whoa, don't shoot." When I didn't lower my gun, he added, "Weird, huh, how we keep meeting in the woods like this."

"How did you sneak up on me?" My heart was beating so fast I was sure he could hear it.

"I spend a lot of time out here hunting. Stealth comes with the territory if I want to eat." His smiled faded a little.

247

I pressed my lips together. A couple days ago, we spent the day together like old friends, but that feeling was gone. You couldn't trust a Dover and deep down, I'd never trusted this one. But I had felt the stirrings of something else and thinking about it made my cheeks warm. I averted my gaze, searching over his shoulder for anyone else. A sneak attack wouldn't be shocking.

"Are you alone?" My sunglasses hid my eyes when they returned to John's face.

His smile was gone, but his jaw was slack and his expression friendly. The denim jeans he wore had a rip at the knee and the logo on the shirt he wore was so faded I couldn't make out what it was. His attire was exactly what you'd expect from a guy who lived at the edge of the wilderness and spent most of his time surrounded by nature.

He hadn't shaved and when his hand cupped his chin and rubbed, I imagined what the bristles felt like, then blinked and exhaled.

"Yep. I've been following you, Sadie. All the way from the hollow. You're in fairly athletic shape and if I wasn't such a good tracker, I would have lost your trail a while ago."

I straightened, lowering my gun a little so it aimed at the leaf-covered ground beside John's feet. "Why would you do that?"

"When you didn't call me this morning, I figured you went to the hollow yourself. That might not have gone so well."

The situation was chaotic and disturbing. I was distracted, but anger flared in my chest. "I have every right to ask the Dovers questions. Frankly, I'm tired of this bullshit where your family thinks they're immune to the law."

"They always have been," John said easily, lifting his chin in a silent challenge.

"Once I find Darcy and Russo and get this investigation wrapped up, things are going to change around here," I promised.

"Your people are missing?" John's eyes flared. The crack of his voice told me it was the first time he'd heard the news.

"No one's heard from them since last night when they were in these parts snooping around about an Amish kid who did some work in the hollow for your grandmother."

The sound of a roaring engine, probably missing its muffler, turned both of our heads. John pushed me up against the tree, his chest flat against mine.

"Shhh." He made a hissing sound as he pressed into me. I could feel the tree's trunk poking into my back and my gun pointed downward between us.

I understand why he had done it, but that didn't make me any happier about having John manhandle me in such a smooth, quick way; I hardly had time to think before I was up against the tree. I had to stop letting my guard down around this particular Dover. In many ways, he was more dangerous than all the others put together.

249

John's face was close to mine and I caught a whiff of cologne, like sandalwood and leather, probably from the soap he'd used that morning.

Because of the way John's body covered mine, I couldn't easily see over my shoulder. "Who is it?" I whispered into the curve of his neck.

"Cooter."

Shoot. I should not have wasted time conversing with John. Staying still, I waited for the sound of the engine to get louder. When it passed by, John shifted his weight and I wriggled away from his body and a few steps around the large trunk.

"He's not alone," John said a little louder. The roar of the engine made it impossible for anyone to hear us.

I peeked around the tree and caught my breath when Cooter parked the truck and Elwood Dover jumped out of the passenger side. Cooter took a little longer to get out of the truck and with his hulking size, he dwarfed the skinny Dover. The two of them walked to the barn. Elwood slid the door open and the pair went inside. The door shut behind them. If they said anything, I didn't hear it.

"What the hell is he doing here?" John muttered, barely loud enough for me to hear.

"I was hoping you could tell me that," I said.

"This isn't good." He leaned in. "We'd better go back to the hollow and let Grandma Gerrie handle this."

There it is. The reason I would never trust a Dover. In their minds, the world revolved around them.

"I'm not going anywhere. Darcy and Russo might be around somewhere."

"What makes you think that?"

"The evidence brought them here, same as me. I'm willing to bet on it."

John backed slowly away, his face turned toward the barn, which was closer than the house. "I have to go, and you should come with me."

Seeing the determined set of his jaw bothered me. He was abandoning me and my mission to alert the Dovers that Elwood could be entwined in something very bad. I raised my gun. "Stop right there, John. You aren't going anywhere."

The corner of John's mouth lifted, but there was no spark in his eyes. "I think you have more important matters to attend to."

I followed his gaze and saw Lita and Kaine come out of the house through the back door. Where Lita's hair was jet black, Kaine had a thick head of gray hair. Lita was lithe and moved quickly across the yard to the barn while her husband moved at a more leisurely pace. Smoke trickled from the cigarette Lita had clenched between her teeth and I smelled it on the breeze. The woman's face and neck were wrinkly, and I knew if she smiled, she'd be missing a front tooth. Lita and Kaine were in their fifties and yet their tanned, weathered faces looked much older.

Kaine had a pistol in a holster on his belt like he'd stepped out of a Wild West movie, and I wouldn't be surprised if there was an arsenal inside the barn.

John pivoted and started walking away at a fast clip. "Go ahead and shoot me if you want, but that'll ruin your chances of sneaking up on any of them." He slowed just enough to look back once. "Stay safe, Sadie."

He was right. I couldn't stop John from leaving and he'd done nothing wrong. Cuffing him was impossible without making noise. If I wanted the element of surprise with me, I had to let him go.

I didn't waste any more time watching John disappear into the thick foliage. Turning on my heel, I took one last look at the barn. The door was closed again, and I didn't see anyone outside. It was a gamble to assume no one else was in the house, but I was confident enough that Lita, Kaine, and Cooter lived alone.

It was now or never.

Sprinting as fast as I could, I ran through the trees, over the gravel drive, and into the yard in front of the cabin. The grass hadn't been mowed in a while and almost reached my knees. Trees shading the house instantly blotted out the sky, making it feel like it was twilight instead of morning.

I jogged up the porch steps, hopping over a splintered one and didn't stop until I reached the open window nearest the front door. A ripped, lace curtain fluttered in the opening, and I paused to listen for any noise inside. The beating of my heart steadied while I took slow, shallow breaths. Damn. I didn't have a search warrant and going into the residence was over-the-top, but the lawlessness that I dealt with on a daily basis in the hills made it seem almost acceptable. I made plans in my head, picking the judge I would call if things went south. The incident between Cooter and Lucinda Miller might give me a bargaining chip if it came to it. But all those thoughts were a blur. I had to see if Darcy and Russo were here or had been recently, and I didn't have time to follow the letter of the law.

When I pushed my finger through a hole in the screen and tore it further, I focused on one thing: getting inside and hopefully back out without being seen. Once the opening was large enough to get my leg through the window, I was able to push the rest of the screen aside before I climbed through. Fried grease and stale cigarette smells made my eyes water while I straightened up and looked around. Several paths led through the front room into other rooms between piles of debris and boxes. A black and white cat shot over a path, jumping from a rusted pet crate to a microwave stacked on top of a pile of newspapers.

So, the Calhouns were hoarders. Not surprising at all. A kitty litter box in the corner had fecal matter spilling over the edges and I wrinkled my nose when that smell hit me. I didn't like the cluttered space that was only lit by the shaded natural light from the windows.

But trusting my instincts, I moved quickly, slowing at the bottom of the staircase.

Pressure on my leg made me jump sideways. It was just another cat. This time a calico tried to rub against me. If I lived in this wreck of a house, I wouldn't lock someone on the second floor, and I was pretty sure the Calhouns wouldn't either.

The kitchen wasn't any better than the front room, and it was even darker. Dishes filled the sink and besides a couple of cereal boxes on the table, I didn't see any other food. There were several bottles of bourbon at various levels of fullness, and a box of Marlboro Lights on the counter. A dead plant in the windowsill caught my eye, but only because it was marijuana.

I was partially holding my breath and even though I'd just snuck into someone's cabin—a hill person's home— I was calm, feeling almost as if a divine entity was guiding me through the cluttered, dirty house. I'd learned a long time ago to trust my gut and this time was no different. Everything pointed to these people not only being involved in Darcy, Russo, and Albert's disappearance, but also the deaths of Liam and Orville. I just hoped I made it in time to stop more bloodshed, and that my friends weren't victims of some sinister backwoods' dealings.

The kitchen gave a view of the barn, and the door was still closed. John had probably crossed the road by now and I worried that if he rallied the Dover troops before my job was done here, their interference might do more damage.

A quick look at my phone told me what I already knew. There was no cell phone reception this far off the road. I was essentially cut off from the world until Buddy arrived. Tanya's face materialized in my mind as I rounded the corner and found what I was looking for—the door to the cellar. My sweet friend was back at the department worried sick about her sister, and now, probably me too. Whatever happened, I had to bring Darcy back to Tanya alive and well. *I had to.*

There was a heavy-duty lock on the latch, making the breath catch in my throat. People didn't lock up their basements unless they were hiding something down there. Which meant that the entire family was in on whatever was going on. I pushed the thought out of my mind and removed the tool from my belt that had a mini bolt cutter on one end. The tool had come in handy on more than one occasion. I cringed, glancing over my shoulder when the snapping noise broke the silence.

I had to shove hard to dislodge the door that scraped the top step. The air was stale and dusty. At the bottom of the step, it was too dark to see more than a few feet into the basement. After one last glance around the kitchen, I took a step down and closed the door behind me to the point where only a sliver of light remained.

A puff of the sharp peppery scent of decay in the air made me freeze. *Oh God, no...*

Still holding the gun in front of me, I turned on the flashlight and descended into the gloom.

27

LUCINDA

I sat close enough to Martha that our sides touched. My friend made small talk with Tina Peachy while we waited for Ezra to come in from the stable where he was helping the younger boys feed the horses.

"We're not too worried, Martha. Albert, like most boys his age, has a rebellious streak. He's a good lad and will come home soon. At least, that's what I pray for."

Tina had five other children, all under ten, and even as she spoke, her eyes were on two of the toddlers playing on the floor on the opposite side of the room. Strands of the woman's brown hair stuck out from under her lopsided white cap and there were smudges of flour on her navy-blue dress. Tina could barely keep charge of her little ones and she seemed to have less time for her oldest—and missing—child.

"What makes you believe that he's with your cousins who left the Order?" I spoke up for the first time.

Tina's eyes wandered over to me slowly. Her pinched mouth made her look annoyed at the question. "Ezra was in Blood Rock. He tells us that he saw Albert there, and that he's safe and with family who went English."

And she blindly believed Ezra? Fool woman.

"How would he have made it all that way?" I pressed. Martha dug her knuckle into my thigh beneath a fold my dress, but I ignored the silent plea.

Tina's mouth dropped open as she grunted. "In an automobile more than likely. Really, Lucinda, you interrogate me like the bishop would question teenagers found kissing behind the woodshed. I am Albert's mother, not you."

I dropped my gaze. *Then perhaps you should start showing the concern of a mother!* I screamed in my head. When I responded, my voice was light and quiet. "He's only fourteen. I would think his tender age worries you. It's quite young for one of ours to be out in the world, don't you think?"

Ezra walked through the screen door at that moment. It swung shut behind him, bringing in a warm breeze and a quick peek of the autumn splendor of the hillside behind the Peachys' farm. The inside of the house smelled like baking cookies that were ready to come out of the oven, but Tina seemed to have forgotten about them. When she saw her brother-in-law, she rose and went to the children. She picked up one hand from each and ushered them back out the door, speaking to us without turning around.

"The children need fresh air. You all can continue without me."

Martha and I looked at each other. Rolling her eyes and giving a shake of her head, Martha stood up and went to the oven. As if it were her own kitchen, she picked up the oven mitts and removed the tray, setting it on the stovetop.

Martha's quick thinking made me exhale in relief. The cookies were safe, so I fixed my gaze on the tall blond man, who remained standing in the center of the room. A portion of his wispy hair fell over his left eye, and he didn't try to move it away. His beard was scraggly and his frown was etched deeply on his face.

"I'm busy assisting my brother with farm chores. What is so amiss that you came here on such a fine morning to see me?" Ezra's tone was polite, yet I saw his tense shoulders and the rigid planting of his feet on the floor.

He didn't want to be here anymore than I did. The way his eyes skimmed over me caused my chest to burn.

"You told Tina and William that Albert is doing well in Blood Rock. What proof do you have of this?" I snapped.

Martha sat back down beside me. Her presence gave me strength. We both looked up at the tall man, waiting for him to answer my question.

He licked his lips and it reminded me of a snake. Ezra's pale skin was an oddity too. Most Amish men's faces were tan from working outside. Just another clue that Ezra was not telling the truth about going back to the Amish.

"Albert hitched a ride with the Masts when they traveled up that way for a horse sale. Because we're family, he reached out to me. I saw him a couple of times. He's working at the metal shop, pocketing some savings."

"When will the boy be back then?" Martha asked.

Ezra shrugged. "I assume when he's good and ready." He took a step back. "If that's all, I'll be on my way—"

"Wait!" Martha bolted upright. "My oldest brother is the bishop in Blood Rock, and he knows nothing of Albert Peachy being in that settlement."

"Hmm. That's odd." Ezra smirked. "Perhaps he's moved on." His gaze landed on me and the raw look in his eyes made me queasy. "I hope James is treating you well, Lucinda. You always deserved the best."

When the door closed behind Ezra, I slumped in the seat, barely able to catch a proper breath. Martha patted my hand.

"No worries, dear friend. All will be well. I have faith in our Lord that he's protecting the boy. And I trust Aaron. My brother is always on top of things. He's also keeping an eye out for young Albert."

28

RUSSO

With much effort and a shooting pain across my back, I managed to roll sideways, bringing me closer to Darcy. I watched her stomach as it rose and dropped slowly and shallowly. She was alive. My head cleared with the shock of relief.

But as my mind sharpened, the stench became worse and I gagged, dropping my head back on the hard dirt. Where was it coming from? I tilted my head slightly, allowing my eyes to adjust to the semi-darkness. Beyond Darcy's prone form was what looked like a small rectangular table. There was a pair of mismatched chairs on either side and a drinking glass was knocked over on its top. Behind it, there was a bare shelf on the wall. I shifted my gaze further down the room. Is that a bed? Yes, a twin-sized bed with a crumpled-up blanket—no, not a blanket—something else. I lifted my head and squinted into the darkness.

That's where the smell is coming from.

God, help me. Judging by the dry smell of the reek and the temperature in the basement, I concluded the decay to be several days old.

Had Darcy and I found Albert Peachy? Who else could it be? I closed my eyes. How stupid of me. My trip home and the visit from Anthony and Jimmy had messed with my head, causing me to act like I had nothing to lose. And perhaps I didn't. But Darcy did, and that's where I'd fucked up. I should have known better than to allow her to get tangled up in this investigation.

Now, she was knocked out and I was incapacitated. We were more than likely going to die. I always thought it would be the Flores family who took my life, but it would end up being some toothless hillbilly.

The roar of an engine reached my ears and I turned to the sound. It had to be a big vehicle, probably a truck. A moment later the engine cut off and it was quiet again.

The minutes ticked slowly by as I wracked my brain, trying to think of a way out of this terrible predicament. I kept going back to only one slim chance of survival—Sheriff Sadie Mills.

Would Sadie figure out where we were before these inbred monsters murdered us like the unfortunate person on the bed? I had been impressed with her instincts and ability to think and work outside of the box, but it could take her days to figure it all out. And by then, we'd be rotting corpses like our roommate over there.

I wondered where my gun was. I thought about Ma and how she'd cry when my body was someday discovered. Dad wouldn't show much emotion, but he would be pissed. Would Tony come back to avenge me? I doubted it. I'd made my own bed and that's where it would end. Darcy's sister would be distraught, and the sheriff would feel guilty. I hated that I would never have the chance to tell Sadie that I admired her, because I did.

What a mess I had made of things. My head became heavy. It dropped to the side as clouds pushed into my mind again. Being unconscious wouldn't be a bad thing. I almost envied Darcy for that.

A burst of light caught the corner of my eye before it disappeared.

Dammit. They were back.

I held my breath and closed my eyes, not wanting to see my captors, hoping it was a shot to the head. That would be quick. For the first time in too many years to remember, I said a silent prayer that Darcy wouldn't suffer—or wake up before the end.

Silence and darkness filled my mind until there was a soft pressing on my arm followed by a touch on the inside of my wrist. My eyes fluttered open and the way the flashlight was angled away, I could only see the silhouette of the person next to me.

"Russo, Russo, wake up!" the whispering voice urged. The tape ripped off my mouth so quickly, I barely felt it. The sound of it was more disturbing than the quick jolt of pain.

God sent an angel in a tan uniform, with her brown hair tucked behind her ears. Sadie had come for us.

"I should never...have doubted...you," I choked out, my mouth so swollen and dry my own words sounded foreign to me.

Gently, she rolled me onto my sides, and cut the binds around my wrists and then at my ankles. Stretching my arms and legs was a joy I would never take for granted again.

Sadie stepped over me and bent down to Darcy. She patted her cheeks and murmured to her, "Darcy, it's me. Come on, you have to get up."

Darcy groaned, which was the first sound she'd made since I'd regained consciousness, but her eyes remained closed.

"Thank God, she's alive," Sadie breathed.

I saw Sadie's face drop to Darcy's and for a second, I thought she kissed the other woman.

"She smells like chloroform. You all were drugged," Sadie whispered harshly. "She's in a deep sleep." She flashed the light over Darcy. "She doesn't look injured. Can you stand, Russo? We have to get out of here."

I inhaled deeply and pushed up into a sitting position. My vision swirled and I thought I'd be sick. Placing my hand to the back of my head, I felt a crusty bump, then wetness. The wound was bleeding again. "Concussion, I have a concussion. But I'll try, Sadie." I reached out to her. "Here, help me."

She left Darcy and wrapped her arm around my chest and under my shoulder. Sadie was stronger than she looked, and managed to get me upright, leaning against her.

"Russo, listen to me. There are four of them. Lita and Kaine Calhoun, and their son Cooter—he's big enough to count for two men. Elwood Dover is the fourth. They're armed and in the barn. I have no idea what they're doing in there, but I'm sure it's nothing wholesome." She sucked in a breath and snorted. "What the hell?"

Sadie braced my arm on the nearest post that braced the beam that ran down the middle of the basement ceiling. She walked slowly toward the bed.

I managed to push away from the post and wobbled after her. It was my job after all.

Sometime between when Sadie had arrived and I stood up, I'd gotten used to the scent of decay. Normally, it didn't bother me and unfortunately, because of my career choice it was a scent I knew well. Now that Sadie was here, I felt a lot braver and I experienced a burst of hopefulness. Though I ached all over and the back of my head throbbed, I was alive.

"Probably four, maybe five days deceased," I said quietly, stepping up beside Sadie.

He pointed the light at the body, hovering over the face, which was bruised and cracked with red lines.

The pupils were light gray, nearly blending in with the irises and the sclera. The skin had already sunken into the body. The boy was shirtless and wearing what appeared to be pajama pants. Blond curly hair, skinny, and a young teenager—I was guessing thirteen or fourteen.

The only injuries other than the decomposition was on the hands. Three fingers were missing on one hand and four on the other. Flies buzzed around the appendages.

Sadie made a grunting noise and her hand covered her mouth. She spoke into her palm. "This must be Albert Peachy."

"That's a good assumption." I started to feel stronger as I took notes in my head about the condition of the body. "Appears to be a teenaged boy, roughly fourteen years old."

The horror was written on Sadie's wide eyes as she handed me the flashlight and turned away, returning to Darcy on the floor. If we'd found the boy alive, I would have had more emotion—sympathy, sadness, fear—the usual feelings, but seeing his soulless corpse didn't illicit those feelings from me. He went from being a human being to a slab of evidence several days ago. If I became distraught every time that I performed an autopsy or prepared a body for viewing, I would be a mental case. Still, I understand Sadie's emotional response to finding the boy dead. She was a mother herself, after all.

"Orville Walker was missing fingers as well—just like Liam McCoy and this poor kid," Sadie said quietly. "It's a sick pattern."

I stared at the body, noticing the black veiny trails leaving the wounds. "Like Liam, this boy may have succumbed to septicemia as well."

"We have to get out of here. I don't have cell phone service this far off the road and I'm alone." Sadie rubbed Darcy's forehead.

"You came alone?" I let out a rough sigh and left the body in the darkness. Standing over Sadie was difficult, but I knew if I sat down, I might not get back up again for a while. "Where's Buddy?"

"In the hospital. He was wrangling cows early this morning that were on the road and a heifer ran over him. He promised me that once his arm is set, he'll head this way."

"What about the rest of the department?" Possum Gap's population was less than six thousand, and I was having a difficult time wrapping my mind around the fact that Sadie was a one-woman show on a day like this.

"Half of our department and most of the city police are at the chief's daughter's wedding in Louisville this weekend." Sadie slipped her arm around Darcy's back, then started to rise. "Here, help me get her up, Russo."

I touched Sadie's shoulder. "No. That's not a good idea. We'll never be able to carry her up the stairs, through the house, and into the woods before any of them leaves the barn." Sadie eased Darcy to the dirt floor and cocked her head to listen to me. "We have to make a stand—take them all out."

Sadie's brow knitted and she rose quickly, standing very close. "What the hell are you talking about?"

"They're serial-killing scum, Sadie. You know it." I lifted my chin towards the dead kid in the corner. "Look what they did to him. Liam and Orville must be their victims. Who knows, there could be more. They would have killed me and Darcy too. The only thing that stopped them is whatever they're doing in that barn."

Sadie thought about what I'd said and remained silent for several long seconds. "Look, as fucked up as this all is, it's not the Wild West." She glanced at Darcy and let out a ragged breath as if seeing her there on the dirt floor had changed her mind. "We only have one gun between the two of us and you can barely stand up. Even if I was open to a gunfight, we're out-numbered, four to one."

I liked that Sadie was at least contemplating my suggestion. That's why I liked her. She was up for any-thing that might save Darcy and get her home safely to her daughter.

"When do you think backup might arrive?" I asked, staring at the ceiling, searching for any sign of dust dropping through the cracks while I listened for move-ment above.

"I would expect the good guys to arrive within thirty minutes. The bad guys will get here in fifteen."

She said it in such a casual way, I remained as calm as she was. "The Calhouns aren't the only bad guys here right now?"

Sadie shook her head. "John Dover left me ten minutes ago. He was heading back to his family to bring reinforcements to get Elwood out of whatever mess he'd gotten himself into."

"And you believe they'll side with the Calhouns going against us?" The conversation would be insane to most people, but I'd actually had similar ones with Tony and my father.

"They'll do what they must in order to save Elwood. That's the only thing I'm betting on." She snorted. "Since he's so friendly with Cooter, I'm afraid, we'll be going up against him as well. Which means the Dovers will stop us."

I nodded as she talked. My mind was clear and my thoughts quick. "With this family, I'd say there's probably another gun upstairs somewhere."

Sadie had also been thinking. She pulled out her 9 MM, along with two magazines, and handed them to me. "I'm going for help." When I started to interrupt, she raised her hand, stopping me. "No, don't argue. This is the only way." She walked toward the stairs, and I followed her, trying to be as quick as her, but limping slowed me down. "If I get a few thousand yards from here, I'll have service again. I'll call everyone, including the Wilkins County sheriff. Once I'm out there, I'll use the trees for cover so they don't know I'm here. I can pick them off one at a time if I have to. Hopefully, Elwood stays out of the crosshairs." She spared a glance for Darcy. "If I'm quick about it, I can get in a good position before any of the Dovers arrive. Stay with Darcy and protect her, Russo. That's your job. Can you do that?"

I ran my hand through my hair, not wanting to see Sadie go up those steps without a weapon. But there was no way I could take care of Darcy without the gun that I had clenched in my hand.

"Are you sure you want to do this?"

"It's the only way for all of us to get out of here alive." Sadie reached out and patted my arm, then shot up the steps.

As the dust fell on my head from Sadie's departure, I dragged a chair closer to the stairway and eased myself onto it. After resting the gun in my lap, I sighed.

All I could do now was wait.

29

SADIE

Cooter was louder than a grizzly bear when he talked, and Lita always had a cigarette in her mouth. I hoped both things would give me a heads up if they were coming around the corner when I slid my leg through the ripped screen. I felt naked without my gun, and that was one of the reasons I relied on speed instead of stealth this time. The other was that I wasn't just in a race against the Calhouns and Elwood; I had to reach the woods before the Dovers arrived.

The rifle and shotgun I'd grabbed had been hanging on a peg in the first-floor bedroom. That room, like the rest of the cabin, was full of junk, but for all the disorganization scattered around, the hunting weapons were neatly arranged on the wall next to the bed.

I picked the .22 semi-automatic because it held ten rounds of ammunition, and the Mossberg shotgun because it had a shoulder strap allowing me to easily carry two weapons, which would come in handy. When I was a kid, I'd go hunting with my dad. I never liked the killing or butchering part, but it was the only time he paid attention to me. The experience prepared me for this moment. The long rifle rested comfortably in my hands. If I'd been in a suburban home, I wouldn't have had a variety of weapons to choose from. The only luck I'd had all week was that this shit was going down in a cabin where a bunch of rednecks lived.

Looking over my shoulder, I checked the barn. The door was still closed. My legs carried me into the shadows of the woods. I ducked behind a straight-trunked poplar, drawing in a huge breath of air into my lungs. The sound of voices reached my ears, and I blew out the same breath carefully, quietly.

I peeked around the tree. There were enough saplings to diminish my view, but Cooter was hard to miss. Lita followed him out, then Kaine. I waited for Elwood.

Where is he?

The cocking of a gun behind me was a familiar sound and sent a shiver through me.

"Lookie here. You spend more time in the hills than you do town, Sheriff Mills."

I didn't turn around. I recognized the voice and made an educated guess that he stood about four feet back.

"Were you out here keeping guard the entire time, Elwood?" As I spoke, my head was spinning. Neither Russo nor I had foreseen this—probably because neither one of us had given the Calhouns credit for having any forethought.

"You're like that stupid person from Grannie Gerrie's storytelling who kept poking the sleeping bear. You just won't let up and now you woke the beast, haven't ya?"

Was he referring to himself as the beast or fate in general? I had no idea. I hated the smug sound of his voice but let the feeling go and focused on the job at hand. "The Calhoun family is in big trouble, Elwood, and you don't have to go down with them. Right now is your chance to make things right."

I didn't look back, instead keeping my eye on Cooter and his parents when they stopped beside his truck.

Elwood snickered, making my stomach constrict. "You aren't in any position to be talking like you're in charge, Sheriff, because you ain't. I am."

I made my move, swinging around as fast as I could, I used the barrel of the rifle as a weapon. I struck out at Elwood's handgun, knocking it to the ground. With another quick jab, I struck his face before he could scream out. But his loud grunt might have been enough to alert the Calhouns of my presence. Elwood was a scrapper, and even with blood spurting from his nose, he rolled sideways and grabbed for his gun, hooking it with his fingers. The next instant, he was on his back, pointing the weapon at me and I was doing the same to him with the rifle in my hands.

"Lower the rifle, Sadie. Please."

I saw them in my peripheral vision. John had returned with Summit and Willow. They were all armed. Willow was the only one pointing a shotgun at me. Summit's semi-automatic was resting in his hands as he looked past me towards the Calhoun cabin. John's rifle was strapped over his shoulder like my second one was.

A blast of white anger pulsed through me from the pit of my stomach outward to the rest of my body. I had been so stupid trusting John Dover and even more so for thinking we had developed a friendship of sorts.

"Can't do that." The words hissed through my cracked lips. "Willow, you're aiming a weapon at a law officer. I'm not going to forget this."

"If you're dead it's not going to matter, is it?" Willow said defiantly. The sneer on her face was at odds with her ponytail and smooth complexion that made her look a lot younger than her twenty-something age.

Summit made a low growling noise. "You're an idiot, Elwood. Put the fucking gun down."

The moment felt like a dream. Sunshine jetted through the branches, dappling the forest floor. A warm wind stirred the golden leaves and a spattering of them took flight, sprinkling around us in what would have been a magical moment if there weren't two guns pointed at me.

Boom. Boom.

The sounds split the autumn air and I ducked, sliding against the trunk of the massive tree. Suddenly, Willow and Elwood were the least of my worries. Willow moved to a slender poplar tree a few yards away at the same time Summit grabbed Elwood, hoisted him up by the scruff of his shirt. Elwood half ran and was half dragged to the cover of a squat maple tree to our left.

When the first shot was fired, John had closed the gap and was now braced against the tree, our shoulders rubbing. There wasn't time to bitch him out or arrest any of the Dovers. We were all under attack.

"What the fuck are you doing?" Willow shouted at all the Calhouns. Her gun was raised and she was ready to return fire.

With a quick look to the side, I saw Elwood now held his pistol close to his side as he peeked around the tree. He started to argue with Summit, who told him to, "Shut up!"

"You're on your own, Sheriff. Grandma Gerrie ordered us not to get involved. We came here to bring Elwood back, and that's all we're going to do," Summit said.

"But they fucking shot at us!" Willow argued.

"There's a rotting corpse of a kid in that cabin and it's probably Albert. And Darcy is out cold in the cellar. I need your help stopping this sick family," I pleaded, my gaze skimming over Willow's conflicted frowning face to lock on the large redheaded Dover.

Summit flinched, then closed his eyes. When he opened them a few seconds later, they were cold and indifferent. I knew his answer before he opened his damn mouth.

"I don't want to see anything happen to Darcy, but it's not our war."

Summit gave Elwood a shove and the younger man stumbled away from the tree. He looked like he was about to say something when Summit ran by him, disappearing into the dense foliage.

Willow cursed again, then she looked straight at me. "I'm sorry," she whispered fiercely, before sprinting in the direction Summit had taken. When she ran by Elwood, she shouted, "Come on!"

He glanced at me with angry eyes. Elwood still wanted to fight but thought better of it. "Try not to die, Sheriff," were his parting words, then he sprinted after his cousins.

"Aren't you joining those cowards," I muttered under my breath, not looking directly at John. I was too busy watching the yard for movement.

"They aren't cowards. This isn't their fight."

Adrenaline rushed through my veins. I still managed to keep my voice level. "Kidnapping and murder in the neighborhood doesn't interest them, huh? Well, Elwood is mixed up in this shit. If I get out of here alive, he's going down with them. And there's nothing your family can do to stop me from hauling his ass into town."

"I wouldn't expect any less of you, Sadie." John's voice was quiet and conversational. He certainly didn't sound like someone who'd just been shot at. I glanced over and the brown strands that had escaped his ponytail were plastered to his forehead with sweat. The run to and from Jewelweed Hollow had been a feat of athleticism. His bulging bicep closest to me twitched, and I stared at the bees buzzing around the roses and their thorny branches. I finally thought I understood the symbolism of the tattoos he chose—that pretty things could be dangerous things.

I heard a rush of blood in my ears and looked away, hating John for his ability to make me lose focus without even realizing he had that effect on me. "Why are you still here?"

"I'm seeing this thing through," he said firmly.

"Aren't you supposed to listen to your grannie?" I couldn't help smirking, but I didn't face him.

John chuckled and the sound was warm and friendly. "If you hadn't noticed, I quit doing what my Grandmother Gerrie said a long time ago. That's why I don't live in the hollow. I wanted my independence, and I have it."

Enough talking. I couldn't see Cooter, Lita, or Kaine. I sucked in a breath and took a gamble. "Cover me!" I hissed. His eyes widened but by the time he understood what was happening, I was already in motion. He reached out to grab my arm and missed.

I was willing to bet that Cooter was the one who

fired on us, meaning that either Lita or Kaine might be heading for the basement. John did what I'd asked, and he was a damn good shot. Several *kabooms!* shattered the beautiful morning. Stretching my legs, I ran as fast as I could toward the nearest junk car. Someone returned fire with John, but I made it to cover, advancing a good distance and clearing the woods.

The silence lasted a moment while I doubled over, catching my breath. I looked back over my shoulder but couldn't see John. If he hadn't stuck around, I would never have made it this far without being shot.

Now, things were going to get trickier.

I shouted and I was sure my voice carried on the wind to Cooter and his folks. "Stand down! This is Sheriff Sadie Mills. You don't need to die today. Throw down your weapons!"

Cooter's grizzly bear voice laughed. It was coming from behind his truck which was ten yards away.

"You dumb bitch! You're the one who's going to die!"

Cooter opened up on the car I was hiding behind, and between the gunshot blasts and the tearing of metal, I couldn't hear much, but it was enough to gauge that a few of the shots had come from the refrigerator on the ground by the barn.

Boom! Boom! Boom!

A dog yelped when the gunshots stopped.

As insane as this all seemed, time moved slowly. I worried about Chloe. If I was killed, she'd be raised by her stupid dad and his fake wife until graduation. For all her grief at my passing, she'd be pissed at me for leaving her in that predicament.

It was John and me against three—that is if John stuck around until the end, which I wasn't convinced he would do.

I wasn't prepared for Cooter's next move or the precision of his father.

An engine roared to life and in the second it took to understand what was happening, the truck was already barreling at the car that I hid behind.

The blue sky disappeared as I tumbled backwards into a dip in the earth, then rolled into a fetal position. The crash sent the car flipping over me as more gunshots rang out.

The world went dark. My last thought was of Chloe. *"I'm so sorry, baby girl."*

30

RUSSO

Gunshots rang out at the same time Darcy began to moan. I wanted to limp over to her but instead, I keep one eye on her slight movements while I stayed put in the chair. I knew what was coming, and I wouldn't let my guard down.

"Russo?" Darcy's voice was nothing but a hoarse whisper.

"I'm right here. Don't move. Stay still and rest," I said in a coaxing voice.

"What's happening?" Her fingers twitched and she stretched out her legs.

"You don't want to know, trust me." Another series of blasts exploded outside, and I found myself holding my breath as I scooted to the edge of the seat.

Darcy's head bobbed side to side as she tried to

push up but failed. "Stop moving, Darcy. Please, stay still. Help is coming. Sadie has it under control."

I wasn't that confident in my words. It sounded like a battle zone out there. Had Buddy arrived or was Sadie holding on by herself? I hated not knowing what was going on, but I was in no shape to make it up the steps with my vision still ringed with blurriness. Shooting at a distance, I would be lucky to hit an elephant in my current condition.

There was an explosion that made me half rise.

What the hell was that?

The door to the basement suddenly scraped across the floor and then there were footsteps. I held up the gun and waited.

When Lita came into view, her light-colored eyes were bloodshot, and her gray hair was sticking out everywhere. Her hands were not empty either. She raised her gun at me.

A strange calmness came over me. Curiosity might kill the cat, but I was a man and I needed answers. "Why did you kill that kid over there?" I asked in a level tone.

She snorted and took a step closer. "What happens to my children are no concern of yours."

I saw it then. The crazed look in her eyes. Before I'd settled on becoming a coroner, I contemplated a career in psychology and Lord knows, I took enough classes to be fairly proficient about the human mind. By the way this woman's eyes trembled and her face twitched, I knew hers was damaged.

"How many children do you have Lita—it is Lita, right?" I offered my smoothest voice.

"Don't go talking to me like we're friends. You're nothing to me and the only reason you're still breathing is because we had to go over the product with our boy Cooter." She tilted her head like she had forgotten what she wanted to say, then she somewhat recovered. "He's our oldest, you know. Eats and drinks too much, but a good boy."

I tried again. "What about your other children. Are they good?"

Lita let out a breath. Confusion wrinkled her face. "Jeremiah was a good boy, better than Cooter even. He never gave me any trouble." She sucked in a gasp. "He died. Cancer took our little boy away. He shriveled up and I watched the life drain from his pale little body." She shook her head vigorously. "No, no. I'm wrong about that. He came back to life, he did—twice, no three times. But he wasn't the same. The devil got into him, and he wasn't the same."

I licked my lips. I started to understand and my skin crawled with it. "Who helped bring Jeremiah back each time?"

"Elwood always brought our boy back to us." She snorted and cocked her head. "Of course, it was worth his effort. Kaine always paid him well." She threw her head back and barked out a laugh. "If his grannie knew, she would have whipped the tar out of him. Geraldine likes to think she knows everything happening in this part of the woods—like she's a queen or something—but she can't keep track of her own kin. First Christine and now Elwood. My children have always been better young'uns, I'll tell you that."

The puzzle pieces fell together, and the horrific picture took form. I felt sick to my stomach.

"Did you punish Jeremiah? What did he do wrong, Lita? Is that why he's over there in the shadows?"

She sniffed the air. "I done told Cooter to clean up that dead cat. They get into the basement and sometimes die down here." Lita glanced down at Darcy who was moaning louder. "What's that?"

I swallowed. The woman was nuts, but she held the gun steady. She didn't need her sanity for her aim to be true. "That's my girlfriend. She's sick and needs to go to the hospital. Will you let me take her?"

Lita's mouth scrunched. "I...I don't know." Our eyes met and a light flicked on in her gaze. She was coherent again—and full of hatred. "You aren't supposed to be here, outsider—"

I fired before she had the chance to. Three bullets hit her in the chest and she fell backward. Blood gurgled out of her mouth. She whimpered as I limped forward and bent just enough to grab her gun, jerking it away from her hand.

She wasn't my first kill, but it was the first woman. My emotions were blank. The woman was a murderous psychopath who'd killed at least one and probably three teenaged boys. It didn't matter to me if she was crazy or if her husband and giant son were involved either. From a practical perceptive, I had just done the world a favor.

"Russo…"

"I'll be back. I promise," I told Darcy.

As she began to cry, I grasped the railing and forced my legs to go up the steps.

If Sadie wasn't already dead, she needed my help.

31

SADIE

The sound of crunching steel exploded in my ears, and I tried to make myself as small as possible. Something struck my shoulder and then there were too many gunshots to count.

Dust billowed and I coughed, blinking. Several things happened at once. I saw some branches, then I tasted dirt in my mouth. When I stretched, my legs and arms worked.

"Fuck. Are you alive, Sadie? Talk to me! Tell me you're alive!"

I recognized the voice. John's words shook with emotion. Opening my lids, I found him hovering over me. Our eyes locked. With his gun slung over his shoulder, he slipped his arms around me and lifted me.

"Probably shouldn't move you, but I have no

choice. No time to wait." His words rushed together as he lurched forward.

I smelled gas and everything registered in my mind at once.

The swell of heat hit us at the same time the car exploded. John was strong. He held me tightly as he jumped. We rolled together. Pain shot through every part of my body. Junk rained down on us as John curled his body around me.

A loud ringing in my ears was all I heard, and I couldn't breathe. John mumbled something but I didn't understand. It was too smoky to see. When he rose, he pulled me with him and my legs hardly worked. I knew we had to move but my body wouldn't cooperate. John wasn't as strong as he was before the car ripped apart almost on top of us.

"Come on, Sadie, we have to get going. Come on," John urged although his voice was weaker than it had been.

My eyes burned as I forced them open. Digging my boots into the dirt, I gave it my all and tried to stand with him.

Cooter and Kaine walked through the smoke. They held their guns and were coming straight for us.

John swiveled and pulled the trigger, but nothing happened. He was empty.

This was it. I might have survived the car going over me and then its explosion, but I wouldn't survive being shot at point blank range. The shotgun and rifle

I'd held moments earlier were somewhere beneath the wreckage.

"It's going to be fun watching you die, Sheriff," Cooter said when he came to a stop a few feet away.

"Leave John alone. He's a Dover and you don't want to piss Geraldine off," I said through chalky lips.

John leaned his head back. "I keep telling you, I'm not a true Dover. Grandmother Gerrie won't care if I live or die."

Kaine spoke up. "That's right. But no reason to take a chance riling her either. Cooter, shoot the cop and be done with it."

Cooter raised the gun and I stared back at him. I was slightly aware of John's arms around me, and though the embrace should have been weird, it wasn't. I was about to die. And Cooter's well-placed bullet in my head would spatter John. He was trying to comfort me for what was about to happen.

I watched my killer's face twist before he pulled the trigger, and I had the satisfaction of not turning away when the blast shook the forest.

32

RUSSO

From the front porch, I saw everything. A giant cloud of smoke billowed through the trees, blotting out the sun, and flames shot out from what was left of the burning car. The black pickup truck was wrapped around a tree trunk. Its hood was popped open and smoke rose from it.

A scary looking black dog ran by, heading for the road. Its tail was tucked between its legs and it didn't even look my way.

Cooter and his father stood close to the wreckage. When I lifted Sadie's gun, it was too late. A shot was fired, then four more in quick succession. I heard the sound of two bodies hitting the ground.

I slumped into the railing and closed my eyes.

The gunning of an engine popped my eyes back open. The black SUV appeared around the bend at a fast clip. It screeched to a stop, and Tony jumped out of the passenger seat a second before Jimmy exited the driver's side.

Tony saw me and lifted his hand. I returned the favor and started down the steps. Jimmy met me at the bottom and flung his arm around me.

"You dumb shit. This is like a scene out of that movie—what was it called? About the hillbillies and the banjo?"

Jimmy's New Jersey accent made me smile. I let him help me up. "It doesn't matter. I'm just glad you guys showed up when you did."

Jimmy snorted. "It was all your brother. You know how protective he is."

"Go to the basement in the house. Darcy—my friend—is there," I told Jimmy.

He nodded, slapped me on the back and jogged up the steps and into the house.

As I made my way closer, I watched Tony bend down to Sadie. With John Dover's help, Tony had Sadie standing when I was close enough to talk to them both. The Dover man had his arm around her, and she leaned into him. I raised my brow and John's furrowed back at me.

"Are you all right, Sadie?" I asked.

She drew in a long, deep breath, cringing as she did so. We were both going to be sore for many days to come.

"I think so." She glanced at Tony. "Thanks to your brother."

Tony beamed and I rolled my eyes. My brother hated cops—really authority of any kind, but he loved being in the spotlight. Have someone in his debt was just icing on the cake for Tony. But in reality, my family was just as dangerous as the Calhouns and the Dovers. Sadie wasn't a fool. She'd let him play the part of savior this time.

Tony looked me up and down. "You okay, bro?"

I nodded and he offered me a tight smile after making a *tsk, tsk* sound.

Sadie's cheeks were smudged but gaining color. A quick glance told me besides a bloody abrasion on her arm and a tear in her pants, she wasn't seriously injured—which was a miracle. The Dover man looked worse. He had a nasty gash on the back of his right hand and most of his hair was singed.

The sheriff shrugged John's arm away and stood by herself, although he stayed close enough to catch her if she wobbled.

She pulled out her phone. "Dammit," she muttered, holding it up for everyone to see. The screen was significantly cracked. "Can I use your phone?" she asked my brother.

He held up a finger. "Not so fast."

Sadie's eyes flared, then she lifted her chin towards the plume of smoke billowing into the sky. "I give it less than ten minutes and half the town will show up."

It was her way of trying to maintain control, even though she had none when it came to Tony Russo.

"My little brother came here to escape being shot at. What the hell is going on?" Tony spread his arms wide.

I caught Jimmy out of the corner of my eye. He helped Darcy sit on a chair on the front porch. When he handed her a water bottle and she began to drink, I returned my attention to the conversation. Sadie's gaze slid past me. She had been searching for Darcy as well.

"It's a long story, but your brother was helping me investigate a possible murder, which might possibly have turned into several murders—"

I interrupted Sadie. "Oh, yeah. Definitely multiple victims. Lita Calhoun wasn't right in the head, but I have an idea what's been going on."

"Holy shit, Ray. This place is right up your alley." He gave a laughing snort and looked at Sadie. "He loves carving up those bodies and it seems you're keeping him busy."

Sadie's mouth dropped open, but Tony turned to me. "You're not going to come home with me, are you?"

I shook my head, avoiding Sadie's hard gaze in my direction. "I have work to do here."

Tony walked up and hugged me. "Watch your back, bro. They might find you, even in this God forsaken place." He kissed my cheek and stepped back, glancing at Sadie. "Hell, it might just be lawless enough around here that you'll be safe. It's been a pleasure, Sheriff Mills. Take care of my brother. You owe me one."

Sadie took a stiff step forward. "We value law and order in Possum Gap, Mr. Russo. You just caught us on a bad day."

Tony chuckled. "Yeah, right." He held up his fingers. "Did Raymond tell you I'm a lawyer?" Tony smiled at the surprised look on Sadie's face. "I might not have taken the Kentucky bar exam, but some things are pretty universal. And I don't have enough fingers to count all the policies and procedural protocol you've broken. So, keep me and Jimmy out of any of your reports. We were never here."

"How am I supposed to explain your bullets killing Cooter and Kaine?"

I held my breath and in a blink of an eye, Tony pulled his gun, aimed and fired at the truck's exposed gas tank. The explosion brought Sadie and John to the ground. I staggered backwards. This time Tony didn't offer to help Sadie up. He wiped the dust and smoke from his eyes with a handkerchief he pulled from his pocket.

The blaze was incredibly hot as I approached Sadie. Sadie swatted my hand away and rose more fluidly than she had a few minutes earlier. It was the adrenaline surge. I didn't feel any pain either.

Sadie half turned, staring at the flames. Cooter and his father had gone down next to the truck. I already knew their bodies would be burnt to a crisp. I would have to wait until the smoke cleared to have my suspicion confirmed.

Two streams of smoke puffed through the trees, joining and blotting out the blue sky, and making it look like dusk instead of morning. I took shallow breaths and still coughed. My throat was raw and brittle.

Sadie would know that the bodies were so damaged, the gunshot wounds wouldn't be easily noticeable. Since I was doing the autopsies, their cause of death would be the explosion. She rounded on Tony as he started walking away, catching up with him, grabbing his shoulder, and swinging him around. I moved as quickly as I could in my wrecked state, positioning myself between the sheriff and my brother. John couldn't move because Jimmy had a gun pointed at him. When he'd left Darcy and joined us in the yard, I didn't know.

"Do you think you can come in here and do whatever you want?" Sadie's voice was scratchy yet firm.

"I just saved you a ton of fucking paperwork." Tony wagged the gun at Sadie like he would his finger. "I don't care if you damn rednecks kill each other. But if anything happens to my brother, I'm coming back and I won't be alone. Your cute little daughter, Chloe, won't be safe if you rat on me and Jimmy or give Raymond here any trouble."

Sadie recovered quickly from the threat. "You are fucking with the wrong person and the wrong town," Sadie said. "If you get anywhere near my daughter, I'll kill you."

I heard the wail of sirens in the distance. "Get out of here, Tony, before it's too late."

Jimmy backed up until he reached the SUV. He started the engine while still pointing the gun at our little party.

Tony lowered his gun and headed towards the SUV. Sadie tried to follow but I held out my arm and shockingly, she stopped. The dirty look she shot my way made me drop my gaze.

"I'll be back to check in on you, Ray. When I do, I'll make sure to cook up some sauce and we'll invite the sheriff and her boyfriend over for dinner at your place. She's probably never had real Italian food before."

Tony got into the SUV and Jimmy did a U-turn practically from a standstill. Gravel and dust kicked up behind the vehicle as it sped towards the road.

Sadie walked by me and said, "You have a lot of explaining to do, Russo. But not now."

When she sped up, she limped badly, but it didn't slow her down. She embraced Darcy and the two women clung to each other. I was glad to see them both okay, but shocked that we all made it through.

"Your family is more fucked up than mine," John said, stepping up next to me.

Judging by the blaring sound of the sirens, there were several cruisers, a fire truck, and an ambulance almost to the driveway. Tony and Jimmy should be clear by now. If they hadn't shown up when they had, we'd all be dead. Hopefully, Sadie would keep that in mind when we finally had our sit down.

I turned to John, whose arms were crossed. He watched Sadie and Darcy closely, and I experienced a pang of annoyance toward the other man.

"At least my family members have all their teeth," I said briskly.

John's gaze traveled sideways to look at me without him having to turn his head. I wasn't expecting to see the twinkle there. He broke into laughter and slapped me on the back, hard.

I doubled forward and he grasped my arm to keep me from stumbling to the ground. God, I was weak, and jelly legged. I eyed the mountain man and realized how ridiculous we both looked, covered in soot, bruised and battered. We had something else in common, I knew John was as relieved as I was to be alive.

"You've just been initiated, Russo. Welcome to Possum Gap."

33

SADIE

"Good grief, Sadie, what the hell happened here?" Buddy scratched his head as David and Bran passed by with Albert's body on the gurney.

Russo was with them. Somewhere, he'd found a notebook and even though he had no business taking notes, he was. He was writing when our group walked by and didn't look up. He had refused medical help for the time being, insisting it was more important to collect evidence, which another coroner would normally be called in to do under the circumstances, but because of the implications of having someone other than Russo handling the case, I didn't say anything. After all, a boy's body had just been taken from the basement and we were pretty sure Liam had met his end below in this same cabin, as did Orville. We just had to construct the timeline and pull the evidence together—leaving Russo's crazy family out of the report.

My head still spun from nearly dying, then being saved and nearly dying again at the hands of my rescuers—who were as bad as the people trying to kill me. The entire thing was like a hazy dream and hardly made sense. One thing I was sure of though: Russo came from a crime family and was hiding in Possum Gap. From whom, I didn't know yet. The thought that there might be worse people than the Russo family out there looking for my coroner was not a pleasant thought. But one case at a time.

"It will take me an hour to explain it all, and only after I've figured it out myself," I said.

"Let me take you to the hospital, Sadie. You look terrible." Buddy never minced words and I was sure he was right. My entire left side was numb and my right throbbed painfully. My chiropractor might not be able to straighten me out this time.

"I'm not going anywhere until the fire is put out completely and we've gone through the cabin with a fine-tooth comb."

"Adam Crawford is on his way over here. Wilkins County is providing assistance. They got wind that their cold case is probably connected to the Calhouns.

"Good. We could use their help." If the forest wasn't damp from all the rain we'd had the last few days, the fire would have spread, perhaps burning thousands of acres. The two trucks and a half-dozen volunteer fire fighters just about had the flames contained. Besides the two vehicles, several trees were lost, but I considered us pretty lucky.

"The KBI is on their way too." Buddy's gaze landed on the barn. The door was open. "Damn, Sadie, I think there are a few hundred pounds of meth in there."

"It looks like Cooter was cooking the crap with his entire family."

"How do you think that figures into the teenagers' murders?"

I exhaled. "It's what lured them here."

Buddy looked over my head, which was easier from his tall height. "What in the hell are they doing here?"

I took a step to the side to see past Buddy and quickly found Geraldine, Summit, Elwood, and John walking in between the cruisers. There was still a smoky haze in the air and the flashing lights lit up the gloom on the Dover's faces. John had disappeared right after the cruisers pulled in. He had time to wash his face but was still wearing the same soot-covered denims and t-shirt. His hair was down and also several inches shorter than when I'd last seen him. He must have just cut off the singed hair to make it even. The shorter locks were wavier and moved with his strides. The tattoos spreading up his left arm caught my eye and I felt my cheeks heat. Not very long ago my face had been smashed against that very same design.

"Looks like Adam has arrived. Why don't you meet him, Buddy? I'll talk to the Dovers."

Buddy sighed dramatically. "Dammit. That's a reporter, isn't it?"

I followed his gaze. Sure enough, right behind the
Wilkins County's Sheriff was the newspaper's van. "I
owe Chrissy Coleman a story. Be nice. Tell her I'll give
her a quote when I'm finished up here."

The Dovers hung back until Buddy was well away.
Geraldine motioned for me to go with them in between
the fire trucks. Curiosity made me follow without com-
plaint. Summit stayed close to his grandmother's side.
Elwood kept his head down, and John took up the rear
of the little group. He glanced back, grinning slightly.
I didn't return the friendly look. If there was one thing
I'd learned today, it was that John Dover was not good
for me. I didn't have time for distractions, and that's
all the Dover man was—a distraction. And a pain in
the ass.

Once we were past the trucks and behind the barn,
beneath tree branches unscathed by fire, Geraldine
stopped and faced me.

"The Calhouns have been cooking meth for years,
but you know that now," she said with a sly smile. "It
started off as a way to bring in a little extra income—
Jimson got them started. Cooter expanded the business around five years ago. That's when the devil came
to call."

Geraldine paused, glancing up. The sky was
smoke-free here and the sun cast long shadows across
leaf-covered ground. The clan's matriarch stood in

one of the shadows, blistering sun lined either side of her, but none of the darkness touched her body. The Dovers like most of the hill people talked a lot of God and praying, even though they made money with their moonshine stills and growing illegal things. They lived violent lives and I'd been told by old timers that the mountains were littered with the bodies of the people who'd crossed them.

Yet, for the trashy homes and illicit behaviors, there was an earthy, almost magical quality to these people that had always fascinated me. Now with the matriarch carefully planning her words, I waited quietly, ignoring the shouts of men and the rumble of the truck's engines. The pain sketched on Geraldine's face was mesmerizing, probably because I'd never seen her look so sad, even when she'd looked at her son Jax's corpse in the mortuary.

Summit leaned against a tree and Elwood's lanky form was slumped. Any fight he'd had earlier was gone. A bruise on his cheek had darkened since the beginning of our walk. It was fresh and it wasn't from our scuffle.

When people like the Dovers talked about the devil, they might be speaking metaphorically or literally. In this instance, I thought she meant the latter.

Geraldine gestured to the back of the cabin through the trees. "This place is cursed. Did you know Lita's mother was only thirteen when she gave birth to her?" I shook my head. "My mama told me it was

Lita's father who had impregnated her. His wife disappeared that same year. Her body was found in the briar patch up yonder on the southside of Black Rock Hill." Geraldine smirked, then continued, "The family said she must have been picking wild blackberries and fallen, breaking her neck."

"I don't recall that—"

"You wouldn't. Emma Jean wasn't taken to town. She was immediately buried by Lita's daddy."

The information made the boy's body in the cellar slightly more understandable.

Geraldine continued, hardly missing a beat. "Lita was a troubled child and had more issues the older she got. When Jeremiah died, it broke her mind. That's when the devil came to call." She paused and looked at Elwood. When he ignored her hard stare, she kicked him in the leg. I jumped a little and Elwood yelped. Summit and John didn't react.

"Go on, boy. Tell the sheriff what you done told me." Geraldine's voice hummed with controlled anger.

Elwood tilted his head back to get his long bangs out of his eyes. "I brought Orville here one day to buy some stuff. When crazy Lita saw him, she thought it was her son. They both had blond curly hair and were skinny. That's where their likeness ended, but not to Lita. It was the first time she'd spoken in an entire year. Kaine saw her happy once again"—he inhaled deeply—"and decided to keep Orville for good."

My mind sunk into a sickening murk that I didn't want to be in. "What do you mean?"

"Kaine and Cooter drugged him up and kept him tied up in the basement. Lita took care of him, fed him chicken and dumplings—Jeremiah's favorite. She washed his arms and face with a cloth. He was so out of it most of the time, he didn't resist." Elwood dug his foot into the ground, pushing the leaves aside until dirt was exposed. "Sometimes, he'd come to a little and try to fight Lita. That's how he lost his two fingers—separate occasions."

When he paused to catch a breath, I asked, "How do you know all this?" My stomach clenched so hard, it was difficult to breathe.

"I visited Orville sometimes. You know, to make sure he was all right and such."

I glanced at John. His lips were pinched and he glanced away. Summit never looked up. Geraldine stood stoically, her face frigid and her eyes cold.

"He was your friend," I whispered. "Why didn't you tell your grandmother—anyone—what had happened to him?"

Elwood met my gaze defiantly. "Cooter paid me with meth money. I drove the shit to Lexington sometimes and Cooter warned me if I told anyone about Orville, he'd make sure I went down with them too. I didn't think it was such a big deal as long as Orville was alive. I figured Lita would grow tired of him someday and let him go. But sometimes Orville woke up enough

301

to understand what was happening. When that happened, he tried to escape and Lita always caught him. She cut his fingers off to teach him a lesson."

I worked hard to turn off my emotions as I listened to Elwood's confession. Orville suffered horribly. I could only imagine how scared he was. The only way I could look at Elwood was to remind myself that Elwood was only a teenager himself when all this was going on. That knowledge didn't erase the disgust I felt for him. "How did he die?" I asked.

"Lita accidentally gave him too much meth. I was here in the barn with Cooter and we heard an awful scream coming from the cellar. When we got down there, Orville was already gone. Cooter threw the body into the river." His voice became unsteady. "Lita was back to not talking again. She also wouldn't eat. Kaine ordered me to bring another boy for Lita to take care of."

My stomach rolled as I remembered the picture of the little blond-haired boy in Paula's photograph. "Liam."

"That's right. He was younger than Jeremiah when he died, but not by a lot. He had the right hair and a girlie face."

Summit groaned, pushed off the tree, and punched Elwood in the face. I heard the cracking noise and blood spurted from Elwood's nose. It used to be hooked, now it was flat. Geraldine didn't move. When Summit went in with another fist, John intercepted his arm, tugging him backwards.

"He won't be able to speak, Summit. Let him talk and get it out for the sheriff to hear," John implored the larger man.

Summit listened and stopped fighting. He walked several feet away and knelt on the ground, covering his face with his hands.

My heart went out to Summit, but my attention returned to Elwood. Tony was right. Possum Gap had turned into a God forsaken place. And I was partly to blame. I wanted to hear what Elwood had to say and even though he needed a medic, I told him to continue.

Elwood wiped the blood that kept falling with the back of his arm and continued his tale in between sputtering blood.

"A-after Joy and Summit b-broke up, she came back. But he wasn't here. She liked heroin and I talked her into coming back here to get something better. She was so out of it. I drove her all the way back to Lexington myself and she didn't even wake up in the backseat. I thought she might die, but I guess she didn't."

"You're the one who brought Liam back here?" I didn't hear my own words. The images played in my mind like a horror show.

"Yeah. I told him he could spend the week with Summit. He was happy about it 'cause he hated his ma." He shrugged, wiping his face again. "We hitched a ride with a trucker to the gas station off the highway near Possum Gap, then hitched the rest of the way in a pickup truck with an old man hauling cattle."

"Liam stayed in that cellar for…nearly four years?" I choked the words out.

"He behaved better than Orville and that's why for all that time, he only lost five fingers. At first, I visited him, but then he started to reek. I couldn't stand the stench."

It suddenly occurred to me that even though Elwood sounded like he had average intelligence, he had serious psychological issues. "How did Liam die?"

Summit rocked back and forth. John stood over him, his hand resting on the distraught man's shoulder.

"After the last time Lita took one of his fingers, the wound wouldn't heal. Liam fell asleep and didn't wake up."

When I let out a breath, I felt hollow. The suffering that poor boy endured all those years. The rest of Liam's horrible story flashed through my mind. "And then Lita needed another boy, right?"

Elwood blinked at me. His eyes were dry, and his face showed no emotion except exhaustion. He nodded.

"Sheriff, you need to come over here. The Amish saw the smoke and heard the explosions. Their bishop wants to talk to you," Buddy said.

Geraldine stepped in front of Elwood. "You deserve what you get, boy."

Buddy's face went slack when he glanced my way.

Elwood still had a lot more to tell me and I didn't know how the poor Amish boy had died, but I wanted to get all this recorded anyway. We had enough of a confession to make an arrest. The rest of the story would be told soon enough. "Buddy, read Elwood Dover his rights and take him back to town. I'll be there as soon as things settle down out here."

Buddy didn't ask any questions and Elwood didn't resist as the giant deputy slapped cuffs on his wrists and led him away.

"That boy doesn't have a soul," Geraldine said to me. "Tell Albert's people, I'm sorry for the part my grandboy took in Albert's death. It's a shame. He was a good worker and a polite boy."

Geraldine pivoted towards Summit who rose slowly, and I reached out, touching her arm. "Wait." She tilted her head and I asked, "How did you get him to confess all that?"

She let out a breath. "I had my suspicions for a while about Lita and the missing boys, I just wasn't aware my grandson was mixed up in it. When John told me what had happened, I promised Elwood that whatever suffering those boys experienced, he would experience it too—an eye for an eye—just like the Good Book says. Summit wanted to kill him right then and there, but I wouldn't allow it. Better to let your justice system work out the punishment. Otherwise, you'd never leave me be. I know you, Sadie. When you get fixated on something, you won't let it go."

"I think Elwood needs professional help. His confession will buy him a shorter sentence with most of the judges around here. He might return to the hollow someday."

"Elwood is no longer welcome among us." She nodded at Summit. "That boy Liam was like a son to Summit. If Elwood came back, Summit would kill him with his bare hands and Elwood knows it."

Geraldine looped her arm around Summit's. They left without a backward glance. John lingered. When I walked after the Dovers, he fell in step with me.

"Now that the case is solved, I guess I won't be seeing you much anymore," he said.

I slowed, the scene around us settling heavily in my mind. Three boys kidnapped, tortured, terrified and murdered. I thought about Paula's and Summit's heartbreak and all the way back to Lita's incestuous relationship with her father when she was a child. Even though the sun shined brightly and the smoke had settled significantly, this part of the forest was still dark and threatening. The cabin's aged wood held decades of wicked secrets, and goosebumps pricked on my arms when I searched the side of the cabin near the ground and found the one small widow that I knew was in the cellar.

A heavy blanket of despair draped over my shoulders and for the first time since seeing Liam's bloated body in the river, I felt like crying.

And then there was Russo's family and some other unknown threat lurking around on the perimeter of his life. To say that I was depressed was putting it mildly. I filled with dread.

When I looked over at John, some of the tension left, and the sky brightened a little bit. Something about this mountain man lifted my spirits.

"Your hair looks good," I said without thinking.

The corners of John's lips rose. "I almost shaved it all off."

"Don't ever do that."

One of his brows shot up and I focused on the fire chief who began rolling one of the hoses back into the truck. "The ladies like longer hair. They won't want you to cut it."

"Is that so? What about you, Sadie, what do you want?" John said in a velvety voice that almost made me forget where we were and Elwood's chilling confession.

I didn't want to answer his question because I honestly didn't know. There was no time in my life for a flirtatious relationship with a Dover whose family I couldn't trust. One day I would come for his grandmother, I knew it in my heart.

But his soft, flirty voice made me feel a little better and that's what I needed right now.

"I want to see your apiary someday, John. That's what I want."

"Done." He started to leave, then stopped. When he lifted his head, he was grinning. "Oh, yeah. You're going to love Dixie."

Emotions collided in my stomach. "You think so, huh?"

John's grin spread into a full-blown smile. "Sadie, Dixie is my eight-year-old coonhound."

The tight sensation in my chest disappeared.

"I can't wait to meet her."

34

LUCINDA

The flashing lights in the woods made me blink and James leaned in close to whisper, "Everyone has a job to do."

Anger flared in my heart as I glanced at my husband's wide eyes while he watched the firefighters and policemen moving about like busy bees. Young Albert was dead and James was gawking, in awe of the commotion. Bishop Zeke was the opposite. He stared at the ground with his hands in his pockets. He'd barely said a word when we drove up to his house less than an hour ago. It took only a minute to explain that the sheriff had called. Our bishop suspected they'd found Albert and he was dead.

Zeke looked up and our eyes met. Many years ago, he'd asked my parents to court me, but I had refused. James was already in my sights and besides being much older than me, the man who would one day become bishop was arrogant, judgmental, and pig-headed.

"Lucinda, why did Sheriff Mills call you directly instead of reaching out to me?" The bishop's question was accompanied by a deep frown.

I licked my lips, trying to focus on our leader's unhappy face. It was hard to do when a tall man wearing a heavy-looking raincoat and a large helmet, asked us to move aside so that he could begin rolling up a hose.

The fire was put out. Only soot, smoke, and red embers remained beneath the metal frame of what used to be a vehicle. I searched past the bishop for Goliath. He was still hitched to the buggy in the yard, standing quietly. The horse was an exceptional animal. Many well-trained horses would be pitching a fit from the flashing lights and loud shouts between men. Giant dogs were apparently the only things that filled that horse's heart with dread.

"The sheriff has stayed in touch since"—I paused, not wanting to say it—"Vivian's death and the kidnappings of my family."

"Do you know the woman well?" he asked.

James lost interest in his surroundings and stared at the bishop, probably thinking the same thing as me—why does he ask such dumb questions when one of our congregation's children was lying dead in the ambulance? My husband didn't understand just how shallow our spiritual leader was. I sighed, disappointed in our leadership.

"Only as well as one can know someone who stops by for an occasional quick visit," I said, trying to keep the agitation out of my voice.

It was a stressful moment for all of us. I was glad Albert's parents had stayed away. The shock of the news was too much for the couple. They may not have feared properly for their child's disappearance, but it was plain to see by their show of grief that they were devastated. Tina fell to the ground and it was all William could do to pull her up and take her back into the house.

James, being a minister-in-training, was expected to accompany the bishop for the tragic errand, but me tagging alone was unprecedented and had only come about because I was the one who received the call. James, of course, welcomed my presence, but the bishop did not like the idea of having a woman present for such a task.

Zeke's hair was almost black with enough gray hairs peppered through it and his beard to show his age. His wiry body was still strong though, and the skin on his face deeply tanned. In his youth, he wasn't so bad to look at. Now, the seriousness of his personality had permanently tightened his features.

"Who watches your children then?"

Zeke's barrage of questions was tedious. "Martha was visiting when the call came in. She volunteered to stay until we returned."

He snorted and gave his head a firm shake. "Ack, that woman stirs the pot."

The time and place were inappropriate for my small smile, but I couldn't help it. Martha would be thrilled to hear she got under the bishop's skin. She was just that kind of a lady.

"Here she comes," James said, flicking his finger to signal the approach of the sheriff.

I drew in a deep breath. The woman's drawn face looked tired. Locks of her brown hair had fallen out of the ponytail and there were sooty smudges around the edges of her face. The sheriff didn't care about her appearance though. Her eyes were focused on our little group, and they were troubled.

The sheriff extended her hand to the bishop and Zeke grasped it. "I hate to see you again for something like this, Bishop."

"We live in evil times." Zeke exhaled and pursed his lips. "Do you know how Albert ended up here?" He extended his hands. "In this place?"

The sheriff didn't hesitate. "I do, and it's a long story." She eyed me and James, nodding. "Where are the parents?"

Zeke answered. "They chose not to come. I will see the boy and carry the information about his death to them."

"You can identify the body, but the information doesn't work that way. I'll need to talk to them in person."

I spoke up before Zeke could argue. "Sheriff Mills, they are distraught, as I am sure you understand. Can you wait until tomorrow? I'll tell them you plan to visit them."

The sheriff nodded. "Of course. That'll work." She offered a small, tight smile. "Thank you."

"Let us get this over with," Zeke said. He rubbed his face and took long strides to reach the ambulance.

We followed behind him, alongside the sheriff. She separated, spoke quietly to the paramedics, then stepped back. The older man signaled for Zeke to enter the back of the vehicle and he walked forward with determined movements.

James dropped his head and closed his eyes. I took a step sideways to see inside, but the door obstructed my view. The sheriff waited with her arms crossed. Another officer—a huge man with white hair—stepped up but remained silent, waiting. I remembered him from before. I thought his name was Buddy.

When Zeke exited the vehicle, his movements were quick and almost bouncy. I furrowed my brow, staring at him as he straightened up and faced the sheriff.

"That is not Albert."

35

SADIE

The words replayed in my mind twice. "Are you sure?"

The deterioration of the body, bloating, and loss of color are all things that could alter a person's appearance as a corpse. The holy man could be wrong.

"Yes, but if you don't believe me, James will confirm what I say." The bishop prompted James with a pump of his hand to enter the ambulance, but the other man stayed rooted in place, scratching his chin through his brown beard.

Lucinda watched her husband squirm in his shoes. The man didn't want to identify the body.

James finally found his voice. "He knows the boy as well as I do." He glanced at me with pleading eyes. "Zeke's word is all you need."

"Under the circumstances, I'd rather have two of you take a look. We don't want make a mistake," I said.

Lucinda raised her hand like she was a schoolgirl in a classroom. "I'll do it. No worries."

James dropped his head. "You don't have to. I'll find the strength."

Lucinda leaned in close to her husband. I heard her whisper, "It's fine, James. It's something that has to be done and I see your discomfort. Let me take your burden."

James nodded and Lucinda wasted no time, stepping into the ambulance.

James slid closer to me and without looking my way, asked, "Who could it be, if not Albert?"

Oh, trust me, James Miller, my mind was already racing with the possibilities.

Lucinda came out quickly. "Zeke is correct. That boy—bless his dear heart—is not our Albert."

Buddy coughed, then cleared his throat. We glanced at each other. The color had drained from his face. We went from closing all the cases to having two more burst open.

I organized my thoughts and my words. "Well then, that's good news for you all and for Albert's family. I'm sorry you had to come out here and see the body like that."

The bishop started to walk away. "We'll be on our way. I'll pray that you discover who this child is with great speed," he said over his shoulder.

James turned to leave, then stopped when Lucinda stepped closer to me.

"Go on. I'll be there in a minute," Lucinda told her husband.

James continued on and the Amish woman who I already knew had many qualities which I held in high regard—bravery, kindness, intelligence—came closer. She was also a conservative rebel of sorts, and I admired her spunkiness.

"I cannot lie. I am relieved that it is not Albert, but I still worry about where he is," she said.

"So do I." I leveled a look at the other woman, who was not much younger than me. She had glossy skin that was slightly tanned, probably from working in a garden. Her blonde hair was tucked neatly in her white cap and although her hunter green dress covered her from neck to ankle, her slim, athletic body was still obvious. "Please keep me posted when or if you hear from Albert. I have a lot to keep me busy with this situation here, but if there's any new developments or you just need to talk about it, you have my number."

"Thank you, Sheriff." She was ready to leave, then stopped. "I will pray for that poor boy's family with all my might. I do hope this marks the end of calamities in Possum Gap."

Lucinda was already walking away when I muttered, "I think it's just the beginning."

The streetlamp spread a soft glow in the inky darkness that had fallen beyond my office window and soft, pattering rain tapped the glass. Leaning back in the chair, I stared at the stack of file folders on my desk.

"It's good it held off until now," Russo said. "Can you imagine combing that property in the rain?"

In the bright office light, the bruising around Russo's eyes was more prominent. The doctor said the raccoon look was from the whack to his head. He wore a long-sleeved shirt so I couldn't see the scrapes that I knew were on his arms. The coroner had also walked into the office stiffly and grimaced when he sat down a few minutes earlier.

"Why aren't you resting as home?" I asked in a mom voice that I didn't intend to use, but it kind of just happened.

The corner of Russo's mouth crinkled. "I thought you might need me."

"You already conducted Liam's autopsy." I shook my head, trying to forget the argument we'd had. "Even though I told you to wait until morning."

Russo shrugged, his cheeks reddening. "Sorry. It was a time is of the essence sort of thing for me."

I sighed deeply, then took a sip of coffee which was almost too cool to stomach. "Yeah, you're right. Cody Willis' family deserves a quick resolution to this madness."

Russo leaned forward with a sharp intake of breath. He was definitely hurting.

"If the kid didn't have that birthmark on his leg, it would have taken a lot longer to identify him," he said.

My eyes traveled across my desk to land on the file with the kid's name on it. He was a thirteen-year-old from Dayton, Ohio who had been missing for nearly two years. His dad was in jail, serving time for attempted murder and his mother had died of a drug overdose the same day Cody disappeared. Talking to the detective in Dayton, there had always been a suspicion that the kid had been sold off for his mother's last fix, but we may never know the exact details of what went down the fateful night when the cops showed up at the public housing apartment to discover his mom dead and Cody gone. The father had entered the prison five years earlier, so no answers came from him. What we did know was that Cody was spotted in Tennessee and then ended up at the Calhouns' cabin during a drug transaction.

The kid hadn't matched on the database because of the five-inch red splotch on his thigh that was absent from Liam's body. At the time of that search, we had no idea that there was another victim.

With his mom dead and his dad incapacitated, we called his next of kin—an aunt living in Phoenix. The woman's voice was scratchy on the phone. I thought she might have shed a tear or two while we talked, but there was not outpouring of emotion. Like so many kids that ended up being trafficked, there wasn't a loving family at home waiting to hear news of them.

That's probably how they ended up in their awful predicaments.

"There's going to be a ton of work to do to piece the entire story together, but I think we're in pretty good shape because of Elwood."

"Do you think he's sincere or simply doing what his grandmother ordered him to?"

"Probably a little bit of both. The more information he gives us, especially the drug contacts, his sentence will get shorter and shorter. Geraldine's not stupid. She knows he has to cooperate to have his sentence reduced."

"How did she take it when you told her the dead kid wasn't the Amish boy? Seems to me, she might have only made Elwood come clean because of an affection a boy she thought had been tortured and murdered in that basement."

Russo yawned.

"Go home. I have a few more minutes and I'll be heading out the door myself. Chloe's coming back in the morning. I want to stop by the grocery store to fill the refrigerator. It's currently empty."

Russo pushed off the chair. "I'll be in first thing tomorrow. I'll have to start the autopsies on what's left of Cooter and Kaine. Lita's will be much easier."

I cocked my head when he hesitated.

"Go on," I urged quietly.

"I'm surprised you're not attacking me with a dozen questions about my family and my history."

My heart and mind were heavy, but I still managed to chuckle. "Oh, we'll have that conversation soon enough. But it can wait until you heal and we get this investigation wrapped up. We both came close to dying today. I think we can take a deep breath and enjoy it before your reckoning comes." I snorted softly. "And Darcy's."

Russo walked slowly to the door. "From the sound of it, Tanya gave her quite the scolding in the hospital." He smiled a little. "She's supposed to be released tomorrow."

"I know."

"I promised to bring her a cup of her favorite brew from the café. I might be a few minutes late."

"I'm okay with that." I didn't return his smile. "I can forgive a lot, but if you break her heart, I'll have your hide. Do you understand?"

"Oh, yes, clearly." He made it through the doorway. I heard him say as he turned the corner, "Tomorrow is a new day."

I slumped back into the seat, crossing my arms over my chest. "And what horrors will it bring?" I said to myself.

A rap on the door brought my head up. A deputy was manning the front desk and if he needed anything, he would have called me rather than leaving his post to walk down the long hallway.

Who would stop by the office at this late hour? I immediately expected the worst when I said loudly, "Come on in."

A woman I'd never seen before entered the office. Cool, nighttime air clung to her and I caught the faint scent of vanilla. She had on a stylish leather jacket over a blue blouse. A pair of jeans and comfortable-looking black suede boots completed her look. The woman's straight blonde hair was shoulder length and although there were no wrinkles at the corners of her eyes, I judged her to be around my age. It was something about the confident way she carried herself and her serious blue eyes. If my gut was right, the rose-colored glasses had been ditched by this woman a long time ago.

She didn't smile when she stepped up to my desk. "Sheriff Mills?"

"Yes. Do you have some kind of problem?"

The woman didn't answer immediately. She took her time looking around my office, then finally returned her gaze to me.

"Yes, I do. His name is Albert Peachy."

My heart skipped a beat. She wasn't southern, but not from the northeast like Russo either. I would guess the Midwest, either Ohio or Indiana. And she was definitely not Amish.

The late hour, combined with the rain pattering the window and the sudden appearance of this mystery woman made a shiver race through me. But it was hearing her say Albert's name that got me standing up and placing my hands on my desk as I leaned forward.

"You're not from around here, are you?"

She gave a shake of her head. "Blood Rock, Indiana. I need your help with a case I'm working on."

"Who are you?"

She let out a breath as if the introduction was taking too much time—and this woman didn't have any to spare.

"Sheriff Serenity Adams."

Sheriff Sadie Mills joins Sheriff Serenity Adams in SERENITY'S PLAIN SECRETS crime fiction/mystery novel, NIGHT SONG! It's now available at Amazon! This book brings the sheriffs together on a dangerous quest to find the missing Amish boy, Albert Peachy. It's a journey that takes the two strong-willed and savvy women from the hills of Kentucky to the streets of New Orleans as they unravel a horrifying tale of superstitions and devil worship. These women are known for getting the job done, but this time, they're outgunned and up against an ancient evil that not only threatens to destroy them, but everything they hold dear.

Thank you for reading!

While you're waiting, you might enjoy the TEMPTATION series, the WINGS OF WAR series, WILLOW CREEK/ONE KISS IS ALL IT TAKES or THE FORTUNA COIN.

You can visit Karen Ann Hopkins and see all her books at https://www.karenannhopkinsfiction.com
& Karen Ann Hopkins at Amazon

Facebook: Karen Ann Hopkins Amish Fiction @ temptationbook
Twitter: Karen Ann Hopkins @ KarenAnnHopkins
Instagram: karenannhopkins

Are you looking for a breathtaking thriller that will keep you flipping the pages for hours past your bedtime? Please consider THE FORTUNA COIN.

Read on to find rave reviews of Karen Ann Hopkins' newest psychological thriller:

Rave Review from Booklife/Publishers Weekly:
"With clear, compelling prose, Hopkins has constructed a seemingly effortless story that weaves together paranormal, fantasy and romance with mind-bending elements of psychological thrillers. Readers will become quickly engrossed in The Fortuna Coin's richly emotional tale of good luck charms, psychic visions, and premonitions...This urgent, personal thriller combines paranormal and romantic elements as a woman out of time faces an agonizing choice."

5 Star Readers' Favorite Review:
"If you're itching for a well-written, character-driven drama that explores a vital social issue, The Fortuna Coin is the book for you."

5 Star Readers' Favorite Review:
"The Fortuna Coin is a very empowering book...This book will surprise you and leave you breathless."

5 Star Readers' Favorite Review:
"Karen Ann Hopkins has taken a sensitive subject and created a magical work of fiction."

5 Star Review from Wine Cellar Library Book Blog:
"It's been a long time since I've read a book that was utterly unputdownable."

Standalone Psychological Thriller

Possum Gap Series

Serenity's Plain Secrets Series

 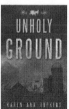